PRAISE FOR

BEFORE MARS

"A psychological thriller wearing the cloak of a gripping sci-fi story . . . delivered in excellently page-turning fashion."
—*Los Angeles Times*

"A thrilling read but . . . also a deep dive into the protagonist's psychology as she grapples with what she discovers on the Red Planet." —*Space.com*

"Part science fiction, part corporate conspiracy thriller; Newman navigates both landscapes while deftly transplanting the myriad social, economic, and political struggles [that] we know on earth, but are grossly magnified in the confines of a Martian colony. . . . [Newman] channels both Andy Weir and Elon Musk to craft a compelling space odyssey."
—*The Mountain Times* (NC)

"A slow-burn psychological thriller . . . a science-fictional spin on the gaslighting theme [depicted in] novels such as *The Girl on the Train*." —*Financial Times*

PRAISE FOR

AFTER ATLAS

2017 Arthur C. Clarke Award Nominee

"Newman writes with exquisite precision of grief, divided loyalties, and the struggle for self-actualization . . . gripping and sorrowful." —*Publishers Weekly* (starred review)

"A lovely locked-room mystery in which the stakes are incredibly high. . . . Emma Newman creates addictive page-turners, and this is another fine example." —*Starburst*

"Newman combines the classic mystery novel whodunit with a frighteningly possible reality of corporate-owned governments . . . keeps the pages turning until the unexpected conclusion." —*Booklist*

"*After Atlas* is a complete and nearly perfectly plotted and paced story." —Books, Bones & Buffy

"The story dug its hooks under my skin so that even now, days later, I'm still reeling from that punch-drunk sensation I get when I finish an amazing book. . . . Emma Newman has written a police procedural like she was born into this genre, laying out the clues and following up on all the leads before pulling everything together for a stunner." —The BiblioSanctum

PRAISE FOR

PLANETFALL

"Gripping, thoughtful science fiction in the vein of Tiptree or Crispin. Unique, timely, and enthralling . . . absolutely beautiful. What a glorious, heartbreaking maze of a book." —Seanan McGuire, *New York Times* bestselling author of *Once Broken Faith*

"Newman has crafted a thrilling tale of murder, mystery, and madness on a world where humanity is still its own worst enemy. Horrifying and heartbreaking in equal measure, the catastrophe driving this narrative will keep you riveted until the very last page." —Kameron Hurley, author of *The Stars Are Legion*

"Builds and builds to this remarkable crescendo. . . . The ending had me breathless . . . an awesome book."

—Roxane Gay, author of *Hunger: A Memoir of (My) Body*

"Think *Interstellar*; think *Prometheus*. . . . Beautifully written: an unfolding alien mystery and complex, utterly believable characters."

—Stephen Baxter, national bestselling author
of *The Light of Other Days*

"Filled with wonders, revelations, and edge-of-the-seat suspense, *Planetfall* is a fascinating, heartbreaking exploration of love and loneliness set against an awe-inspiring backdrop. An instant classic of the genre."

—Gareth L. Powell, BSFA Award–winning author
of *Macaque Attack*

"A strange but mesmerizing book in which almost nothing is as it seems . . . reads at once like a character study, a mystery, a hard-science-fiction tale about the colonists on an alien world, and a surrealist science fiction about alien life."

—RT Book Reviews

"This heartbreaking adventure is a tragedy of science and faith."
—*Publishers Weekly*

ATLAS ALONE

A Planetfall Novel

EMMA NEWMAN

ACE
NEW YORK

ACE
Published by Berkley
An imprint of Penguin Random House LLC
1745 Broadway, New York, NY 10019

Copyright © 2019 by Emma Newman

Library of Congress Cataloging-in-Publication Data

Names: Newman, Emma, 1976– author.
Title: Atlas alone / Emma Newman.
Description: First edition. | New York, NY : Ace/Berkley, an imprint of
Penguin Random House LLC, 2019. | Series: A Planetfall novel
Identifiers: LCCN 2018050764 | ISBN 9780399587344 (paperback) |
ISBN 9780399587351 (ebook)
Subjects: | BISAC: FICTION / Science Fiction / General. | FICTION /
Psychological. | FICTION / Science Fiction / High Tech. | GSAFD: Science fiction.
Classification: LCC PR6114.E949 A95 2019 | DDC 823/.92--dc23
LC record available at https://lccn.loc.gov/2018050764

First Edition: April 2019

Printed in the United States of America
1 3 5 7 9 10 8 6 4 2

Cover art by Anxo Amarelle CGI
Cover design by Adam Auerbach

For Bobbu. They know why.

1

THE TRICK IS remembering that it's all a game. Somewhere along the way I seem to have forgotten that. I don't even know what the rules are anymore.

"So, the rules are very simple," Travis says, smiling as he shuffles the playing cards. "We each start with ten cards and—" He fumbles, scattering a few of them across the table. He laughs, dragging them back into a pile. "This is harder to do in real life than in mersives."

Travis brushes a lock of auburn hair back from his face, one that is too handsome to be believable in real life. He looks like he should be a nonplayer character in a mersive, the sort a creative director would choose as the dangerous lover in a spy story. Or the romantic lead in some soft porn made for lonely hearts. And I can see how looking that way has made Travis's life easier. How he merely chuckles at his own ineptitude rather than rushing to hide or downplay it.

"Right, let's try that again. Beggar-my-neighbor is a really easy game in which . . ." He pauses, looking across the table at Carl. "Are you with us, Carl?"

Carl is resting his chin on his hand, eyes glazed over. His black hair, still thick even though he's in his forties, is now peppered with gray. It's like he's aged ten years in the last six months and lost a stone in weight that he really needed to keep on him. Poor bastard. I've known him for over twenty years now and I've never seen him look this bad. Not even when we were being hot-housed.

He blinks. "Yeah, sorry. Just a bit tired."

"Have you eaten?" Travis asks softly.

Carl just glares at him.

"We're worried about you, Carl," Travis says. "Aren't we, Dee?"

Inwardly, I groan. This is not the way to handle Carl. There *is* no way to handle Carl when it comes to his hangups about printed food. And dragging me into this is not going to help either.

I look at Carl, then back at Travis. "Don't bring me into this."

"Into what?" they both say at exactly the same time.

"Into this"—I wave my hands at them—"intervention."

"Eh?" Travis cocks a perfectly shaped eyebrow at me. "This is just a card game, Dee."

"No, it isn't," Carl says to me. "This *is* an intervention, but one for *you*, not for *me*."

Carl directs another glare at Travis. "At least, that's what I was told."

Travis sighs, resting the pack of cards in the palm of one hand. "I'm worried about you too, Dee. I just thought that spending some time playing something easy and relaxing together would be good for you."

I fold my arms and sit back. "And there was me thinking you had a sudden hankering to play shitty old games in a state-of-the art spaceship. I thought you might have found it funny or something."

"Well, I did have a 'sudden hankering' to play it," he says with a shrug. "I was playing a mersive and there was this family and they were playing beggar like my gran—" He waves a hand. "It doesn't matter. What matters is that you haven't played mersives with us for . . . months. You keep canceling plans. And when we finally persuade you to come and join us, you drop out."

"He has a point," Carl says, his voice softer. "We haven't shot the shit out of stuff on Mars since . . . since a long time ago."

How much is held, left unsaid, in that pause. And the irony is, the thing he won't say, that he is skirting around like an arachnophobe locked in a room with a tarantula, is the reason I don't play games anymore.

But I won't say it either. I can't. So I end up just sitting there, staring at my best friend and his sort-of lover, none of us mentioning the thing that is slowly killing us.

"I just haven't fancied it," I finally say, drenching the words in nonchalance in the hope the two of them will just slide off and we'll talk about something else.

Travis and Carl exchange a look. I swear, if either of them says another word about this bullshit, I will walk out of this crappy communal eating area, find an air lock and chuck myself out into the void. We're six months out from Earth now, and the cold vacuum of space is more appealing to me than this room's depressing functional furniture and 360-degree display of whatever sentimental view of Earth has been called up by the last people in here . . .

And then I don't see the table, the chairs, the others. I see a huge bed with luxurious dark gray cotton sheets, the bright colors of the communal room fading to the muted tones of my parents' bedroom.

"Can you put the mountains view on the wall for me, Deanna? You know the one—the one I like."

Picking up the remote . . . cycling through the interface to display the mountains for him on the bedroom wall. The smell of vomit lingering even though I'd scrubbed the carpet twice. Watching the huge television display change from a sunset over New York to a mountainous landscape that was always his favorite. "There you are, Daddy."

"Thank you, Button. Oh, that's so beautiful. That's better."

Turning around, noticing his eyes swollen shut so he couldn't possibly be seeing the view, the crusted blood, the way his forehead seemed to curve inward above his right eye and the terror of it! The terror of seeing the towering man I adored lying on the bed. Dying.

"Dee?" Carl takes my hand. "You with us?"

I blink. There's a forest showing on the walls around us. Not mountains. There's the background hum of Atlas 2's life support. We're not even on Earth anymore. And I'm not a child.

"Sorry," I say. "I was miles away."

It's then that I notice how bloodshot his eyes are, and the scattering of burst capillaries around his eye sockets. He could get those sorted out, if he wasn't so terrified of a stranger touching him. Shit. I should have done something sooner.

"Carl . . . have you thought about getting some help with the food thing?"

He pulls his hand away and picks up the small pile of playing cards in front of him. Shit, there's a pile in front of me too. When the hell did Travis deal those?

I pick up the cards I've been dealt and start to spread

them out like a fan. I've done this only a few times in mersives, and my fingers feel clumsy holding the real thing. The design is quite bizarre, now I'm looking at them, especially the royal cards. So stylized, so . . . old. They're not newly printed, and the edges are worn soft from handling.

"Where did you get these from?" I ask.

"They were my grandmother's," Travis replies, sorting his cards too. "She taught me how to play all sorts of games with them."

"Did she not like tech or something?"

He laughs. "She was the lead programmer on Bright Purple."

I lean back, impressed. Bright Purple was one of the most disruptive, radical crowd-sourced AI projects of the early twenty-first century. Arguably, their work made the interface with our Artificial Personal Assistants what it is today. And as their work was unassociated with any corporation or single government, they could take the research in directions that no one else thought were profitable, leading to breakthroughs that made neural chip technology possible. I know about it only from work; one of the young up-and-coming mersive directors wanted to find something edgy to make a documentary about, but we couldn't even get her proposal past Legal. Someone in the Noropean gov-corp really didn't want that story from the time of democracy and wild crowd-sourced activism to be dredged up again.

"What happened to that project?" I ask. "It never made it into the post-riots history mersives."

He nods, not looking up from the cards. "Well, it didn't fit the post-riots narrative, did it? Couldn't have people remembering that some really good things were happening before the collapse of democracy. That maybe the gov-corps weren't the magical, fair solution they wanted everyone to think they were."

I'm surprised by the bitterness in his tone. He's usually so . . . positive. So eager to be liked.

Carl has noticed it too and is looking at him over the top of his cards. "Was she still alive when . . ."

"No," Travis says quickly. "She died when I was at university."

The atmosphere, not great to begin with, sinks even further. We all spend far too long arranging our cards. Travis turns over the top of the remaining cards in the center of the table between us as I think a command to my APA: "Ada, show me the rules of beggar-my-neighbor."

A few lines of text appear overlaid across my vision. Travis was right, thankfully—the game is really simple. "Oh, wait a minute. We're not supposed to look at our hands," I say, and the other two groan. One read-through and I blink the rules away. My APA interprets the movement and the words zip up into the top right, forming an icon I can select if I want to refresh my memory during the game.

"Well, this can be a practice round," Travis says, back to using that disarming smile. It doesn't work on me though.

"And the first card turned over and put in the middle is from your own hand," I add. "We're just supposed to have our cards facedown in a pile in front of us."

Carl collapses his fan of cards and dumps the pile down in front of him. "This game had better be worth it."

"You're just hangry," Travis says. "Why don't you eat something and then you'll enjoy it far more."

I sink a little in my seat, waiting for Carl to blow up at him, but the poor bastard hasn't got the energy for that. "No, it's fine."

Travis puts his cards down too, looking at him. "It really isn't, Carl. Look at you. You're wasting away." He looks to me for support, but I keep my eyes on the cards.

"All right," Carl snaps, holding his hands up. "What do you want me to do? Admit that I've been struggling to adjust to life on board? I can't be the only one!"

"Why don't you talk to us about it? We want to help. Right, Dee?"

I want to punch Travis so hard right now. This is not my style, nor is it Carl's. This is the sort of "friendship gets us through everything" bullshit sold by twats marketing nostalgic mersives that hark back to a time when people socialized outside of work. But if I say nothing, I'll look like a bloody drone. I look at Carl, meeting his eyes, hoping I am conveying a silent apology well enough.

"We won't judge you," Travis carries on. "Why don't you tell us about what you're struggling to adjust to?"

Is he fucking joking? Does he want Carl to mention the thing we haven't talked about for months but have thought about constantly?

Carl slides down in his chair. "Just . . . I mean, c'mon, living in a giant . . . metal . . . skyscraper ship thing flying through space . . . It's . . . unnatural." So he still can't talk about it either.

It's getting harder for Travis to hide his frustration. "But what about the food thing, Carl?"

There's the twitch, the one by Carl's left eye, right on cue. "I . . . I don't like printed food."

"You don't like the taste?"

He presses his lips together and shakes his head. "It isn't that," he finally says. He rests a hand on his stomach, drawing in long, slow breaths through flared nostrils.

"Give it a rest, Travis," I say sharply.

"We can't just keep ignoring this! Look at him!"

"It makes me throw up," Carl says quietly. "You know that."

"Yes, but why do you think that is? The printer that serves your row has been feeding dozens of people for the past six months and none of them have been ill."

Carl scowls at him. "Why? It's fucking obvious, isn't it? It's me!"

"Why are you angry?"

"Because you're being such a twat!" I snap at him. "He doesn't want to talk about it, Travis. That's up to him."

"If you don't want to talk to us, then talk to a counselor," Travis says, refusing to get the idea, like so many men.

Both Carl and I bark out a bitter laugh, and we both know exactly why we did. "Yeah," Carl says after glancing at me. "They make it all better."

"I mean a proper counselor. A trained professional whose job it is to make sure people on this ship don't fall apart—for their own good, not for those money-grabbing bastards who wanted to make as much money out of you as they could."

So he knows Carl used to be indentured? But they must have met when Carl was still a specialist detective for the Noropean Ministry of Justice, and it was part of his contract to never tell anyone about his status as a corporate asset, just like it was in my contract. Did he break that rule before we left Earth, once we were with the Circle, those contracts paid off? Or was it confessed here on Atlas 2, when Earth and its horrors were far behind us? Regardless of when it must have happened, I never thought Carl would ever share that with anyone except me. He's opened up to Travis far more than I thought.

"For our own good?" Carl scoffs.

"And for everyone else's too. We're all on this ship together. If someone goes Trafalgar Square on board, it's a lot worse, right?"

Carl frowns at the mention of that massacre. One lunatic

with a dirty bomb was bad enough in a huge city; it would be so much worse in a spaceship. "Now, I'm not for a moment saying that you're going to lose it like that man did," Travis continues, "but . . . you are losing it. And it's going to kill you if you don't sort it out."

"They won't let it kill me," he says with a bitterness I understand all too well. He's still thinking like someone classed as a corporate asset, like I was. But that debt was wiped the moment he made the deal with the Circle to bring us onto Atlas 2. Somehow he got the funds to pay off my debt too.

It will never leave us, the memory of others having power over our bodies, over our lives, but it's still gnawing away at him. I refuse to let it do that to me. They took enough years of my life. But I don't think he's in a state to see it the way I do.

Then again, I suspect he sees very little the way I do.

While I don't agree with how Travis is doing this, I do agree with his appraisal. I've been keeping Carl together since we were classed nonpersons over twenty years ago; there's no way I'm going to let him die now, not when we've finally gotten away from that shower of shit that was corporate slavery.

"No, they won't let it kill you," I say, "just like anyone else on this ship. I guess they'll fuck with your brain even more, without your permission, if it comes to it. Look, Carl, this is serious shit. Talking to someone about this food thing could make your life here so much better. We're stuck on this ship for another, what, nineteen and a half years? Your chip has already done all it can to keep you alive. It's not enough. Antiemetics and uppers and downers can only go so far, and they're not a long-term solution anyway. If you don't find help, they're gonna have to get more invasive." He remains silent. "What's the worst that can happen?"

"I could say too much."

"They know you're fucked up, Carl. And whoever it is

will know your background. It's in your medical file." I don't say anything more, not being certain of how much he's told Travis. We had so many learning acceleration drugs pumped into us back then, they'll know he's been hot-housed, even if he doesn't disclose it. Our brains don't look normal anymore.

"I'm not worried about that." His voice is quiet and his body is still. "What if . . . what if I start to open up and I just blurt it out?"

"Blurt what out?" Travis asks, as I scream at him in my head to shut up.

"That everyone on Earth is dead."

I wait for the rest, for the fact that not only are they dead, but someone on this ship must have given the order for the nukes to be fired from America into Europe. That someone else breathing the same recycled air as us right now is responsible for the deaths of billions. But he doesn't say it, even though we're all thinking it.

There's a fly on one of the cards and then I can hear them buzzing.

What is that sound coming from the bedroom? "Daddy?"

The buzzing gets louder. Is there something wrong with the wall?

Pushing the door, revealing him on the bed, the buzzing louder. His eyes open, his mouth open, the flies coming out of his mouth—

"I *can't* stop thinking about it!" Carl shouts, and there are no flies here, of course there aren't, we're in space, thousands, if not millions, of miles away from every bug known to humankind. "Every single fucking time I try to eat I think about the food I used to cook, about the gingerbread . . ."

"Gingerbread?" Travis asks, but Carl is crying into his hands now. Shit.

"Look," I say, getting up to rest a hand on his back. "Cry

it out if you need to, but you have to . . . to . . ." What can I say here that won't make me seem like a monster to him?

He drags his hands down his cheeks, sniffling, to look at me. "How are you coping so well?"

Oh, Carl, if only you knew.

"We all deal with things in different ways, mate."

"Yes, but you're not dealing with it, are you?" Travis says, looking at me. "You've closed yourself off from us, you don't play mersives anymore and your gamer score was insane when I first met you."

"Been snooping into what I do in my private time, have you?" I fire at him, Carl sitting up as he wipes his eyes.

"I'm worried about you too!" Travis says, spreading his hands, looking for all the world like a bloody middle manager trying to keep the board happy. "Why aren't you playing anything anymore, Dee? Why aren't you—"

"Because what is the fucking point?" I yell at him.

Confused, Carl twists round to frown at me. "It's gaming, Dee. There doesn't have to be a point."

And he's right. He is completely right, and I feel like an idiot. Why did I say that? Why am I letting them see any of this after I've been working so hard to keep it away from them?

JeeMuh, I swear there is a fly in here.

"Look . . . all of us are struggling to adapt," Travis says gently. "We just have to make the most of it."

"What the ever-living fuck is that supposed to mean?" Carl shouts. "Make the most of what? Of being stuck in this tin can for the next twenty-odd years while everyone we left behind is either dead or dying and whoever did it is on this fucking ship with us?"

His voice rings off the plastic table. I am so grateful for the soundproofing on this ship. The designers wanted to make sure that people living in close quarters wouldn't drive one another mad, with the added bonus that we're not likely to get killed thanks to Carl and his bloody anger issues.

Travis looks away, attending to something in his visual field. Probably checking that no one else was walking past in that moment. The communal area we're in has been booked out for our use, but still, Carl shouldn't have put us at risk like that. "Thankfully, I know how to make sure our conversation is actually private, rather than just looking that way," Travis mutters, adding, after a beat, "What else can we do but make the most of it?"

"We can find out who gave the order," I say.

"And then what?" he asks, all the pleasantness gone from his tone.

"And then we tell everyone else on board what they did," Carl says. "And we . . . we make sure they're prosecuted."

Travis laughs. At first it's cold and sarcastic; then he draws in a breath and starts laughing even harder. "Seriously? According to whose laws are we going to do that? Don't you think that whoever gave that order is going to be pretty high up on this ship? Do you really think that anyone will believe us?"

"You didn't keep the footage we watched?" I ask.

"Since when has anything like that ever been used in a successful prosecution, Dee?" Carl mutters back to me. "They'll claim it's faked."

"And I didn't save it anyway!" Travis says. "I never wanted to watch that again and I definitely didn't want it to be found in my private space!"

"So we just do nothing?" Carl says. "We just—"

"Yes!" Travis says, standing up. "Yes, we just move on and be grateful that we weren't one of those poor bastards down there when it happened!"

"You just don't have the guts to do something about it!"

Carl yells, and Travis gives him a look that I simply don't understand, something that speaks of betrayal and disbelief and . . .

He walks out, leaving his playing cards on the table. The door slides shut behind him, Carl sitting back and folding his arms like a petulant child.

"Well . . . as interventions go, that one was pretty shit," I say, and then we both burst out laughing, feeling the release of tension.

I lean down and wrap my arms about him. He rests his head on my arm. "What the fuck are we going to do, Dee? I miss you. Come and shoot aliens on Mars with me, like we used to. We can make the settings as ridiculous as you like. Horny scientists? I know they make you laugh. Don't you need to have a laugh? I know I sure as fuck do."

I think about it. But I know what will happen. It'll be the same as every other time I've immersed. I'll end up standing there, seeing, smelling, feeling and hearing every damn thing in the mersive exactly as I should; and I'll just stand there not caring. Or actively hating it. Killing zombies, or growing as many bloody carrots as I can in a square meter on some fantasy farm, or whatever puerile shit I've tried always suffers from the same problem. Me.

Where is the joy in postapocalyptic survival horror when you've only just escaped it yourself? Where is the joy in any environment that reminds you of an Earth you've left behind, dying? Where is the fun in shooting stupid fake aliens on Mars when you know the real people in the base there are stranded and condemned to a slow death?

But I can't say that. I can't tell him how I feel. I never have. All these years I've known him, I've propped him up. I've been the one who doesn't let anything get to her, not even being rounded up by those corporate-sanctioned slavers and being hot-housed and sold to a gov-corp. It was all water off a neoprene suit to me. I never let it bother me, and if something had, I'd never have let Carl see it. Not the only person in the world who actually means something to me. Nothing ever did bother me though. I killed off that sentimentality a long time ago.

And the irony is, I never even liked anyone we left behind. I never went out into nature, or loved any of the cities I lived in, or even cared that much about anything other than surviving and finding the latest game to help me escape it all. I thought I was invincible.

Turns out that watching thermonuclear war from space in real time didn't just run off me like water. Maybe I am human, after all.

"Talk to me, Dee," he says, squeezing my arm.

"I'm fine, seriously," I say, pulling away, marveling at how easy it is to lie to him. "I just don't fancy it anymore, that's all."

"How about we just try going to Mars? Tomorrow, maybe? No pressure. Even if we just sit there and take potshots at rocks for a while. Nothing too intense."

I can hear the need in his voice. "All right. Throw a time at my APA. It's not like I have anything else going on." I point at the cards. "What should we do with those?"

He starts gathering them up. "I'll take them back to Travis. Peace offering."

I nod. "Tell him not to do that to me again, will you?"

Carl gets up, looks me in the eye. "I will. I got your back, Dee. Always."

2

MY CABIN IS only a few meters away, and as the door slides
shut behind me, I feel both the relief of solitude after Travis's
clumsy interference and the familiar faint disappointment at
my living space.

The ceiling, a creamy white printed sheet of thick plastic,
stretches above me, merging seamlessly with the walls. The
door to the tiny bathroom is shut, as is the one that leads out
onto the corridor. Carl's room is on the other side of the wall
that my bed extends from and I can't help but wonder if he
is feeling the same relief as I am. Is he going to try to eat
anything? What can I do about it?

I lie down, there not being any space for a chair in here,
and squeeze the foam of the mattress with my hands. I
think about the bed I lie on, about the floor my bed rests
upon, about the other cabins beneath mine and the many
floors of the ship between my cabin and the engines. It helps
me to ground out in my body when I feel unsettled, but it
worked better when I was on Earth and lived in a normal

apartment. It was far easier to feel like I was at home, in the real world, when I lived there. That building made sense and I understood it.

There are many things I don't understand about Atlas 2. I know that antimatter powers the engines, and that there's some sort of clever gizmo that makes it in the quantities required to maintain our speed, but I don't understand how either of them actually works. That means of antimatter production was one of the major technological breakthroughs the Pathfinder made all those years ago. Apparently she woke up out of a coma, knew where to go to find God and then figured out a revolutionary way to fuel interstellar travel in less than a month. Bloody overachiever.

I know that those engines create a huge amount of heat that has to be sent somewhere; otherwise it will melt the ship. I know that a tiny fraction of that heat is used in life support and that the rest is removed by means of "droplet radiators," which are basically two jets of superheated molten sodium that are sprayed out from the sides of the ship. The sodium is piped past the engines, taking in that waste heat, which melts it; then it gets sprayed out. The cooled droplets are caught by pipe catcher things near the base of the ship and pumped back into the system. If the little mersive I watched about the ship is to be believed, the cooling sodium fanning out from the spray jets on either side of the ship looks like giant glowing wings as we travel through space. I would love to be able to see that. Apparently, you can see a sliver of that spray from the viewing window, but my time slot hasn't come up yet. We're only allowed a very small amount of time looking out of the only window on the ship because of the radiation (or so we've been told), and there are about 10,400 people to share it with.

I understand the principle, sort of, behind those droplet

radiators, and I don't need a greater knowledge of it than I have; there are other, far more qualified people on this ship who have got that covered. I'm happy with my rudimentary understanding of how gravity is generated by the fact that we're accelerating at the equivalent of one g, but I did get a bit lost when the mersive explained that gravity is actually falling. Again, I don't need to be able to do the calculations there; I can just live here, walk around, run, lie down, jump and land again just like I did on Earth. At the halfway point in the journey we'll temporarily lose gravity and have to strap ourselves to our own beds to prevent injury. It's something to do with having to turn around and decelerate or something, so we don't eventually hit our destination planet at just below the speed of light. Never a good look.

No, what really bothers me is that I don't understand how the ship is structured *socially*. Pretty much every organization I've ever interacted with, from an apartment block residents' association to a huge gov-corp, has had a clear hierarchy of roles with easily accessible information about who is employed in them. Military vessels have command structures and everyone knows who the captain and first officer and all the other critical members of the crew are. But not Atlas 2. Someone is in charge of this ship, and I don't have the faintest clue who that is.

It seems absurd to me. Surely if there's anything that thousands of years of human history has told us, it's that people like to know where they stand in the pecking order and whom to depose if they want to climb higher. I have no idea whether the average peasant in ancient China knew who the emperor of the time was, nor whether the peasants of medieval England knew who the king or queen was, but I reckon it wouldn't have been difficult for them to find out. Someone in their village would know, surely, because there would have to have been someone connected to the wider machine of society. Those poor bastards couldn't have been adequately exploited without it, after all.

Even if a person has no hope of climbing their respective social ladder, they want—no, *need*—to know the name of the one at the top so they have someone to blame for all the ills of the world. A name to curse while bemoaning one's lot. Is that why this ship's captain has kept their name secret? Because they don't want to be seen as the one responsible for all of the bad as well as the good? Unlikely. In my experience, the sort of people who pursue roles at the top of the ladder actually want everyone else to know their name. And this is a historic trip, one that will form the foundation of the new civilization we're going to build at our destination. The captain will want to be remembered long after we have arrived.

This ship is similar in size to the original Empire State Building, protects what is literally the last group of human beings that will ever leave Earth and is more technically complex than anything the US gov-corp has ever built. Simply the Rapture itself was a remarkable feat; being able to build over a hundred spacecraft in secret, recruit all the people for the project and send them all up into orbit around the moon on the same day was incredible. And no one knew about it until they saw our vapor trails. At least, no one who lived long enough to blow it all open. And then there's the fact that they built Atlas 2 on the dark side of the moon without anyone knowing. That's . . . insane. The number of satellites they must have either shut down or hacked to hide it beggars belief. After achieving all that and getting the ship under way without a single accident, they weren't going to just leave us all to our own devices for twenty years. Surely there is a command structure of some sort, whether it's based on a naval carrier military structure or the usual corporate hierarchy—how could a ship of this size be flown to another planet without one? Which raises the question, why isn't that command crew public knowledge?

I'd ask Travis, but he just made it perfectly clear that he is happy to just ignore everything difficult for the rest of the trip. Carl is too unstable to talk to about this, and besides, his status is just as dubious as mine. For a while I thought I was hitting a brick wall whenever I tried to find information on how Atlas 2's social structures work because, like Carl, I'm an ex-asset. Both of us arrived on this ship still wearing the security bangle designed to keep us off the Internet entirely. It was only after we complained a week into the trip that they removed them. Then there was some debate over whether I had the correct clearance on Atlas 2's servers. I wasn't known by the Circle—even though I came aboard with that weird group of scientists masquerading as a cult— so I hadn't got anything except swift, last-minute permission to come on the ship from the US gov-corp and was effectively an unknown quantity. I still have the feeling that if it had been several months until Rapture, instead of only days, Carl and I wouldn't have got our places here at all. They would have had the time and resources available to kill him and keep the secret of Rapture safe without his father's knowledge.

Cheery thought.

I sigh. Even now, several months into the trip and with the same security clearance as the average Circle member, I still can't get a sense of my place here. If I could lose myself in mersives like I used to, it wouldn't bother me. But I'm aimless, drifting, trying to find a way to fill all this unstructured time I used to crave having. Any queries regarding contacting anyone related to command simply result in the ship AI directing me to Carl's father, the de facto leader of the Circle. Any attempts to find other passengers online are quickly shut down by the AI, citing strict privacy rules. There's no crew or passenger manifest that I can find online, and even the booking system for the rare public spaces on the ship isn't designed in such a way that allows me to see who else has booked individual slots; they're just listed as "unavailable."

If I hadn't seen the other shuttles on the way up to the ship, I'd have suspected that the Circle was the only group on board. But I also saw the size of Atlas 2 and there's no way any gov-corp would have built something on this scale if it wasn't meant to be packed full of people.

But it isn't just a desire to find some way to understand life on board. Like Carl, I want to know who was responsible for what we saw happen to Earth. Unlike him, I don't feel any desire to press for prosecution; I lost faith in any sort of gov-corp justice many years ago. I just want to know, to have someone I can focus all this nebulous, miserable pain on. Someone I can point to in my head and say, "It was your fault." Not having that is surprisingly hard to cope with.

Without the names of the people in charge, I'm stuck. They are the most likely to have given the order to start that nuclear war, or at least to know who did. Though with the way information is locked down on this ship, I'm not sure how far I'll get without better access privileges.

It would be easier if the ship was organized differently, but it's been designed to keep people in the groups they arrived in without any opportunities to mix with anyone else. Carl's father, Mr. Moreno, said that it's to keep the social focus around established communities, to keep a sense of continuity from Earth, throughout the journey, to the destination. I wish I could agree with him. It seems that whoever runs this ship wants to keep us all apart from one another. Considering we're going to be arriving at the same planet and that we're all, hopefully, making a new life there, this seems spectacularly shortsighted.

Perhaps there is something to be said for the approach if you are actually properly part of one of those communities. But Carl and I aren't. And he has the tie to his father to help him. I feel like the awkward ex-girlfriend dragged along to a family event, without the relationship part, thankfully. But it feels the same, everyone pegging me as the one Carl brought with him. They're nice enough, but I haven't clicked with any of them. I don't expect to. Making proper friends is something other people do. At least I assume they do actually feel things for them, rather than just going through the social motions like I do. I have Carl, and he is what I'd call my friend, and then there is everyone else. Travis . . . Travis isn't a friend, but he doesn't exactly fit easily into the category of "everyone else" either. That shared experience only hours after we came aboard, the simple fact that we were together when we watched everything we had ever known being obliterated, binds us whether we want it to or not.

Everyone else in the Circle has known one another for years, all working toward this trip. Even Travis seems comfortable with them, though he was only with them a little while. And there's something about Travis I don't trust. I'm not sure of the deal he cut to get into the Circle, but seeing as he was once married to the notoriously shady Stefan Gabor of GaborCorp fame, there must be something dodgy involved.

I sigh, knowing I can't just lie here feeling miserable. I have to take care of the meat that carries my brain around. It's not just for my own self-care, however; it's a stipulation of the contract I signed to come aboard. There's an entire page of health commitments that I've promised to adhere to, and I signed it without any bitterness whatsoever, unlike the last contract I signed that had dictated how I cared for my body. Back then it was because I was expected to put in the requisite care of a corporate asset. Now it's simple common sense. No one wants the ship's complement to arrive on the new planet and be too weak and unfit to cope.

I'll be sixty-three when we arrive. There was a time when that sounded so old to me, but now? Now one's sixties are seen as a halfway point. Maybe a third, if you're superrich and can afford all the replacements and maintenance. Travis's ex-husband famously boasted that he would live to see three hundred. I remember commissioning mersives about the tech being developed to achieve that. There are rumors that the knowledge the Pathfinder left behind includes life-extending technology. I'll believe it when I see my two hundredth birthday.

Right now, my forty-three-year-old body needs some damn exercise. I open the one storage cupboard I have, containing the only pair of shoes I own other than the soft slip-ons I'm wearing now: running shoes. There are two shallow drawers, containing the bare essentials for daily life and the only necklace I own. I haven't worn it for over thirty years. Above the drawers are two shelves upon which rest all the clothes I own save the joggers, T-shirt and sweatshirt I'm wearing. There's another set, exactly the same as these, in there, plus pajamas I have no intention of ever wearing and an extra blanket. It's taken me all of these six months to stop viewing them as prison garb. They were waiting for me, packaged in bioplastic when I arrived, just like the toothbrush and everything else in the bathroom. It makes sense that they mass-produced them on that lunar base for use on the ship. We weren't allowed to bring any clothes other than the ones we wore on the day of Rapture. Every kilogram of weight that wasn't part of our bodies had to be strictly accounted for. It doesn't bother me as much as I thought it would.

Just as I'm lacing my shoes there's a knock on the door and I freeze. Has Travis come looking for reconciliation already? "Who is it?" I whisper to my APA.

"Gabriel Moreno," Ada's voice "whispers" back to me.

"Come in," I call, and Carl's father enters.

He's the kind of man my old manager would have called a silver fox; old enough to be distinguished and respected, blessed with a full head of white hair, and still attractive. The resemblance between him and his son is obvious enough; the same big brown eyes and Spanish set to his jawline.

His smile is brief and he slides the door shut behind him to stand just inside the room, clearly not wanting to invade the tiny space too much. "Hi," he says, gaze dropping to my running shoes. "I won't keep you long." There is only the slightest hint of a Spanish accent in his voice now.

I smooth the Velcro closure of the left shoe and stand. Just as I'm about to say something, I close my mouth again. Thinking that he's here to ask what is wrong with his son is childish speculation. We're all adults here and I am not his son's keeper.

"Take a seat," I say instead, waving a hand at the bed in the absence of a chair.

He perches on the edge of it. We're all getting used to this now, most of us adopting that slightly uncomfortable position to show that we're aware we're in someone else's sleeping space. I sit on my pillow, leaving as much of the length of the bed between us as possible.

"I've been thinking about a conversation I had with Carl a couple of days ago," he begins. Something about the way he is looking at me, slightly nervous, makes me wonder what the hell Carl has been saying about me. "And . . . and he said that he felt that you need a purpose here."

I fold my arms. "Oh, he did, did he?" I try to hide my irritation behind a veneer of wry amusement. I can't believe

Carl would say that. But I can believe his father would have interpreted some vague concern he may have expressed about his friend and translated it into this. Carl and I understand each other. We don't tell other people about what we need. His dad is just really bad at trying to find an excuse to "help" me.

I doubt this is going to turn into anything interesting anyway; I can't see how any of my former skills could be put to use. There's no entertainment network on the ship producing new content—at least, as far as I'm aware—so I can't commission new material as I used to on Earth. Sure, I have transferable skills, no doubt. But with no idea what most people do with their time on board, that's just an assumption.

Not that I want to be plugged back into some corporate hierarchy. Maybe I should shut this down before it goes too far. I hated my old job. I never chose to do it, in any sense, and I resented every moment of my life that it stole from me to pay the debt that had been forced upon me by the hothousers.

But if there's a transferable skill I do have in spades, it's keeping my thoughts to myself and hiding how I feel while I work out what the best possible outcomes are. If he does have an idea of how to give me something to do that can change my status here, maybe I can make some progress on finding the ones responsible for the war. I can't find the information I need while stuck in the liminal space I occupy on the fringes of the Circle. If I can find a way to be useful to more people on this ship, I'm more likely to get better data access privileges.

Of course, Gabriel has no idea what my true motivations are, so I fix a hopeful expression on my face, playing the part of someone who believes this kind, fatherly man has come to fix a little problem that his son kindly brought to his attention. "I must admit, I have been . . . finding it challenging to have so much time on my hands," I say, choosing the words carefully. I don't want to tell him how unfocused I've been, how despondent. And I want him to think I'm enthusiastic, but not too much. "It would be good to feel useful again."

"Oh, I understand. To be honest, I would be worried if you didn't feel this way. I'm sure this is the reason Carl is struggling so much. But he won't talk to me about it."

I see the opening, the hope in his eyes that I will give him enough information and insight into his son's problems that he'll be able to build a bridge with them. Carl rarely talks about his father and never about what happened between them in the past. At some point, the man sitting on my bed must have screwed up so catastrophically as a parent that his son fell into slavery. Is he even aware of that?

I know his son far better than he does, and there is a value in knowing something another is desperate to understand. I pull the pillow out from under me, taking my time repositioning it against the wall to give me the chance to weigh up the transaction opportunity laid before me. Keeping this man on my side, making him believe he can trust me, will serve me well. Gabriel has the highest status of all the people I know here and most probably has access to all the information I need too.

But I'm not willing to sell Carl's trust in me. At least, not for something as minor as his father's goodwill. That said, Gabriel's seen how much weight he's lost. That's no secret.

"Carl is in a really tough place right now," I say. "I just don't know how to help him, to be honest, and it's so hard to see him suffering."

Gabriel nods, his shoulders slumping. "It is hard, yes. And even harder when you are the reason why he is the way he is."

"No!" I say, pretending to be aghast at the suggestion. "He's a grown man and he has to find a way to move forward, regardless of what happened in his past. And it's complicated with him. The food thing . . . I don't know where that comes from. And you're completely right; he has too much time on his hands. Carl has one of the keenest minds I know. I've seen the way he solves puzzles, how driven he was bringing people to justice. He's floundering without that purpose in his life."

I don't tell him the reason why he is that way. That his son was conditioned, sometimes violently, to be unable to leave a case unsolved. Even though he seems to feel culpable for his son's problems, I don't know if Gabriel is aware of the indenture we both suffered under. If he isn't, and Carl realizes that I told his father, he'd never forgive me, just as I'd never forgive anyone who gave that away about my past without my permission.

"He is very lucky to have such a good friend," Gabriel says.

"I just wish I could do more," I say. Was that too much? No, he seems to have bought it.

He clears his throat. "I haven't managed to find anything for Carl yet, but I have found an opening for you. I asked around and had a chat with a few people about your skills. Told them you were keen to contribute. Americans like that."

Asked around? How did he do that? How did he chat with people who were presumably outside of the Circle? I'm desperate to ask, but I keep that desire in check, concentrating on channeling that hunger into the portrayal of an underemployed woman waiting for good news.

"I can't promise it will be as interesting as your last job," he continues. "And of course, if it turns out to be something unsuitable, there's no obligation to carry on . . ."

"Mr. Moreno," I say with a smile, "just having an opportunity is wonderful. What is it?"

"Just analysis, to begin with, rather than anything creative." He says it apologetically, but my breath catches with excitement. Analysis means data, and that's the only thing I'm interested in. "They want a second opinion on mersive consumption trends from someone with experience."

"What's the analysis for? Are they making anything new during the trip?"

He shrugs. "I have no idea, sorry. If you're interested, I'll let them know and they'll tell you more."

"I'm more than interested! I'm thrilled!" I don't have to amp up the enthusiasm very much at all. Analysis of consumption trends inevitably means information on the people consuming the mersives. Even if it doesn't lead me to my targets—and there's every chance it could, depending on how they process the data—it will give me an insight into the other people on board. That's something.

He beams at my excitement and claps his hands. "¡Muy bueno! I'll let them know." He stands and I do too, shaking his offered hand with both of mine.

"Was it hard to set up?" I ask. "It's just that I've tried to find other people to talk to, just socially, and I've been getting nowhere."

"Social contact is deprioritized between groups, but this was different. Just a couple of chats, as I said, and then final sign-off before I could offer it."

Final sign-off. So there *is* a hierarchy. "Well, thank goodness for a chief media officer who's willing to give an unknown like me a chance." I bait the hook . . .

And he bites: "Oh, there's no CMO; it was Commander Brace who approved it."

"Well, thank goodness for her!" Another little conversational maggot goes on the hook.

"Him," he says, reaching for the little hollow handle in the door, ready to slide it across. He pauses. "You . . . you will tell me if there is anything I can do to help Carlos, won't you?"

I rest my hand on his shoulder. "Of course, Mr. Moreno."

"Gabriel," he says, glancing at me over his shoulder. "Call me Gabriel, please."

"I'll see you soon, Gabriel. And thanks again."

He slides the door open and I close it after he has left to rest my forehead against it, grinning into the plastic.

Travis may not be willing to do anything, but I am. Finally, I have a purpose again. Not to make people higher up the gov-corp ladder richer, not to pay off a debt, but instead to get an answer to the question that's been plaguing me since I watched everything end. But there's another question close on its heels, one I am incapable of answering yet. Will it be enough?

3

AFTER REMEMBERING THAT I need to go for a run and doing some stretches, I receive a notification from my APA just as I'm about to leave my cabin. My user privileges have been changed, giving me access to a new set of data. There's an e-mail from someone called Carolina Johnson, introducing herself in the briefest of terms as a former entertainment executive of Knifepoint, a high-profile subsidiary of the US gov-corp that produced some of the most successful media franchises of the past twenty years. She's sketchy on what her role is here, simply explaining that she wants me to take a look at the consumption data she's linked to and give my first impressions.

It's so broad a request I suspect this is actually just a test of my ability. I wouldn't put it past her to seed some rogue data in there just to see how I respond to it. She says I can take a couple of days if I need to. I decide I'll get it to her in half the time.

I'm not concerned about whether I'll be able to do it; this

was one of the core skills in my previous position on Earth. AIs are great for crunching data, for giving pointers at where trends are. Any crappy machine intelligence can generate pretty graphs, after all. Where the skill comes in, and critically where the need for a human being comes into play, is the interpretation of all that data. AIs can do it in lots of industries, but when it comes to entertainment, to predicting what people in their millions will want to consume, there haven't been any reliable AI results. Not that there have been many reliable human ones either; we all accept that we can only make educated guesses. But there are a couple of things that AIs fundamentally don't have that we do: instinct and empathy, and both are needed in my old line of work. If you're incapable of understanding how it feels to have an emotional reaction to something someone else has created, you're screwed. If you can understand it well enough to not only commission great entertainment but also get what you want in meatspace, life is so much easier.

It makes me wonder whether Johnson is planning to commission some new material from people on board the ship. There must be creatives among the thousands of passengers. Of course, there will be limitations on what can be produced. No hugely expensive director-vision pieces here, filmed with actual real-world sets, unless there's someone who wants to make something set on the ship. Those pieces appealed only to a small audience anyway, relegated to catering to a wealthy niche of people who swore you can tell the difference between a real tree and a genned one. But I'm thinking too far ahead. I'll get the report done first and then see what she really has planned for me.

I go out into the corridor and walk briskly to the end so I can start jogging along the main passageway that runs around the central accommodation blocks. There the corridor is only wide enough for two people to walk side by side—and still close to each other even then—but back where my cabin is, the corridor is even narrower. This route is better for running and has the added advantage of forming a circuit that is just under half a kilometer in length. While my APA keeps track of my time, it still gives me a sense of satisfaction to mentally tick the distance off in the old-fashioned way.

I stretch out my hamstrings one last time, my APA detecting the cue to start up my physx program. My heart rate appears as a small green number in the top right of my vision, along with a timer. Then there's the bark from the end of the wide corridor.

I can't help but smile; I always do when I hear Dragon's Ghost. I look over my shoulder as I finish the stretch and the husky is there, tail wagging, front paws bouncing up and down off the floor in his excitement. He barks at me again, as if to say, "Come on! Let's go already!" His eyes are the color of a clear sky on a cold winter's day and the fur of his muzzle is a brilliant white, darkening into grays and charcoal black over the rest of his body. His paws are white, and a little patch of fur on his chest too. He tips his head to the left as I look at him, the sharp excited bark from before now turning into a low meandering note, closer to a quiet howl that sounds like he's trying to talk to me.

I know he's just an Augmented Reality construct, generated by my neural chip, which is tricking my brain into thinking I can see and hear him. But it still makes me happy. And it makes these tedious daily runs bearable. I set off and he yelps with delight, dashing off round the corner, leaving only the sound of his claws on the hard floor echoing back to me.

It's impossible to catch him, but I try anyway, the AR running in concert with the physx program, ensuring that Dragon's Ghost behaves in exactly the right way to keep me motivated and my pacing optimal. He's always just ahead, close enough to trick some part of my brain into thinking that I can catch him if I just pick up the pace a little. When he disappears around a corner, I want to keep running to keep sight of him. If I slow down too much, he'll poke his head back round to bark at me. If I stop, he'll whine and stare at me judgmentally. That husky is a better personal trainer for me than any human could ever be.

Three kilometers into the run I've only seen one person, Geena, heading back to her cabin. We've said hello to each other a couple of times but nothing more. She's also from Norope, despite being a member of the Circle, but she doesn't seem very interested in getting to know me. It looked like she was coming back from the lab on the other side of the accommodation blocks, one of the many rooms I don't have access to as a peripheral member of this group. I have no interest in labs, so it doesn't bother me, but it does make me wonder what it would be like to have another place to go to in meatspace.

My APA flashes up a notification of a new message. I usually ignore them until I've finished a run, but it's another message from Carolina, so I ask Ada to read it to me.

Hi Dee,

I noticed from your profile that you were a serious gamer back on Earth. If you're interested in a challenge, there's a locked server for leets who don't need in-game enhancements to win. I've given you access if you're feeling brave.

CJ

I stop, too distracted by the prospect of finding an actual leet gaming space to keep my legs working at the same time.

Dragon's Ghost peers back round the corner he's just whipped round at full pelt, giving an uncertain whine. I raise a hand, patting the air to tell him I'll be with him in a moment without really thinking about what I'm doing. With a tiny groaning growl deep in his throat he lies down, head on front paws, watching me.

I'd heard about elite servers before, back on Earth, but could never find anyone who'd give me an in. They'd had an almost mythical status, dropped into online conversations in passing with the same mixture of reverence and disbelief in their existence as an ethical gov-corp policy maker. Just like them, whenever anyone asked the person mentioning it for a concrete example, a link to a specific place to find one, it was all hand waving and "Oh, I heard about it from a friend of a friend."

All the rumors coalesced around a central idea: that of playing a game in which the difficulty level was determined not by the game's AI but by the player's own real-world ability.

When I first heard about it, I scoffed at the idea. Surely the whole point of gaming was to experience being better than we are in meatspace? What would be the fun in surviving a zombie apocalypse if my avatar had to stop and catch her breath all the time? How could I play my favorite ultraviolent shooters when my body and brain didn't really have the ability to pull off a decent long-range head shot?

But then the more I thought about it, the more I could see the appeal. It was the ultimate ableist velvet rope, for one thing, the sort of space that fitness freaks could go to and show off in. But more than that, it was the ultimate rejection of the idea that meatspace and gamespace were separate things. Turning the appeal of immersive gaming on its head, it combined the desire to be physically fit with the need to be seen to be the very best in a gaming space as well as in some tedious real-world gym. And it had to be for the purpose of being seen by other players; there are countless games designed to increase fitness, after all. AR has been around for bloody ages. But there's a world of difference between being able to jump over obstacles projected onto one's vision—or chasing an imaginary dog—and being able to keep up in a mersive where everyone knows that you are able to outrun slavering mooks because you are that fast for real.

I'm fitter than I've ever been, desperate to find joy in gaming again, and keen to meet other people on this ship so I can find my targets. Damn, I am tempted. After months of metaphorically banging my head against data barriers, I suddenly have new data access privileges and an invitation to a leet space. This is turning into a good day.

"Show me the leet server entry requirements," I tell my APA. A list of criteria appears, floating over the corridor in my vision. They're not the usual fare; no mention of pay grades or subscription model options. Instead there are blood pressure ranges, a requirement to be able to run a kilometer in less than six minutes, optimum VO_2 max measurements and a string of other measurement units I don't even understand. There's even stuff about reaction times and links to AR training games that can be used to measure them.

"Do I meet these?" I ask Ada.

"You have a ninety-one percent match with the required criteria." A dialog box from MyPhys appears, listing the supporting evidence for the statement.

"Can you design me a training program to get to the standard required to meet them?"

"I can. Would you like me to replace your current daily training schedule?"

"Yes. How long will it take to reach the standard required?"

"Based on current fitness levels, I estimate you will reach

the required standard in fourteen days with a two-day margin of error, if the new training program is followed every day."

"Two weeks? Bloody hell, that's far too long. I'm not that unfit!"

"Your cardiovascular fitness already meets the required level. These are the criteria that are not currently met."

Ada highlights the relevant entries in the list and brings them forward, fading the MyPhys evidence and dropping it behind.

"I have no idea what these refer to. Summarize for me."

"Reaction times, core strength and calorie consumption rate."

"Bollocks," I mutter. No shortcuts there, at least not that I'm aware of. I review the new training program and see that it still includes a daily five-kilometer run, so I start moving again, much to the husky's delight.

Carolina's invitation seems to fly in the face of the strict boundaries between the different groups on board. But then maybe I've simply been stuck in a status no-man's-land and things will start to change now. Gabriel said something about social contact between groups being deprioritized. Was that an order from the command crew or the way this ship has always been planned?

At least I know that there is actually a command crew, rather than a corporate structure, which is something. It makes me wonder whether the military have always run the project and simply exported their model to the ship, or whether the US gov-corp decided it would suit the mission better. Either way, I need to think of a way to find out more about Commander Brace without leaving a massive bread-crumb trail of searches. If he does turn out to be one of the people who gave the order to fire the nukes, he will be security conscious and I don't want him to know I've been snooping. I must not give away that we know what happened. When someone is willing to murder billions, making three people who aren't critical crew disappear would be as easy as chucking a food tray in the recycler.

Then it occurs to me that Carolina must have checked out my profile and seen my gamer scores; otherwise she wouldn't have invited me to the leet server. I open the message from her again and laugh out loud at my stupidity. Just like all messages, hers has her name at the top, which is also a link to her profile. We've made contact, she's sent an invitation . . . it would be totally legit to check hers out too.

I finish the run in record time, Dragon's Ghost yelping with delight at the speed he has to go to keep ahead of me. I end the program and he runs off down the corridor, the sound of his paws fading as the program does all it can to make the transition to plain reality as seamless as possible.

Post shower and changed into fresh clothes, I sit on my bed and open the message again, scanning the words that appear to float in front of the cupboard door. Then I tap my finger on Carolina's name and her profile loads.

A lot of it is private, the settings retained from a former high pay grade by the look of it. As far as I know, I don't have an actual pay grade or any sort of corporate position here. Absurdly, I haven't even considered it, despite the fact that if we were on Earth, I would be officially classed as a nonperson again. I guess I just assumed that all of that bullshit was behind us now, but judging by how much of her profile is locked out, maybe some of it has come with us. Maybe she is just old-school private.

There's a bare-bones curriculum vitae detailing not only an impressive career but also evidence that she was born into a wealthy family with good connections. I push away the bitterness that rises. It won't serve me here.

The gaming subsection of her hobbies and interests is far more interesting anyway. She is obviously pretty hard-core, some of her scores making me ~~feel horribly~~ inadequate. But then I look at how young she started playing those games and the insecurity eases. If I'd been playing *WorldAR* at the age of fourteen instead of fighting to survive, I'd be just as good at it as her. Fucking privilege.

I've looked at this long enough for it to be of interest to the ship AI, so I reply to her message.

Hi Carolina,

Thanks for the data and the opportunity to do some interesting work again. I'll start working on that report right after this message. It won't surprise you to know that I am excited about the invite to the leet server and I've already started training to bring up the couple of stats that need improvement to meet the entry requirements.

Looking forward to working with you (and fighting off mooks with you!),

Dee

I send it, ignoring the mild disgust that writing such false cheeriness gives me. All part of the game, sweetie, I remind myself.

Now that it's been sent off, I can go back to her profile and look at the friends she has linked to it. This is where the gold could be.

A lot of the names, and the little circles above them containing the profile pictures, are grayed out. People from back on Earth? Presumably so, now out of contact. Of course, she'll think they're grayed out because of the distances involved, not because those poor bastards are probably dead, or even worse, slowly dying. I deleted everyone on my

Earth-bound friend list the moment we left Earth and I'm glad I did. Otherwise I would have had to look at their faces when I knew what had happened to them, each deletion feeling more like a declaration of actual death, rather than merely a severing of an obsolete connection.

Carolina looks like the kind of person who friends people readily and doesn't delete for fear of hurting feelings. There are so many grayed-out people on the list that I'm sure they could populate a few floors of this ship.

I filter them out, confident that this won't be flagged as suspicious activity, given that there has been correspondence between us and that most people find others to connect to through friend lists. Over two hundred people remain, all on this ship right now.

The faces are varied. Male, female, nonbinary. Most are white faces. The names mean nothing to me. She doesn't seem to be connected to anyone in the Circle. Not even Gabriel. There must be some common link between them, but maybe that's within the ship's hierarchy, not necessarily the same as people she hangs out and games with.

Then I see it: William Brace, a man in his late forties, early fifties, wearing a US naval uniform.

Is he the Commander Brace that Gabriel mentioned, who signed off on giving me this opportunity?

I'm desperate to click on the profile but don't, thanks to the same fear of that digital trail coming back to bite me in the future. Perhaps there's another way around this.

I go back to Carolina's core profile and navigate to the list of games she plays. None of that is behind any sort of privacy line; she's obviously proud of her scores. I click on the one she's played recently, a colonization game with the standard combinations of resource management and military encounters. In seconds I find the list of people she regularly plays with, the smart profile connecting their gaming data and cross-referencing it with hers. It's designed to make it easy for her to contact those players outside of the game but it has also made it easy for me to see that Commander Brace plays this game with her. On the leet server, no less.

I punch the air in triumph. Finally, I have a lead. This Brace guy may have had nothing to do with nuking Earth, of course, but at least I can see a way to find out more about him. I'll improve my stats, join the leet server, make sure I play a game with him, giving a legit reason for me to check out his profile and then boom! Access to not only his information, but also to that of the rest of the command crew he'll be connected to.

I close the profile and lie down on the bed, tucking my hands behind my head to take stock. In a minute I'll start working on that data. It will take a matter of seconds to instruct the AI, giving it a variety of different ways to crunch the data and give me something I can work with. It will be the interpretation that will take the time. That and trying to work out the angle. Usually these reports are commissioned for a very specific purpose, like "Can we justify spending a crap ton of money on a new season of this mersive to support a new gaming module designed to increase the audience of the previous seasons?" and "Are citizen-employees in the lowest three pay grades consuming more violent mersives than those in the top three pay grades, and, if so, why?" That sort of thing.

I guess not giving me a specific purpose for the report is part of the test. Carolina will want to see what catches my eye and how I interpret it. The only thing that bothers me is whether all the years of experience I have will be of any use here. This is a strange sample group after all. The only ones I know anything about are the members of the Circle, and they are hardly average people.

"Sod it," I say to the ceiling. "I'll do my best."

It takes less than a minute to instruct Ada to carry out the first batch of data crunching. I pop out to the communal food printer before the lunchtime rush, print myself a goulash with pasta, Croatian style, and eat it alone. A glass of water later, I'm ready to dive in.

It's much easier to play with data in a virtual space, so I go in for full immersion. After the usual checks from my APA that I'm not about to try to do this while standing up, driving machinery or any of the other dumb things it already knows I'm not doing, I'm in my office.

I say office; it's more a blank slate. Literally. I've made myself a giant slab of dark gray slate that stretches in all directions as far as I can see. Above me is a night sky filled with stars. Nice and spacious, a comfortable twenty degrees Celsius and no wind.

"Okay, give it to me," I say, and Ada drops in three-dimensional graphs and Venn diagrams around me. Each one is as tall as I am and lands with a thud that I find very satisfying. I can walk up to them, pull out data points and examine outliers, all by grabbing them with my hands or simply pointing to them.

There's demographic data, a variety of graphs on consumption behavior including level of immersion, duration and other standard criteria, and on categories of mersives. There are at least ten of those and that's just for starters. Being such complex things, mersive categories can span factors as diverse as age suitability, level of realism (the definition of which is constantly argued over), whether they are recorded and replayed by the consumer or created by a third party, and level of neurophysiological integration. The latter can be a very telling metric, as it indicates the sort of experience people are looking for. In the simplest terms, it shows if they want to watch something passively or feel like they are inside the story, with different levels of immersion between the two.

Back on Earth I worked with creators of all types of mersive. Some were purely focused on the story, aiming to give the audience as much freedom to explore it in as many different ways as possible. For them, the variety of routes that people can take through a story was far more important than anything else. If there was a scene in a forest, they didn't care what species of trees were there, or even what season it was, necessarily. What mattered was what was happening there, who was saying what and how the plot was being advanced—be it through conversation with NPCs or through finding key objects or other types of information, if it was more interactive. That meant they could build the mersive using instructions to neural chips with greatly reduced cost, the chips being instructed to create the experience of a forest by triggering whatever had been encoded in the consumer's brain already. Depending on where someone had grown up, or the media they'd consumed the most, they could experience a chase through a Nordic pine forest or a dense jungle. To the creators it didn't matter, as long as the story was cohesive.

Other creatives found this approach abhorrent; for them, it was just as important to control the aesthetics of the experience. They argued that relying on a person's prior experiences to create art was elitist; what about those who'd never experienced a forest, or those for whom such environments were encoded so differently that they would negatively impact the story? Their critics in turn said that the cost of the mersives created using real locations was prohibitive to those in lower pay grades. I don't know how many hours of my life I wasted listening to advocates of each approach arguing it out in bland virtual conference rooms.

I wonder if any of those creatives are on board. It's impossible to tell without knowing the selection criteria for the other people outside of the Circle. If there's a military-style command structure, they may also have been in charge of passenger selection. JeeMuh, am I on a ship filled with thousands of soldiers? But thousands of soldiers would mean invasion . . . was the US gov-corp planning to invade the Pathfinder's colony? No, surely not. Why would—

A "new message" ping interrupts my thoughts. I accept the invitation to read it.

<I hear that Carolina has invited you to the leet server. Kudos! Want to try a new game before any of them has had a chance? I'm looking for playtesters and I think you'll like it.>

I groan at the cheesy sales tone and am just about to delete it when I remember that I haven't had any sort of spam like this for months. Somehow Carolina's message has put me on the radar. Haven't I been craving information about the people outside the Circle?

There's no signature, but there is the option to reply. I look for the profile of the sender and the lack of it confuses me. Online anonymity is illegal. Then I realize it's not a standard e-mail, but some sort of live chat that looks . . . weird.

"What the hell is this person using to talk to me?" I say aloud to Ada.

"A person-to-person chatbox."

"But how?"

"A person-to-person chatbox is—"

"No, I mean . . . is this new software?"

"This has never been used to contact you before. Would you like me to block its use?"

"No. Is it legal?"

"I cannot determine that."

"What?"

"I cannot—"

"Oh, shut up." I frown at the message. If I can't determine the sender, surely it must be illegal. I grin and rub my hands together. Brilliant.

I tap my finger on the reply option and have my APA turn my speech into text. <I'm listening.>

<Free right now?>

<*If* I decide to play, it'll be in a couple of hours. I have some work I need to do first.>

<K. I'll send you a key. Eat and drink first. It'll be intense and you won't want to stop in the middle of the story.>

Whoever this is, they are one cocky bastard. Intense? I'll be the judge of that. <Who are you?>

<A friend.>

I actually laugh out loud. They've played too many spy mersives; that's for certain. <So it's like that then? Okay.>

<You gonna play?>

<Maybe. Would help if I knew who you are and more about the game.>

<I told you: a friend. What do you have to lose? The game will help you achieve your goal. It won't be a waste of time.>

<It helps with training?>

<Yeah. You in?>

<K. Send me the key.>

<Look behind you.>

"You are fucking joking," I whisper to myself, but still turn around. On the floor behind me there's a box made from solid black glass. It's only the size of my fist, but it freaks me out.

"Ada, did you give anyone access to my mersive?"

"No access has been requested."

I point at the box. "Then what the cocking hell is that?"

"A box."

"Jesus fucking wept," I mutter beneath my breath. <How did you do that?>

<I'm leet, baby.>

Must be a bloke, and a young one at that. Do I really want to play in a mersive created by someone who clearly has dodgy opinions about boundaries?

Of course I do. He can't do anything to me in a mersive. And who knows? It might break me out of my gaming slump. <You show-off. Okay, I'm in.>

4

IT'S HARD TO work with that black box behind me, tempting me, but soon enough I am so absorbed in my task that I actually forget about it. Even though I thought I wasn't missing my old job, there's no denying that digging into the data, making notes, testing theories and seeing if the data bears them out gives me so much pleasure. It's the sense of total mental absorption that I love, the fading of my own noisy mind into the background with only the work filling the space. When I'm looking at the data, finding different ways to slice it up and examine it, there's just the right balance of total objectivity in the form of the numbers and the subjectivity of my interpretation. The data is both rigid in its accuracy and malleable in my hands. The thrust of the report soon coalesces in my mind, so swiftly, in fact, that I hold off writing it for a while. I'm always suspicious when the data seems to support any prediction made before I start the work.

The prediction as it stands is also too simplistic: that

people will be using mersives more than usual and that they will be favoring personally recorded mersives rather than consumables. Any idiot could hypothesize that, and it would be embarrassing to send that in to Carolina, even with a stack of evidence behind it. Of course people are spending time in their recordings of home. We're all crammed into a huge traveling skyscraper, hurtling through space at terrifying speed, for heaven's sake. We're homesick. Well, they are, anyway.

What's of more interest—and will make a better report—is an analysis of the elements these personal mersives have in common. It would be impossible for me to download one of their recordings and experience it myself, as neural chips simply don't work that way, partly because of the distribution of memory across the brain and the fact that that differs from person to person, and partly by design. In the early days of immersion technology, people did attempt to share personal recordings, driven inevitably by the porn industry. But then people started sharing murders, violent attacks as both the perpetrator and the victim and even heart attacks. Human beings are mostly garbage, after all. When one particular recording caused the death of thirty men in one night, the firmware was radically overhauled. Part of the problem was the very fact that the recordings could not be experienced in exactly the same way as the person recording them had. The neural chips were simply doing their best to reproduce the physiological experience, and when that was someone dying of a coronary in a bootleg mersive with dodgy settings designed to override a person's MyPhys safeguards, that meant driving heart rates and blood pressure to dangerous levels.

Now the firmware has been updated many times, and the software is far more sophisticated too. I can't walk around a room someone has recorded, experiencing it like they can, but I can look at the raw code used to re-create it. All the little markers such as "temperature twenty degrees Celsius" or "Walls: emulsion paint #3498DB" are encoded in each recording. It is possible to make a nonimmersive render of another person's recording, but it's never accurate and doesn't give sensory feedback—feeling more like a cheap game render. And of course, it has none of the emotional attachment, or the unique perspective given by looking through that person's eyes.

With the help of my APA, I start calling up all these tags, the AI automatically sorting them into broad categories. I look at the frequency and range of elements, across individuals and different chunks of population. Then I get that tingle, that sort of flutter in my throat when I know I'm onto something. This data looks weird as fuck.

I knew that the demographic data would be unusual; there isn't a single person on this ship who is over sixty-five, and there are only a handful of people over sixty, Gabriel being one of them. Ninety percent are between the ages of twenty and forty. Fine, that's to be expected. The youngest people who have data here are nineteen, but there's every possibility there are children on board. They won't be chipped until their late teens though, so they wouldn't appear in this data set anyway.

But what's strange is the massive difference in element tags for those under forty. A look at the frequency and range of the elements in personally recorded mersives consumed by people aged forty and above shows a very broad distribution. They incorporate a vast array of environments, from deserts to forests to moorland. Lots of coastal element tags too. There is a normal range of solo and group mersives too, and while I can't see who the people are in those mersives, I would guess they are recordings of parties, special occasions and perhaps large-scale public events. For individuals, it's even possible to deduce when they found out they'd made the cut and got a place on board Atlas 2, by noting the sudden increase in number of recordings, particularly those made in natural environments. They were building a bank of perfectly recorded memories of Earth to take with them. In short, the same sort of data I'd expect to see in a population of people who knew they were leaving Earth for good.

But the data for the under-forties is bizarre. It's an incredibly limited range of element tags. In the younger people's mersives, the trees are less diverse, but that could be because they are limited to one continent. That's interesting too; they all seem to be American. Only species of flora or fauna indigenous to North America have been tagged. Okay, fine, the US gov-corp picked the younger ones from the home crop, unlike the Circle, who cherry-picked their members from all over the world. Given the way the US has been since the 2020s, it doesn't surprise me that they haven't ever traveled outside of their home country.

It's when I look at the data for individuals that I start to feel really freaked-out. The first thing that leaps out at me is the lack of the "Oh shit, I'm leaving Earth forever, I better go record everything" spike. Not only is it nonexistent, but the sheer number of personally recorded mersives is way below average. I pluck out ten individuals at random and expand out their data. Each is characterized by low numbers of mersives, an impoverished environmental tag range (implying that these people didn't travel much at all) and zero mersives featuring other people.

Surely that's an error? I carry out a quick analysis of that specific data element for that population, and only ten percent of them have personally recorded mersives that feature other people.

Am I on a ship full of introverts? It wouldn't be a bad thing. But Americans tend to prefer the extroverted approach to corporate life. Lots of socializing within your corporate department or where you live—often both are one and the same thing. Lots of meetings. Lots of talks and outreach programs to spread best practice and religious ideals.

I twitch. I haven't noticed anything that suggests churches or religious iconography, but that wouldn't be something I would look for unprompted, being the filthy atheist that I am. With a smirk, I remember the interview when they were evaluating my suitability. The data from my chip had already told them I didn't practice a religion, which for some Americans would have eliminated me entirely. Perhaps the people in charge of my fate back then reasoned that no religion was better than one of the long list from other cultures that they really didn't like. By the time I was in the tiny town close to the border of the Circle's land, waiting in a frigid air-conditioned room for the interviewer to arrive, I'd already worked out my angle.

The US gov-corp's evaluator had the archetypal strong American jaw, bronze tan and incredibly white and even teeth. His name was . . . probably Chad or Brett or something. I remember him lacing his fingers together and leaning forward, taking a breath before asking the next question. His hesitation told me that it was going to be about faith. It was the critical divider between our formerly close nations, after all.

"So, I see that you don't practice a religion," he said.

"It's difficult to go to church in my corporate sector," I said with a sprinkling of sadness. "It's actively frowned upon," I added sotto voce.

He shook his head sadly. "I know it can be tough over the pond. Would you go to church if it didn't reflect badly upon you?"

I paused, pretending to be nervous about my reply. "Is there any way this interview will get back to my employers?"

He leaned in, lowered his voice too. "No. It will be shared with my boss, but no one else."

"I would," I said, looking down as if it were something to be embarrassed about. "I went when I was really small, to a church that still did services regularly. I still think about it."

He smiled. "Tell me about that."

"My grandmother took me. She was Polish—well, her mother and father were. She moved to Norope when she was a babe in arms. I can remember incense . . . the sound of the voices . . . like everyone's singing was lifting something to God. I felt safe and happy there. Held, I suppose."

His eyebrow had twitched at the mention of God. "So you're a woman of faith, then?"

"I could never admit it at home, but here, I feel I can." I looked him in the eye then, portraying a woman who had carried that terrible, shameful secret all her adult life and could finally set it down at his feet. "I do believe in God. And I pray, often, but inside my head. You know what I mean?"

And he looked at me with such sadness and such . . . what even was that? A strange sort of joy, I think. "I think there are a lot of people in England who feel the same way."

It was hard not to yell at him about crappy assumptions. "It can be hard to keep it private," I said, bedding into the lie to stop myself from ranting about how everyone in England was getting along just fine without all their hypocritical religious bollocks. "And to live by my principles in a place like that. If you note the mersives I've personally commissioned, none of them explore religious themes at all."

"I did notice that."

"It's because the network has an antireligious agenda. There's no way they'd let me put something together that was unbiased, let alone faith positive. I guess it was cowardly of me, but I worked damn hard for that position and I didn't want to be ostracized."

"They do that there, for real?"

I nodded. "I would have been sidelined, maybe even sacked, if I made a fuss about it."

He said nothing for at least a minute. I think he was genuinely shocked. I knew then that he believed every steaming lie I'd just spouted at him. Like most people, he was happy to believe whatever confirmed his view of the world. Once I'd made him think I was a victim of that godless hellhole England, he was on my side.

"Do you believe the Pathfinder knew the way to find God?"

"I don't know what she thought she was looking for, but it always seemed strange to me that she built a spaceship to go to find him."

"Why do you say that?"

"Because God is here," I said with a shrug, as if it were the most obvious thing in the world. "I feel like he's always with me. Why the need to travel such a long way to find him?"

He sat back then, and I worried I'd taken the lie too far. I do that sometimes, even believing what I'm saying in the moment. Like assuming a character and starting to forget I'm just role-playing. "If that's the case, why do you want to join the new mission to follow her?"

I brightened then, making my eyes sparkle with enthusiasm. "Because it's the only way I can see more of what God made for us."

I'm laughing now, at the memory of all that bullshit. But hey, it worked. They let me in. And that guy—JeeMuh, why can't I remember his name?—even gave me a hug at the end of the interview. It was so hard not to push him away, but I endured it. I wonder if he's somewhere on the ship now. Not everyone made the final cut; I know that from overhearing a conversation between Gabriel and someone else I didn't see as they talked around a corner on one of my runs. I kind of hope he didn't make it; otherwise he might seek me out to go pray together or something equally awful.

All of the Americans I met before Rapture were very open about their Christianity. Most wore a cross either on a necklace or on a ring or a tiepin. There was iconography everywhere, creating a genuine culture shock when I arrived at the airport and saw a twenty-meter-high mosaic of Jesus welcoming all visitors with a glowing, holy smile. That's why the lack of element tags relating to Jesus, to crosses, to church, in the people under forty is really confusing me. To be American is to be openly, passionately religious. As far as I knew, all the people who were uncomfortable with that emigrated over fifty years ago. Lots of them came to Norope, in fact, and were welcomed into communities built around the other major religion: corporate profit. The only difference was that in England and indeed Norope, it was possible to worship at that altar alone, without paying any attention to God. I had a good friend whose parents had left New York when the religious Far Right made life unbearable. "There's a strange symmetry to it," I remember him saying as we discussed it over wine one night. "I mean, all those hundreds of years ago people left England because they were too hard-core for the religious folk here. Now people are leaving the US because they're not hard-core enough!"

Even though I'm confused by the way the data doesn't match my impression of Americans, I'm kind of relieved. I was worried that once we reached the final destination, we'd all be forced into church every bloody five minutes. But judging from this data, ninety percent of the people on board don't care enough about all the trappings of Christianity to revisit it in their mersives. Of course, it could be that they still have faith; they just don't depend on memories of churches. No, it's more than that; the element tags for the iconography should at least be there as background features; it's so hard to record anything in the States without picking up something religious in the background. Even on hiking trails, there are crosses carved into signposts and Bible quotes at the tops of maps. Wherever these people recorded their mersives, it wasn't in the usual places.

How should I handle this in the report? If I was of a higher pay grade than Carolina, I'd be able to find her data and see whether she's one of the over-forty-year-olds who like going to their local church from back home when they're feeling homesick. But as I have no pay grade to speak of, all of the data I can see is anonymized.

It's too glaring a fact to ignore. Perhaps I could mention it, but focus instead on what they are consuming. Then it gets even weirder.

These people either have a really small number of personally recorded mersives, or simply favor a very select few of them. I can see that most of them are replaying the same mersive once or twice a day. The over-forties are playing a far wider range and spending at least two hours a day in them. The freakish demographic only spends thirty minutes a day immersed, at the most. Then I drill down into that data. All of the mersives they are consuming are exactly thirty minutes long.

"Who the fuck are you people?" I mutter to myself.

I turn my attention back to those element tags, and filter out the people who don't show this limited mersive consumption behavior. My APA helps me to sift through the categories and different ways of organizing the data until I see groups of people consuming mersives with exactly the same collections of tags. From those, I can tell which environments each set of people lived in. Examining the broad categories in greater detail, I can divide those people into more distinct groups, each one formed of approximately 150 people.

Groups of people who lived together before Rapture? Maybe they trained together for the trip. Yeah, that makes sense. So why does this make me feel unsettled?

Looking up Carolina's profile again, I see that she is in her fifties, making it pretty much impossible that she is in one of these groups. I double-check the ages of the people who show that pattern of mersive consumption and element tags, and confirm that the eldest of them is thirty-nine years and nine months old.

Then it hits me; they were all born after the Pathfinder left. A coincidence? Or evidence that the US gov-corp had the data from the Pathfinder's capsule pretty much from the time she sealed it, and started planning straight away, setting up training camps for the people they planned to send after her? There needn't be anything sinister about that, of course. It's efficient. Keeps costs down. Like specialized schools, I guess. But what about the families of these people? Were kids recruited and the parents told they would be ultimately sent to another planet?

I try to shrug off my worry. Who cares how the US gov-corp prepped their passengers? But the fact remains that twenty years from now, I'll have to live with those people in a potentially hostile environment, light-years away from home.

The report is almost a secondary concern now, but I have to do it nonetheless. What have I missed? I go back through my workings, then do one last analysis looking for any under-forties who don't fit into those strange groups. There are thirty who don't. Only thirty? JeeMuh.

I pull the information on them and it couldn't be more different from that on the others in their age bracket. There are dozens of trappings of wealth in their mersives: interiors of private jets, particular brands of bags and clothing and jewelry, and a far wider range of environmental tags than in the mersives of many of the over-forties on board. These people were well traveled. Adventurous, one could deduce, given that several of them have mersives that look like they've been recorded in places all over the world. Though I bet if I rendered some of these to have a poke about, the environments would be different six-star hotels, rather than places where real people live.

Less than a minute of reading through the lists of mersive element tags and I know those thirty people fit into another demographic, one that is not well represented in the total data set I've been given; they are superrich. Or were, on Earth. They probably bought their places on board. Maybe I'm doing them a disservice, but by the look of these lifestyles, it's unlikely that they were world-class scientists or moral philosophers or any other kind of person who may actually be useful. Fucking parasites.

They're consuming slightly more mersives than average for that demographic, though interestingly fewer personally recorded ones. Are they less homesick? Or are their third-party mersives so bloody good they pick those to feel better instead of memories from home?

Thinking about my tiny cabin, its plain plastic walls and ceiling, I can't imagine anyone who came from their world being able to cope. I'd expect to see far higher levels of mersives—right up to safety limits—but they seem to be coping fine. I laugh, bitterly, as I realize that those people won't have the same sort of cabin as me. For all I know, they're living on some swanky deck with huge suites of rooms with champagne fountains and plants everywhere.

"It's all just a game," I whisper to myself. It's just that some people are born with cheat codes.

It's all grist for the report mill though. I decide to write it all up. Sod it. If I leave any of this out, I'll look incompetent, and I'd rather look like I know how to do my job. If any of this is news to Carolina, then she may help me to find out more. Though with that said, if she games in the leet server with Commander Brace, she's likely to know all this stuff already. My report won't offer any judgment, nor will it express any of the feelings I have on these groups of consumers. The only place I'll get creative is where I suggest ways to use this analysis. I'll stick to targeting the over-forties for that. They are the greatest consumers and could well benefit from some new material, something to wean them off hankering for home and get them looking forward instead. Yeah, that's the thrust I'll make.

An hour later it is done. I take a moment to enjoy the sense of satisfaction that floods through me as I send it off. Only then do I allow myself to turn around in my virtual office and pick up the obsidian box.

It's been coded to be heavy and cold to the touch, the sort of box that a director I once worked with would have used as a prop in a mersive to hold the horrors of the world or something equally pretentious. I lift the lid and it even squeaks menacingly, making me laugh. There's an old-fashioned metal key inside, the sort I've handled only in historical mersives. It's the size of my hand, chunky, bronze, with an ornate bow molded into the shape of the letter *A*, replete with tendrils and flowers weaving around it.

As soon as I take it out of the box, the outline of a door appears in the slate floor ahead of me. The line becomes more defined, taking on depth as an actual slate door forms, then rises until it stands in front of me. This is pretty slick. Of course, I can't stop myself from peeping round behind the door, but the floor is just plain slate once again.

There's a keyhole, obviously, in a plate also made of bronze. I put the key into it and turn, feeling a solid clunk as the mechanism tumbles within. Opening it reveals a dark corridor, too dimly lit for me to be able to see anything more than the suggestion of a way ahead. I set the box down and step into the corridor. A couple of paces in I turn and note that my office space is no longer behind me. Instead there's just a long, dark corridor that stretches back, lit at the far end by a flickering lightbulb. There are no doors off it.

Okay. This is creepy and atmospheric. Good use of lighting, slight smell of mold, which is a nice touch, and it's darker ahead of me than behind, which is always enough to get the heart beating faster. Maybe this is good enough for me to actually get into it. JeeMuh, I hope so. He didn't mention genre, but I'm guessing this is horror. Doesn't usually work on me, but I'll give it a try.

I walk forward, the sound of my shoes on the floor suggesting it's made of concrete. There's a rattling sound as I move, and I tap my pocket, feeling something inside. I reach inside and pull out a small box with a rough edge that feels familiar, but I can't place it. I shake it and hear . . . matches! That's what they are. I haven't used these since I was a kid! Striking a match and smelling the aroma that soon follows make me feel small again. I use the light from the lit match to look at the box and shudder when I see it's exactly the same brand as I used back then.

Taking a breath, I tell myself that he must have coded this with element tags, rather than a designed render, and my chip has simply re-created the specific brand—only brand— of matches it has seen. I look at the silhouette of the dancing lady on the box until the flame burns too low and I have to strike another. The smell tugs me back, but I resist the memories and look around. I've been given the matches to create light, so he must have put something worth seeing in the corridor. First basic rule of gaming; if an interactive object is placed in a pretty featureless environment like this one, it's for a reason.

Something pale and thin is lying on the floor near my feet. A candle! There's a holder next to it, so I light the wick, drop the box of matches back into my pocket and press the candle base into the holder. It's one of the really old-fashioned ones, with a small black metal plate to catch dripping wax and a little loop of metal for me to put my finger through so I can hold it steady.

The increased light reveals the end of the corridor in front of me, opening out into a bigger room, rather than ending in a door. There's paint on the wall, flaking in places, and I brush my fingers over it, feeling it crumble away. There's something so horribly familiar about this place, and I keep telling myself it's just the way it's been coded, but it feels like more than that.

Pushing on, more to shake off the horrible sense of knowing this place is bad in some way than for any other reason, I reach the end of the corridor and see that the room opens up into a basement filled with pipes. Before I can stop myself I am turning to my right, unable to resist looking for the nest made of cardboard boxes and biofoam that I know is there. At the sight of it, I drop the candle, plunging the room I know all too well into total darkness.

5

WHEN MY THOUGHTS finally order themselves, I find myself pressed against the wall between two massive pipes with no memory of moving here. The concrete is cold at my back; I can hear the familiar sound of water moving through the pipes . . . it's all too accurate for a memory, let alone a bloody mersive! I'm on the brink of ending immersion but I can't come up from this yet, not less than a minute after I started. I'm too proud for that. So I take a couple of deep breaths and remind myself that it's a game. A totally fucked up one, but a game nonetheless.

It takes two lit matches to find the fallen candle and a third to relight it. The shadows cast by the pipes, the rough gray concrete floor, the way the nest sags to one side like it's about to topple over at any moment . . . shit, it is so real. Even the smell—a mixture of machine oil, damp and the grease used around some of the pipe joints—is exactly as it was in the real basement this replicates. The dimensions of the space, the way the footprint of the building has been divided up, creating this smaller area for all the pipework and waste processing . . . it's absolutely spot-on.

How has he achieved this? How has he made a game feel as authentic as a personally recorded mersive? Even if he had a list of the element tags one would use to create the basement and instructed my chip to use only versions I'd personally experienced before, the render wouldn't be this accurate.

Still pressed against the cold and damp concrete blocks, I run through different possibilities, eliminating each one as soon as I consider it. He couldn't have hacked a mersive of this place; I was chipped years after I last stepped foot in this room and I never brought my bear down here, so he couldn't have found a recording of it with just visuals and sound. I mean . . . fuck . . . only two people in the whole world knew about that nest over there, and the other one is dead. The only explanation that survives through lack of contrary evidence is that the one who made this game is a genius. He knew about Carolina's invite to the leet server. Did he find out about that because he is part of that community and had a say in inviting me? This makes me think he's not only a leet gamer, but a leet programmer too.

Closing my eyes, I listen to the knock of the pipes, the sound of water and waste moving through different parts of the system. Opening them again, I look for flaws, for some sign of a weakness in his programming. It's so disgusting in its perfection, this re-creation of a place I haven't thought of for over twenty years. That I trained myself to never think of again, in fact.

It feels like I'm being violated on some level. It doesn't feel like a game. It feels more like a . . .

A light shines from inside the nest. I am powerless, rooted to the spot, staring at it, feeling as confused and afraid as I would seeing a ghost walking through the wall of my cabin.

It's pale blue and shimmers, unlike a constant light from a bulb.

I don't want to crawl inside that nest. I don't want to see how accurately the interior has been rendered. But, damn, do I want to see what that light is coming from. It has to be the instigating incident of the game, or at least a way to get to the place where the plot is going to be revealed. At least I hope it is. I can't stand those purely "experiential" mersives that are claimed to be games but have no goals or progression through a story.

It's no good; my need to know what it is outweighs any fears about the nest's interior. It's just a game, after all. This place in the real world is gone: the nest over twenty-five years ago and the building itself was probably destroyed by nukes six months ago. The person I was when I lived in that pathetic pile of cardboard and foam is gone too.

I cross the space quickly and set the candle down outside the nest, well away from all the flammable materials. Not giving myself a chance to dither and question my decision, I drop to my knees and crawl in, assaulted by the smell of unwashed bedding. I freeze at the sight of the faded duvet cover and its repeated motif of three penguins in different dance poses. I run my hands over the worn fabric. I can still remember when it was the softest brushed cotton money could buy, how it used to feel to be tucked up in bed, safe beneath it. The bellies of the penguins look blue in the ethereal light, but still I can't tear my eyes from it, no matter how much I want to move on.

Then I'm looking at the piles of scavenged clothes, drifts of detritus hoarded by the terrified child I was back then. No dolls. No bear or others. A knife. A tool set, stolen from another part of the basement. Half-empty bottles of vitamin tablets years out of date. A tub of engine grease, a bottle of machine oil and a pile of filthy rags. A clouded bottle of water. My view of it all blurs and I realize I am welling up, overwhelmed by how that time is expressed so perfectly in these little piles of smelly crap. My gaze drifts to the bundle of discarded carpet offcuts that formed my pillow and I wonder whether the necklace is underneath it.

My hand is halfway to it before I stop myself. It really doesn't matter if it is there or not. It really doesn't. I tell myself a third time, just to make it true.

Instead, I focus on the source of the blue light. It looks like a gemstone the size of my fist with a bright blue flame dancing inside it. It's held in a rudimentary wire cage suspended from the roof of the nest and fills me with relief, rooting me back in the sure knowledge that this is the start of a game. A rectangle of card is tied loosely to one of the wire bars and I pull it free to read the handwritten message.

If you want to know the answers you have to grasp the fire

I smirk. Okay then, so we're bringing a bit of old-school fantasy in? I'm cool with that. The bars of the cage are made of such thin wire it's easy to prize a couple of them apart and fish out the gem inside. It's pleasantly warm to the touch and the movement of the flame within is quite hypnotic. The gem feels solid and heavy in my hand. Do I take it out and throw it onto the concrete to release the flame? I crawl out of the nest and stand up, weighing my options. Grasp the fire . . . I squeeze the gemstone and it shatters in my hand.

Shards of crystal puncture the skin of my palm and I yelp in pain, opening my hand to pull them free. There's nothing there. No crystal, no flame, no light. Just my own blood oozing from a deep gash. Well, shit. I grab one of the rags and wrap it around my hand, watching the blood soak the cloth. It's throbbing a bit too realistically for my liking. I try to call up the settings in the usual way by flicking my right index finger up like I am scrolling an old tablet screen, but nothing happens.

"Ada?" My APA doesn't respond. Now, that just isn't right. Locking me out of standard interfaces without warning is a shit move.

"Dee Dee?" A voice calls my name from the other side of the room and from thirty years ago. My bear is there, waving, looking ludicrously cute. Without even thinking, I find myself waving back eagerly, like I did as a child.

"Do you need help, Dee Dee?"

This is the help interface? Jesus and Muh—

"Yes!" I hurry over to him and pick him up, crushing him to my chest. He's smaller than I remember. Or am I just bigger? Then he feels just right. I bury my face in his brown fur, my tears soaking into it. "Bobby Bear," I whisper. "I've missed you so much!"

"I'm here now," he says. "What did you need help with?"

"Oh . . . I . . ." Struggling to recall the reason, I sit on one of the low horizontal pipes that was usually warm and find that it's another detail perfectly reproduced. I position Bobby on my knee, like I would a child who wants to see the room we sit in. He looks up at me with those huge eyes of his. I see that they are plastic, that they are merely child-friendly covers for the cam lenses behind them, but to me they are just his eyes. The tiny motors beneath the fur of his face move his features into a smile and I return it. Then the throb in my hand reasserts itself. "Yeah, I wanted to take a look at the settings, see if I could dial down the pain." I show him my bandaged hand.

"Ooooh, that looks like a bad boo-boo," he says sympathetically. "There aren't any settings to make that less painful. Actions have consequences, Dee Dee. Didn't we talk about that a lot?"

His words chill me. It really is like my Bobby Bear. But how can it be? The data he gathered over my childhood was never uploaded to my first neural chip. But then, bears probably talk to kids about consequences a lot.

"Seriously? Isn't this supposed to be a game?"

"Ah, but the best games have risk, Dee Dee. You know that."

Risk? "This hasn't hurt me in meatspace, has it?"

Bobby laughs, the perfect reproduction of that low growl and childlike giggle I loved so much. "Of course not! Are you scared?"

I find myself pouting like I did as a child. "I am not."

Bobby pats my arm with a paw, just like he used to. "That's my Dee Dee."

"How do I leave the game?"

His little fur eyebrows knit together in the middle. "You want to?"

I shrug, undecided. "I dunno. It's . . ."

"Don't leave yet, Dee Dee. You have important things to do here. You want to know the answers, don't you? Otherwise you wouldn't have hurt your hand."

I look at the blood drying on the bandage. Like some fucking n00b I smashed it with my right hand. Should have used my left. Like those idiots in mersives who have to make a blood sacrifice and slice open their palm, where the wound will be the most inconvenient, instead of the outside of their arm or something. "But I can leave when I want to?"

"Of course you can. Just ask me and I'll show you the way out. But don't run away. Choose to leave when you're done here. Okay?"

This is too serious. Too real. I'm about to tell him to show me out when I hear a shout from up the stairwell in the next room. My first instinct is to run back into my nest, to give the automatic lights time to dim back out before anyone appears at the doorway. I'm flooded with memories of keeping the pipes in order, of greasing up things that moved and squeaked, knowing that if they wore through, maintenance people or drones would come down and investigate. Eventually there were no staff or drones to worry about, but I didn't know why. And that had nearly got me killed.

"Aren't you going to see who that is, Dee Dee?"

Ah, the NPC is steering me toward the next plot point. "I'm not sure I want them to know I'm down here."

"Why not?" he asks, and then points at the nest. "You don't live there anymore, remember? You're not doing anything wrong."

This is so fucked up, but I stand and set him down on the floor. "You coming with me?"

He smiles, showing off those pointed felt teeth I remember so well. "My legs are shorter than yours. You go on ahead. If you need me, just call."

I don't want to leave him. I never wanted to the first time. How many times did I imagine him calling for me after I abandoned the apartment? How many times did I sob in that nest, worrying about what had happened to him? "Bobby . . . what happened to you, after I left? Were you okay?"

"I was fine," he says softly. "I went and had adventures."

I burst into tears. What the fuck is this shitty game anyway? "I'm sorry I had to leave you behind." I sob like a child, like the child I was back then, all raw and far too emotional. "There were flies . . . everywhere . . ."

He comes over and wraps his arms around my leg. "I know you had to and it's okay. It kept you safe. I understand that. And I wanted you to be safe. So everything's okay. Isn't it?"

I couldn't have stayed there. Of course not. And I was a

kid; I had no idea what would happen to my father's body and— I cut the thought off as quickly as I can. "Yeah," I say, wiping my wet face with the backs of my sleeves. "Yeah, I guess it is."

He lets go of my leg and I can't reconcile the need to leave with the desire to stay with him, making me hesitate until I finally force myself forward. Then I feel better. This is what I've always done, forced myself forward, no matter how much some childish, weak part of me wanted to stay with whoever made me feel safe at the time. It's probably good that I left Bobby behind. That way I never grew out of him. He never had the chance to disappoint me, or betray me, or simply let me down like everyone else.

I go through the door in the far corner on the opposite side of the room from my nest. The space beyond is as I remember: a storage area for the huge barrels of chemicals used to purify the water, and the machines used to maintain the building's air-conditioning system. At least, that's what I thought those chemicals were for; I could have been wrong back then.

Light is spilling down the concrete steps at the far end of the room, the ones that lead up to the ground-floor lobby, through the open door leading to the concierge's office. A shadow in the doorway makes me pause. I spent so long trying to avoid the man in that office, the instinct is still strong.

"Hello? Is there anyone down there? I need some help."

It's not the concierge's voice. But it is familiar. The temptation to come up from this mersive is strong again, but I want the answers that gem promised, so I step forward to the edge of the light and raise a hand. "Hi."

"Deanna? Is that you?"

The sound of my full name makes my body jerk in surprise. I haven't heard it for so long. And never in a game. I don't play games to be myself, for fuck's sake! I'm going to have some sharp feedback for the game designer when I am done!

"Yes, it's me," I reply, walking to the steps. With the light behind him, his face is in shadow. "I'm sorry, I can't see who you are."

"I'm Kam, from number 22. We check the postboxes at the same time. Remember me?"

And then I do, in a rush of memories filled with him lifting me up so I could tap in the key code on my parents' postal box up on the top row. A kind man who wore a turban and carried a kirpan tucked into his belt, who on his birthday gave me special handmade sweets that were sticky and moist with sweet syrup. He was the first one to come and check on me when the riots started. "Kam!" I cheer, racing up the steps to embrace him, his beard tickling my neck. I am nearly as tall as him now, his broad shoulders no longer as impressive to me as they once were.

"Little Deanna, how you've grown! What are you doing down there? That's no place for you!"

I study his face, looking for some sort of detail that's out of place. I don't find anything, but then, I only knew this man when I was a child. I wouldn't know if this representation has inaccuracies. He has the same kind eyes that I remember though, and I check that his steel bracelet is there as I remember. It is. Has the programmer found mersives recorded by the people who lived in this building? How was consent obtained to view them, let alone use them this way? Besides, they were likely lost in the nuclear war. But now isn't the time to figure it out; I'll play through and then quiz him. "I was just exploring. What do you need help with?"

"Something bad is happening on the top floor, but I can't get up there to help."

I shiver. "The riots?" The electricity was cut and the adults barricaded the stairwell when those were at their worst.

"No, no. They were a long time ago. When you were a child, remember?"

He's acting like he's known me as an adult. This weird mix of accuracy and inconsistencies feels dreamlike. "I remember," I say, hoping it will unlock some more dialog.

I remember those riots all too well. How quickly they got out of control, how there were sirens and the smell of smoke for days before things got really bad. Now they're just a footnote in history, mentioned in passing when people talk about the end of democracy. Or rather, the final nail in its coffin. Society had been breaking down for a long time. The riots were just its last rattling breath before the corporations made their final play and bought out the government. Like well-dressed vultures, they tore the carcass apart and gobbled it down in pieces, locking us all into their vision of how society should be: hierarchical, with clearly defined pay grades and no place for anyone who didn't want to be a diligent consumer. "So, someone has barricaded the stairwell?" I ask, not wanting to brood upon all that shit right now.

He doesn't answer that. Strange—even the most basic gaming AIs can adapt to conversations far more sophisticated than this. Then I realize he hasn't responded because whatever is in the stairwell has made him uncomfortable. Not afraid though. "The lifts aren't working," he finally says. "There's no electricity."

Another shiver. It's sounding more like the time after the riots, and I don't want to experience that again. I look behind him and see that the light is coming through windows that never existed in the real concierge's office. This gives me hope; if the building isn't an exact replica of the one I grew up in, it won't be as bad as I fear.

But why put real people I used to know in this game? There are rules against this sort of thing, but then again, those rules only apply to those who are famous enough to need to legally protect their own likenesses and who have the money to pay lawyers to defend them. Shouldn't there have been some sort of warning, at least? Some guidance in the loading area to prepare me for all of this? If that starting corridor even was a loading area. I don't like how it keeps me off-balance all the time; there are none of the usual markers that ease me in and out of games. Games have evolved an incredible amount in my lifetime alone, but the foundations have stayed the same, the underlying framework. This "game" has pulled that out from under me. I hadn't appreciated how much my comfort depended on those behavioral cues until now.

Then I remember the way that box appeared in my virtual office and the designer's obvious disregard of boundaries. I knew it would be problematic, based on what I saw in our brief interaction, and I went ahead anyway. I don't have the right to complain. Do I?

Kam is waiting for my answer. "You want me to go up and take a look?"

He nods.

"How many floors up?"

"Twenty."

Just like where I grew up. Filled with too much energy for apartment living, I used to run up and down the stairwell when I collected the post. The designer said this game would help me to reach my goals. Is it set up like a leet server game, where my own fitness will determine my progress up those stairs? At least it won't be so tough now, as I am much fitter than I was a year ago. Only one way to find out.

"I'll do it," I say, expecting some sort of ping from Ada to tell me that a new quest has been added, but there's nothing. It's been set up like one, from those old-school games that have endured for decades, so it surprises me that nothing appears. Perhaps Bobby has stored it, ready in case I ask him. Yeah, that makes sense. It would be more internally consistent. "You stay down here, Kam, okay? It seems safe. Can you tell me anything more?"

He shakes his head. Just an intro NPC, then. "Be careful. It's dangerous."

I give him my best brave smile and he steps aside. I emerge from the stairwell entrance into the concierge's office, confused by the fact that the windows are too high to look out of, as if they have been placed there for letting in light alone. Normally such a minor detail wouldn't bother me, but it's jarring when juxtaposed with perfectly reproduced environments.

There isn't much of note in here. A couple of comfortable chairs and a smart wall, which is dead. There's a cupboard with closed doors. The concierge managed everything through his chip, so there was no need for any paperwork. It was only because of the fact that this was once an exclusive apartment block that he had a job here at all. Most blocks didn't, the building residents more than capable of living a privileged life without an actual human being as their interface. I know my mother hated the fact that there was a human concierge here; she always complained about how nosy he was, how much he tried to weasel his way into the lives of everyone here. I recall my father having a very different view of it all. But then, he was born into that world where keeping human staff was a sign of status, and he couldn't understand why my mother thought it was crass.

It's been so long since I thought about them together and alive, I find myself just standing here, staring into space. This feels more like a bloody flashback than a game. I shake my hands and arms, roll my shoulders. Come on, your memories aren't that interesting, I tell myself. I'm not going to stand here wallowing.

I march out of the room, coming out into the lobby with

the correct marble floor, the correct windows, the entrances to the elevators right where I expect them. But the view outside the windows makes me do a double take. It's not the one that should be there; it's the one from the network headquarters I used to work in before Rapture. There's the Thames, Blackfriars Bridge stretching across it on a misty morning. There are no leaves on the trees. Did the designer just not have footage of the other apartment blocks that I should be seeing out of these windows?

"Oh, just fucking leave it," I say to myself. The worst thing about this bloody game is trying to figure it out on a metalevel. I need to knuckle down and get on with twatting whatever it is upstairs.

Kam said it would be dangerous, which usually means I need a weapon. There's nothing useful here, unless I try to smash up one of the nice sofas and salvage something. Then I remember the cupboard in the concierge's office. "C'mon, Dee," I say to myself. "Stop playing like a bloody n00b."

It's not locked. There's a first aid kit, a toolbox and a torch. I laugh. Now it feels like a proper game.

I clean up my hand, put some numbing wound sealant on it and pocket the torch. There's a hammer in the toolbox, and a large wrench, but both require getting up close and personal with the big bad and I'm not too keen on doing that. I take the hammer and tuck it into my belt. Only then does it occur to me to look down at what I'm wearing.

Jeans and a black T-shirt I haven't worn for twenty years. The belt is black leather, with a simple buckle, the jeans baggy with the ends of the legs dipped in a pearlescent dye that was the fashion then. The T-shirt says, in small writing, "If you can read this you are a) too close and b) staring at my tits. Fuck off." I had stolen it from one of the apartments on the third floor. Its former owner's body had been in the bathroom, slumped over the toilet. Some sort of overdose, I reckon; I didn't go to check. All I remember thinking was that it was a shame she'd died wearing the T-shirt with a fairy-tale princess flipping the bird at a knight in shining armor; otherwise I would have nicked that one too. I'd been stealing from her for months by then, ever since the day I'd found one of her wigs in the trash and realized I could get to her door and open it without worrying about the cameras if I wore it and kept my head down. I already knew the codes to all of the doors by then. Her printer kept me fed for one more week after I printed a stack and carried it down to the basement, the cameras nonfunctional by that point. When I went back for more, the smell had alerted the neighbors, her body had been removed and the door code changed.

The hammer tucked into my belt, the wrench in my good hand and the torch in my injured hand, I close the cupboard door, as kitted up as this level is going to get me.

The door to the stairwell is on the other side of the lobby. I cross to it, put a hand on the door to check for any heat and then slowly push it open. No fire. Good. I couldn't handle that again.

It's so dark in the stairwell, devoid of windows and electricity as it is, that I can't see even the first step. Switching on the torch, I go through the doorway and sweep the beam up the first flight of stairs. It isn't the slick of blood I find myself standing in that makes me yelp, or even the sight of the dozens of bodies littering the stairs. It's their eyes. Open, all of them, and staring right at me.

6

I DROP THE wrench. It lands with a sickening spattering noise in the pool of blood. It's flowed away from the bodies, slid in rivulets down the walls and still drips from the balustrade. "Shit!" I can't help but look at them, my eyes darting from one face to another. As if the whole dead-body thing isn't bad enough, they're all people I recognize. I look away from them, up at the ceiling, anywhere that there isn't blood so I can pull myself back together.

"Okay, okay, okay." I suck in a breath. Push it out again. In. Out. I can handle this. It's just a game. A really fucked up unethical shit show of a game, but a game nonetheless. Anyone would be shocked. It's nothing to be ashamed of. I tell myself that three times, breathing deep.

Sod the wrench—it can stay there in the blood; I am not touching that shit. I still have the hammer and thank God I didn't drop the torch. As the shock recedes, anger takes its place. There should have been a warning, dammit! Even just a horror genre tag. What kind of sick bastard would make a game where you have to climb twenty flights of stairs covered with dead people? What the hell is waiting for me at the top?

"B—" I stop myself from calling for my bear. I've never come up from a game because it's scared me, and I'm not going to do that now. Another deep breath and then I look at the nearest corpse.

It's the woman who lived two doors down from me last year. I only recognize her because she came to my door once, asking if I knew how to use the food printer. She said it was a different model from the one she was used to, but it was a flimsy excuse. She'd obviously tumbled down a few rungs of society's ladder and ended up in an apartment without a kitchen. I showed her, just so I had an excuse to see what her place was like. There were pictures of a fluffy white dog everywhere, displayed on the wall-art screens and arranged in photo frames that cluttered the tiny place up. She still had over a dozen boxes to unpack, but those pictures were up already. She noticed me looking at them and said, rather tearfully, "That's my MuMu. Isn't he beautiful?"

I don't remember what I said back, but I do remember how lost she seemed, even after I showed her how to print dinner. "And does the management company keep it . . . filled up? How does one give them access to the flat?"

"It's a communal system here," I said. "There are tanks for each floor. The building management company maintains those so no one has to worry about access."

"Tanks?"

"Yeah, that hold the protein and the chemicals they pipe through those nozzles to make your food." I pointed at the plasglass cover. "They're in there, the nozzles." But then I realized her confusion wasn't related to their position. "It's like the water in the taps, right? There's a giant system of pipes that run through the building, bringing fresh water to your sinks. It's no different. Nothing to worry about."

She burst into tears and I just stood there, not knowing what to say to a woman I'd only met ten minutes before. "So . . . I'll get going now . . . now you know how to use it . . ." I made it to the door and let myself out before she even noticed I'd gone.

I saw her a few times after that, passing her in the corridor or stepping into a lift she was just coming out of. Each and every time she blanked me. Which suited me fine. I didn't want to become her dog replacement, or her designated guide for life in the slums. Which they weren't anyway, but she would have seen them like that.

Now, looking at her body lying broken on the stairs, wearing the same cashmere coat she'd worn that day I showed her how to use the printer, I feel a flicker of guilt. I could have been a friend to her. But then again, she was obviously a walking disaster. She wouldn't have been any use to me in that state. The guilt is extinguished. She's dead now, anyway. My being around to listen to her crying about the life she had lost wouldn't have done anything to save her.

I tell myself that three times. Just to make sure it is true.

There's a space on the lowest step, next to one of her legs, that's big enough for me to put my foot onto the concrete. Trying my best to ignore the bodies to my left and right, I look for a point on a higher step that I can reach without touching anyone.

My gaze rests upon the man who was in a car one night when it was raining and who offered me a lift, which I declined because even though I was young, I wasn't stupid. He'd looked so hurt. "I'm not like those other men, you know?"

"Then you won't mind if I say no," I said. It wasn't as if there was anywhere to give me a lift to, at that point, but the last place I'd been dossing in had become unsafe and I had to look like I was going somewhere; otherwise the authorities would have picked me up.

"Can't I at least buy you a meal? You look freezing."

"No, thanks." I was starving. I hadn't eaten for three days and had only drunk rainwater. In a society filled with food that required an identity to purchase it, I was in big trouble.

"Listen, I work for an organization that helps people like you. People going through a hard time. Please, let me help you." He rolled the car forward, keeping up with my brisk walk, even though it risked being flagged up as potentially criminal behavior. "Look. Here are my credentials."

He brought up his profile on the windscreen, flipping the display and dialing up the brightness so I could see it from the outside. I didn't recognize the organization's name, but it looked legit. Enough for me to point at a restaurant down the road. "You can buy me dinner there, if you want. But only dinner. Get it?"

And he did. And he gave me his coat to keep. And there were no nasty sexual undertones to it at all. He called his husband from the restaurant to explain why he'd be late and asked him to join us. I was twelve and it was still a year before the nonperson policies became really hard-core. They talked to me. Gave me advice. Asked if we could meet every couple of days for a meal, just so they could check in with me.

It took three months of that to convince me they genuinely wanted to help. Another three months before they asked if I wanted to stay with them. Then I ran away. I never saw either of them again. I have no idea if it would have been as safe as I'd hoped it would be. I just couldn't make that final leap. I couldn't trust them. No, I couldn't let myself love them, or trust them. They would only leave me, or hurt me, in the end. So it was better to end it when it was still good.

His dead husband is lying crumpled next to him. Staring at me, like the rest, and when I look down at that woman, she is staring at me too, even though I've moved. And it isn't a glassy, empty stare. There's an intensity to it, not of the living, but it still feels like they want something from me.

"Fuck. This. Shit," I say, and make myself look for the gray of the concrete steps, steadfastly avoiding looking at anything that could be a face. I gingerly pick my way up, from empty patch to empty patch, sometimes having to climb three stairs in a single step. Why did he code this experience into the game? For maximum psychological damage? To see how far up the stairs I could go before having some sort of breakdown? Well, I'll show that bastard how strong I can be.

I get up ten floors before I need to take a brief break, which I spend staring up at the ceiling as I catch my breath. My theory about it being a leet server training game is gathering supporting evidence with each step. My body here feels like it's at the same level of fitness as mine in meatspace. All sorts of explanations have raced through my mind on the way up here, but the one I've settled on is that this is some sort of test—or an initiation, maybe—for people approached to play on the leet server. They want to see what I can handle. Right? Whether I've got the chops to cope with psychological horror. Well, I'll show those fuckers that it'll take more than this to freak me out.

Then, on the eighteenth floor, after picking my way through this emotional minefield, focused on those tiny islands of gray concrete so I can cope, I see a pair of shoes that makes me stop. I didn't know I was afraid that she would be here until now, when there is a sense of bitter relief that I no longer have to brace myself.

I tighten my hand around the torch, feeling the pain of the wound deep inside, beneath the numbed exterior. Good. Yes, I'll focus on that.

The shoes are electric blue, made out of an artificial material that looks like polished metal yet is flexible. The heels are low but spiked, and even though I can't see them because she is lying faceup, I know there is a tiny shark logo on the back of each, near the top where it meets the rest of the shoe. I never saw anyone else wear a pair of shoes like those. Never saw them in online shops. Never looked for them though.

I squeeze the torch handle as I force my attention to skim over the tight designer suit, the oversized jewelry, to her face. I used to call her the vampire, but only in my head. And only when she wasn't around. Just in case. Her lips are deep red, her skin just as deathly pale as when she was alive, her black hair perfectly straight. When my gaze meets hers I start shaking. I can't help it. I can't undo all the knots she tied in me.

"Ha!" I shout at her face, the noise bursting from me before I even knew it was coming out of my lungs. "I won! I won, you fucking bitch! You're dead and I'm on my way to another planet and nobody owns me anymore, so fuck you!"

The triumph doesn't last long. She's still staring at me, like she did back then, standing next to the Machine, ready to recalibrate me. What a euphemism that was. They had good words for all sorts of terrible things in that place. *Realignment of values. Reaction refinement.*

"Just place your chin here, look at the blue dot." Such a soft, gentle voice. Such a calm, reassuring tone, even though she knew what she was about to do to me. "That's it. I'm just going to pop this into your mouth to protect your tongue. Open wide. That's it. Now hold still while I strap your head in place. Don't pull against the wrist restraints—they're there for your protection."

The hammer is no longer tucked into my belt. It is in my hand. Then it is plunging down into her face. Again. And again.

She doesn't look like herself when I'm done; she doesn't even look like a person anymore from the shoulders up. There's blood spattered all over my hands. I can feel it drying on my face and throat. She's not looking at me anymore though. That's the most important thing. Good. Yes. That's better. Time to move on.

I get three steps up before my legs buckle underneath me and I can't breathe. Wracking sobs seize up my chest and I drop the hammer and the torch to wipe my hands on my jeans again and again. There's too much snot and there's too much pain in my chest to even feel anything emotional, but slowly, slowly, things rise to the surface. The withering tendrils of the rage that took over, relief, exultation, but mostly a cavernous grief that I could fall into and never escape from, if I'm not careful. I've been so angry for so long, but I put that anger in a box and hid it away from myself so well that I forgot it was there.

JeeMuh, I feel like shit. I cough a couple of times, wipe my nose on the bloody rag I stuffed into my pocket earlier and pick up the torch. I look at the hammer, the gore slowly dripping off it, the chunks of brain and skull, and then I'm heaving, like I need to be sick but there's nothing to bring up.

Just as a miserable whimper escapes my lips, there's a thought that cuts through it all. Are we having fun yet?

And then I'm laughing. Hysterically, admittedly, but it's better than the rest of the shit that I've just splurged over these steps. I don't even know what's funny about any of this, but I'm doubled over, my hooting laughter echoing up and down the stairwell. It feels so wrong, so desperately inappropriate, and that in itself makes me laugh all the harder.

I am a fucking monster.

I have to blow my nose again, wipe my eyes, pick up the torch once more and then the hammer. I wipe the remains of her head on the trousers of a man who used to live in this building and never smiled once, not in all the years I saw him. Fair play, bro, I think. Not like there was much to smile about back then. Now he has filthy trousers to add to the misery, but at least I have a hammer I'm willing to hook into my belt again.

When I get to the nineteenth floor, there is a new sound. Thuds and sounds of things being broken are coming from the floor above. This is it, then.

Kam said he couldn't get in . . . He didn't mention the bodies in the stairwell though. I pick my way up the last flight of stairs, expecting to see some sort of barricade; even a wall of piled-up dead bodies wouldn't have surprised me. But there's nothing in the way of the door that leads to the top floor. There is, however, a security pad to the left of it, one that was never in the original building. Oh, so it's a puzzle of some sort?

Taking care to be as quiet as I can be, I get to the pad and examine it by torchlight. It has a touchscreen and looks too modern for anything that would have been installed in the original apartment block. I touch it with the pad of my forefinger, mostly just to wake it up and see what kind of biometric it wants to interrogate to allow me through. A string of digits and letters appears and I tut to myself. At first glance there doesn't seem to be any obvious pattern. I hate these sorts of puzzles. They're such a bollocks kind of hurdle when your APA can—

Oh. Yeah. No APA to run a calculation for me. So this is what it's like in Leetsville, then?

At least it doesn't want a palm print. I was worried it was going to make me drag one of the corpses over, or worse, cut off one of their hands to press against it. Same for a retina scan, though that sort of thing is so cheesy, I should have known the programmer wouldn't have gone for it.

I need to bring my brain back into gaming mode. Not dredging-up-irrelevant-emotional-bullshit mode. That's no use to anyone.

I frown at the numbers; it's clear to me that I'm not going

to crack this code and be able to input the last numbers and letters in the sequence without some sort of assistance, even if it's just a bloody pad and pen. Then it occurs to me that there's no obvious way to input anything, even if I did know what it was. I tap the screen again, hoping that some sort of keyboard will appear, or that it will trigger a v-keyboard prompt in my own chip. But no transparent virtual keyboard floats across my vision, and the screen doesn't change. There's just the string of characters and a logo.

Okay, the logo is the most important thing here. It's there for a reason. I don't recognize it, which makes me even more certain that it's a game element, rather than a bit of decorative detailing.

It looks like a stylized globe with the North American continent featured prominently, rather than the usual view of multiple continents. Wrapped around the bottom of the globe are the letters *CSA*, but it's not an initialism I'm familiar with.

A quick flick around with the torch beam shows me that the logo is not present anywhere else on the door. Then the cam in the upper corner above me is lit up by the beam and I see that it's active. Shit. I pull the bloody rag from my pocket again, find a bit that's still damp and smear the blood over the lens, even though the big bad probably knows I'm out here already. It's too small a unit for me to tie the rag to and is recessed into the wall. Just a piece of chewing gum would sort it, but I don't have that.

What I need more is an APA that actually works so I can look up that logo.

No, that doesn't feel right. That's me thinking about this like it's a normal game, which it obviously isn't. Taking a figurative step back, I consider the clue again. I've been cut off from my APA, so I'm expected to only use what I have at my disposal or what I can find in the environment, right?

But the only thing that's in this environment is all the bloody bodies.

Oh shit.

I laugh. "You clever, sick bastard," I whisper, as if the game designer can hear me. Perhaps he can, for all I know. "You don't want me to ignore the bodies, do you? You want me to look at them. Well . . . fine."

All of the corpses on the landing with me here are dressed in casual clothes. I need someone with a uniform. Or even just a badge. Something with that logo on it. Damn. They could be wearing a badge even with casual clothes. There's no avoiding it. I start examining each one.

It turns into a litany: a gruesome cataloging of all of the deaths that touched my life, no matter how insignificantly. All of the residents I ever noticed in the original version of this building, or the ones I subsequently lived in, or other victims in the hot-housing center, or work colleagues from the network. Hundreds of them.

I try not to care. Some I can barely remember, their faces just vaguely familiar. Some were bullies. Some were tedious, boring people and I'm glad I'll never have to suffer their dull conversation or entertain their mediocre ideas at work ever again. But it isn't enough to armor myself against all feelings, no matter how much I pride myself upon my ability to switch off that emotional bollocks whenever I need to.

It's the anger I can't shut out. These are just an infinitesimal fraction of the dead we left behind on Earth. All those lives, snuffed out in moments, just because some fucker in power—undoubtedly on this ship—didn't want anyone to follow us. That must be the reason why they did it. It just doesn't make any sense otherwise.

It could be a woman who ordered it, of course, or a nonbinary person, but in my mind it's a man, at the head of a table in a room full of men. White, middle-aged men, so terrified of not being the most powerful people on Earth that their fear stalked them onto this ship and made them destroy any other culture that might dare to challenge their vision on the new planet.

Three floors down I have to stop and lean against the wall, covering my face with my free hand and trying to breathe as steadily as I can for a while. I don't want to cry. Fuck tears! Fuck that weakness!

How could I have thought that just finding out who did this would be enough? I don't just want their names; I want their bloody hearts in my hand after I've ripped them from their bodies, smiling at them as I did it. There's no such thing as justice to be found in any system that exists on this ship, which they will no doubt have power over. I have to make my own justice; I have to find them and make sure they pay for what they did, with their own blood. And I will sleep well afterward.

And it won't just be for my satisfaction, or some bullshit karmic rebalancing; it will be to protect the people who got to our destination long before us, led by a woman of Korean heritage who was always careful to talk about finding God without any mention of a specific religion. Surely that will stick in their craw just as much as the risk of anyone chasing us there? Yeah, this is a better purpose than just giving us a name to curse, a face to blame, some release valve for our grief. Names are just the beginning, and their deaths will be the only acceptable end to this.

And it feels better, this focus, this determination after months of drifting. My motivation renewed, I crack on with looking for the logo. I'll beat this game; then I'll know I can cut it on the leet server and that will help me find out more about Brace and whether he was involved.

I finally find the logo on the tiepin of a young black man on the fifth floor. I'm not impressed with this game design.

I had to get all the way to the top to find the logo, then come all the way back down again to find it on something else. And the tiepin is tiny too!

Looking at the man's face, I struggle to place him. All I can remember is his being involved in something technical at the network when I started my first job there. He was nice enough, into sport, and left a couple of months later for another job. JeeMuh . . . how the hell did the designer find him to replicate? Employment records?

No, stop thinking about that! I pull the tiepin free. It's enameled metal as far as I can tell, the logo faithfully reproduced with the same colors. I turn it over, hoping for some sort of code that can help me predict the next numbers or letters, but it's plain. Perhaps it's chipped though.

Back I go, all the way to the nineteenth floor. This will help me to achieve my goal, I tell myself. JeeMuh, I hope he wasn't lying about that. Once I'm on the leet server with him, assuming I find out his identity, I will have a new goal: kick his arse at as many games as I possibly can, and then laugh right in his stupid face.

At least this time I can ignore the bodies. But it's too late now anyway. I seethe as I march up, the rage making my breath shorten. What about the people who didn't die? What about the poor sods trying to survive a nuclear winter now, while I'm here, playing stupid games when I really should be hunting down those responsible?

But then I'm at the security pad and the lure of getting through the locked door is enough to distract me. I hold the tiepin up to the screen, press it against the plasglass and the picture of the logo on the screen. Nothing happens.

"Shit," I say, pressing my forehead against the screen and banging gently against it. "What am I missing?"

I put the pin through my T-shirt, push the clip onto the

back of it and then feel something brush against my leg. I nearly cry out, but it's only Bobby Bear.

"Hi, Dee Dee," he says brightly. "Would you like some help with that little pin?"

I chuckle. This is so damn old-school in the midst of what must be the most advanced neural chip mining I've ever seen. "Yeah, Bobby, I would."

"The pin is a key, designed to be used in concert with your neural chip. I can help to trick the AI into thinking you have permission to wear it, so it will sync with you, but to do that, I need access to your neural chip. Is that okay?"

I shrug. "Sure."

An icon appears in my vision. That's better, something I can work with at last. It's the logo, only three-dimensional, the little globe spinning around. "Bobby, what does CSA stand for?"

"The Christian States of America," he says. "Look at the screen now and tell me if it has worked."

Won't he know if it has? I do as he asks, and now the string of random characters has been replaced by a sentence: "We walk in God's light."

"I can read it now. But I still don't know how to open the door."

Bobby Bear tilts his head to the side, considering me. "Oh, Dee Dee. You've got lazy! *You* have to do the work, not an APA."

It stings because it's true. I'm used to running through games, simply chucking any sort of mental puzzle at my APA, who only needs a bit of direction. That's what it's specced for, after all. That, and data analysis. I've been doing both for so long now, I barely think about how it does things. I've been reduced to the role of conductor of an orchestra of one, playing whatever tune I like at the mere wave of my hand.

"Right," I say, focusing on the task to get away from the shameful realization that I wouldn't last two minutes on the leet server, and not just because of my body's limitations. "So there's a religious group involved here. Great. I know nothing about hard-core religious shit." I look at Bobby Bear. "Do you have all the data you used to have—I mean the default stuff?" When he nods, I grin. "You've got all the major religious texts stored, right?"

"Yes," Bobby Bear says. "You used to ask questions about them. Don't you remember?"

"No. Okay, call up the Bible then . . ."

"Which version would you like to explore?"

Oh bollocks. I didn't think about that. "Whatever the most popular version of it was in North America just before we left. Just the straight Bible, not one of those ones with study notes all over it."

"The most popular Bible in circulation was the King James Version."

"That one then. Is there anything about opening doors? Or . . ." I look back at the door. It's not just about that though, is it? "No . . . about gaining access to someone important."

"Proverbs 18:16: 'A man's gift maketh room for him, and bringeth him before great men.'"

I look at the door and then tentatively push against it. Still locked. Then I repeat the verse myself and there is a clunk from the internal lock. I smirk. Let's finish this.

7

I WAS EXPECTING a corridor, like on all the other floors of this building, with doors to apartments running down both sides. The occasional potted plant, maybe, that looks good at a distance but is plastic close-up. Not this.

It's a single apartment, taking up the whole of the top floor by the look of it, and there's a party going on just out of sight. I can hear piano music tinkling away, some fancy affair with the murmur of conversation and occasional laughter. There are no signs of violence. Confused, I take a step farther into a huge lobby, my shoes making a crisp tapping sound as I walk. I look down to see the shiny black brogues I used to love to wear with my tux clicking against the polished marble tiles. I'm wearing the tux too, my favorite cummerbund made of the most ridiculous iridescent material, which looks like someone wove it out of rainbows and stardust. It matches my equally ridiculous bow tie.

I wore this to an awards ceremony in Paris three years ago. I didn't want to go but had no say in the matter and spent most of the evening stuck at a table with a bunch of horrendously dull people. Their astounding lack of social charm and storytelling skills could make the tale of a trip through piranha-infested waters in a leaky boat seem boring. I was up for an award in an industry I didn't care about, for a job I was forced to do and hadn't chosen to take in the first place. Thinking there was no chance I would win, I'd downed half a bottle of champagne before my name was read out. It wasn't nerves; it was the fact that I'd never tasted real champagne before. Carl, snob that he was, always drank red wine, which did nothing for me, and anyway, I didn't have the heart to drink something I was indifferent to when I knew how many hours he'd prolonged his contract to pay for it.

There was no speech to read, as I hadn't bothered to write one. It was hard enough standing up, with that real champagne doing very real things to my body. By the time I'd reached the podium, my APA had temporarily shut down notifications on my media feeds, as so many messages of congratulations were flooding in at once, and MyPhys had started to undo the champagne's work. With each step up the little stairs at the edge of the stage I was feeling more sober and horribly aware of the giant cock-up I was about to commit.

I can remember a moment of awful clarity, as MyPhys artificially flushed out the last traces of drunkenness, which I hadn't instructed it to do. At no point since hearing my name did I tell it to clean me up quick.

Someone else had.

As I shook the hand of the presenter and took the heavy piece of crystal, all the icons usually in my visual field faded out. I was cut off from making any sort of contact with anyone else. Even though it confused me, the sheer social pressure of having someone shake my hand and then gesture to the podium to signal it was time for me to make my speech kept me moving to the right spot to set the award down and look out over the room as the applause died down.

All I could see was wealth. Half-eaten plates of food made by artisans, left abandoned as if it were junk from a street printer. I hadn't left a speck of food on my plate and had eaten the dessert rejected by the man sitting next to me. "The ganache here is nothing compared to my own chef's," he'd said. "I wouldn't bother." When I'd asked if I could have it—my pride not getting in the way of a good meal since I'd known what it was like to experience real hunger—he'd looked utterly appalled. I just grinned, took the plate and tucked in.

None of the people I looked down at from that podium had ever experienced anything like I had. I could see it written all over them without any need to check what their publicly available profiles said. Their privilege was written in the way they treated the serving staff with utter disdain, the ease with which they sat at tables covered in porcelain crockery and silver cutlery and didn't give any of it a second glance. None of them had had to depend upon their APA to run an Augmented Reality guide during the meal to show them which bloody fork to use for each course. They were too confident, too unimpressed by it all, to be someone like me.

And I hated them. I was going to tell them some truths, I decided. I was going to tell them what their industry was really like. I even took a breath to say it, to speak the words that would have given me at least three black marks and possibly a prosecution, to tell them that I was owned by the network and all of the work that they were acknowledging with this award was effectively forced labor.

But then a sentence appeared across their expectant faces, the text too large for me to ignore. "This is such an honor, thank you."

I knew then that my boss, my handler, my jailer, was

sending that message to me to read out as the beginning of my speech. He knew I hadn't thought I'd win. He'd been watching and waiting to step in if I did.

I had no intention of reading that bastard's words out. I grabbed the award again, fully intending to hold it up as I spoke my own words, but then I saw a little blue dot floating over the ballroom floor. The one burned into my brain by the Machine, the one the woman in those electric blue shoes used to "realign my values."

"This is such an honor, thank you!" I said, as if I meant it, as if it would stop the pain that I still believed would inevitably follow if I hesitated further. And I read every word of it, thanking my boss for his guidance, his support of my career, expounding upon how I could never have got this far without his faith in me. The audience thought the tears were of happiness. That I was so *authentic*. I spent the rest of that evening hiding in a service corridor in the bowels of the hotel, shaking, trying not to think of electric blue shoes. And when I went back to the office, that same boss gathered everyone together so they could applaud me, saying how moved he was by that damn speech. He put the award on the shelf in the entrance lobby, with the others won by employees, so every morning I could look at it and "feel proud," he said. All it meant was that every morning I had something to look at to make me hate him just that little bit more. But no one would have ever known I felt that way. The same training—or should I say conditioning—that made it impossible for me to resist when the blue dot was invoked made it easy for me to hide my feelings. They trained me to hide what I thought and felt, and the whole time they thought they were removing those feelings altogether. Like all things put under threat, my emotions simply went underground.

Why the fuck am I wearing a tux that I left in a hotel

along with a note saying that it could be given to anyone who wanted it? And the hammer is gone! Fuck! I hate this game so much.

I turn to see that the door has closed behind me and that Bobby Bear has followed me in. "My hammer has gone," I say to him. "This is a shit game. No narrative flow, no environmental consistency. I need to find another weapon. A decent one."

"Are you sure about that?" my bear asks.

I frown at him. Is this some sort of in-game assistance? "Kam said there was someone causing trouble on the top floor . . . it's the last place to go in the building and the most obvious place for the boss fight."

"I don't mean do you need one. I mean: do you need to find one? Haven't you already got the most dangerous weapon there is?"

Just as I'm about to ask him what the hell he is talking about, a memory surfaces, nothing more than an impression of being in my bedroom when I was small, cuddling Bear. There was rain, on the window, yes, that was it, and I couldn't go out to the park and I was grumpy about it, in the way that only children with the happiest lives can be.

I can't remember the conversation well, but I do remember him talking to me about something in the world that was bad. I was small, so it was probably something stupid like an ice cream flavor or—

No . . . it wasn't something stupid at all. It was the fact that some children didn't have parents and that was why my parents were working with someone to . . . to make it better in some way. It must have been that they were getting ready for some fund-raiser, yes, that makes sense. And I was moaning about the fact that I wouldn't be able to go with them and Bear was reasoning it out with me.

"I do . . . I remember something . . ." I say to him. "About how horrible the world was and . . . and something about bad people." Even as I speak, more of it comes back to me, with such clarity I start to wonder whether Bear is making me remember somehow. Is that even possible?

"Yes, we talked about bad people and what we can do about them. Do you remember what I told you?"

And then I see it, clear as day in my head. "You told me that my father said in a speech that we were the best weapons against bad people." I frown at Bobby Bear. "But that was . . . figurative. Some bollocks to make rich people feel good about giving money they didn't need to Dad's favorite charities."

He just looks at me. Slowly, one of his little fur eyebrows rises. "C'mon, Dee Dee. Do I need to tell you everything?"

"Am *I* the weapon here?"

"You can be," he replies. "But it's a big responsibility. And there could be serious consequences. Are you sure you want to accept those?"

The way he talks to me makes me feel like a little girl again. Everything he says feels like it's designed to push me along, to make me figure things out, think carefully. Just like he always did. "Yeah, course I do! I'm not here to have a cup of tea with the big bad, am I?"

"All right then, if it's really what you want." Bobby Bear's right paw touches my hand. I feel a slight tingle, which swiftly fades.

"Is that it?" I flex my fingers. "Can I shoot lasers out of them now or something?"

"You'll know what to do when the time is right."

Clichéd, but judging by the rest of this game, it's the only explanation I'll get, so I take in my surroundings. Aside from a huge silk rug, there are planters with huge ferns and more exotic plants sprouting from them and a console table that looks like it's made out of pure crystal. Nothing that could be used as a weapon, so hopefully whatever he did to my hand will work.

An honest-to-God butler walks past with a tray of canapés, ignoring me. Hang on. I came in here expecting a fight, a huge, dramatic confrontation with the big bad. Not a bloody soiree.

"I'll wait here," Bobby Bear says. "I'm here if you need me, Dee Dee."

I give him one last look, wondering if I'll be able to say good-bye to him once I've defeated the boss; then I march out of the hallway into a gigantic split-level room. It looks like it was made from an amalgam of every single high-society murder mystery mersive I have ever played in. It's so big it makes the full-sized grand piano in the far corner look small. It has floor-to-ceiling windows giving panoramic views of London, the same cream marble flooring as the hall, but with a luxurious carpet on the upper area. There are sofas as big as king-sized beds, with beautiful people draped over them like they're in the middle of some fashion shoot with no photographer.

There are serving staff of all genders and a few drones too, some of the latter on wheels, some in flight, delivering top-ups to glasses and trays of exquisitely arranged chocolates. There have to be more than a hundred people in this room, all of them familiar to me, the guests being various media stars I met in the course of my work. Just as they were on Earth, they are too wrapped up in garnering the most admiration they can to even notice me. The serving staff are made up of people who were at the fringes of my job. The guy who organized catering for those crazy-expensive old-style shoots is serving canapés to a group of actors and it's the first thing I've seen that makes some sort of sense.

A cluster of guests is standing on the upper level, laughing, their attention focused away from the main area of the room. Perhaps there's some sort of game going on, or an entertainer. Uninterested, I scan the room for anything that hints toward a final boss fight. Nothing. Not even a disagreement between guests. Confused and disappointed, I'm about to leave to see if I can find another room with some sort of glowering monster in it who needs a good twatting, when I hear a voice that stops me dead.

"Oh, darling, sometimes you are just so ultra!"

My father. That was my father's voice, coming from the upper level! I run across the room, push past the human coat hangers and there he is, with my mother, holding court. They are lying back on a circular sofa, supported by dozens of cushions in shades of brown, my father's feet being massaged by a young man who in the real world was a trainee director. Dad looks like he did when I was a child: tanned, his blond hair swept back, his eyes—my eyes—that glacial blue of our family.

My mother sits next to him while another woman— someone who was involved in special effects in the real world—is massaging my mother's hand. She too looks like she has stepped out of the memories of my childhood before it all went wrong, her dark brown hair long and straight and glossy. Oh, but they are so beautiful, so perfect, that my breath catches in my throat.

I want to throw myself onto the sofa like I did as a child, wriggling my way between them to make sure that their love still encompassed me even when they were so deeply focused on each other. They'd laugh every time I did it, and make mock groans and then tickle me and—

But I don't move. I can't let myself do it. This isn't right. They're dead. They died a long time ago and I am not going to throw myself through the wall I've built between that perfect memory of them and the reality. They haven't noticed me and I back away before they do, reeling, trying to shore up my crumbling resolve as my father laughs again.

I should have expected it, given the stairwell, the nest, the sheer emotional hurricane this gameified hazing has battered me with. Their bodies weren't on the stairs; that was a kindness, I'd thought, something too brutal for even this arsehole to code in. But somehow this is worse. He must have found the data from Bobby Bear. Must have—

Then suddenly it makes sense. I'd been thinking, like a total fool, that the data on all these people and these phases of my life must have been destroyed on Earth and lost forever. But the people in charge of this trip let me join the crew. They would have mined the entire Internet, trawled through data farms and warehousing to find out everything they could about me. That data must be on the ship server, ready to be exploited by this sick genius. Is he just using the US gov-corp's thorough research to initiate me into the leet circle? Or is he telling me that they know everything about my life, even the parts I thought no one knew about, like the nest in the basement?

I leave the room via a door to the left of the grand piano, barely taking in the person playing it. Ze is very talented; I absorb that much on the way into the adjoining hallway.

It strikes me that no one has offered me any refreshments or talked to me. Another member of serving staff passes without even glancing in my direction, and to be honest, it's a relief after the silent stares from the dead bodies on the way up here. I feel like I am invisible, or at least so far down the social ladder that no one deigns to look at me.

Feeling unfocused, I drift to the next room and find a huge kitchen full of caterers. It's homely though, not made of the industrial steel units found in the top-class hotels, and it's vaguely familiar. However, I can't remember ever being in a place like this before. There are pots on a six-ring stove bubbling away, huge trays of ingredients being made into canapés by three cooks working in an assembly line along one of the counters. Thinking that I'd like to try one of them, I head over to steal one of the assembled ones from the final tray, only to find they aren't food at all. They are electronic components of some sort.

"What the . . . ?" I pull back as one of the waiters collects the tray and carries it balanced on the fingers of his right hand out of the room in the opposite direction from the party.

"Why are you here?" says one of the cooks, right at me.

I blink at her, thrown by the sudden loss of invisibility and the fact that she looks like a woman who sat at the same table as me at that awful awards ceremony. "I'm looking for someone," I say. "Someone causing trouble up here."

Then they all turn and look at me. I take a step back. Every single person in this room was at that ceremony. I'm sure of it.

"He's not in here," the cook says. "You can't be looking very hard."

I ignore the spark of hurt pride the comment causes and scan the room. "I heard something when I was downstairs, but nothing seems to be wrong up here."

She laughs; then they all start laughing, as if I'd said the funniest thing in the world. "Everyone's going to die," she says, still chuckling and wiping a tear away from the corner of her eye. "He's going to kill them."

This is the weirdest lead-in to a boss fight I have ever experienced. "Okay . . . so . . . what the hell is going on?"

The cook points out of the room with her knife, in a way no sensible person would in a busy kitchen, in the same direction the waiter just took the tray of components. "He's through there. We've all known it was going to happen.

Even our parents and grandparents did. He's just getting it all set up now."

I look at the trays in the assembly line. "What is he setting up? Some sort of weapon?"

She nods.

"Well, shit, why are you helping him?"

The look on her face makes me feel stupid. "Do you have another job you could give me? And all my staff?"

"What about the people through there?" I point toward the party. "Do they know?"

"Know about what he's going to do?" She laughs again, and all of the other staff laugh too, all stopping their work to look at me and laugh, like this is some sort of weird arthouse play about social embarrassment or something equally tedious. "Do you think that would make any difference? They don't care."

They all have knives. Every single one of them. Even the ones stirring the pots on the stove have knives in their free hands. I look at the racks on the wall, hanging down from the ceiling over the central work top and in the blocks on the countertop that they are normally stored in. Not a single free knife in the entire room. I don't want to go rooting about in the drawers, not yet anyway.

Shit, am I supposed to deal with the boss with nothing more than a saucepan and enthusiasm?

"If you're not going to do anything, you may as well leave," says the cook. "Go outside and get killed with the rest of them if you like."

"No," says the cook next to her. "She's allowed to be here and watch from the window if she likes."

"Watch everyone in London die?"

"Not just London, darlin'," he says. "The 'ole bleedin' world, innit."

This is too close to the bone to be coincidence, surely? Is

the game designer trying to tell me he knows what they did to Earth?

No, that's ludicrous. How many games have I played where I, as the hero of the piece, have had to stop the big bad from destroying the world? It's a trope, nothing more.

I have no intention of just sitting back and watching mass murder happen all over again, game version or not. I march out of the room, heading in the same direction as that tray of components was taken, my thoughts bouncing between seeing all of this as a message buried in a sick initiation and trying to work out how to handle it. Pretty much any other game that ends with a violent final boss tools you up as you progress: armor, weapons, whatever. And if it isn't a violent confrontation, there are usually all sorts of clues and story elements along the way to give an insight into the enemy so they can be defeated in some other, dialog-heavy way.

But this game? This game chucks all of that out the window and then pisses on it. I mean, what kind of thought process went into this? "I'll make a game. Let's set it in the player's old life and visit all those juicy traumas along the way. Hello, player! Welcome to hell. If you look on your left, you'll see the pathetic attempt to make a home in the basement of the building you once lived in. And if you look on your right, you can see your dead parents, laughing again. Don't look down! There's dead people there. All the dead people you ever knew. Ha! I am such a genius!"

Of course, the lack of the usual narrative supports could be his way of trying to make this seem more realistic, admittedly in the most unrealistic way possible. Life in meatspace doesn't have the same rules, doesn't lay out the right way to go as clearly as lots of games do. The figurative armor and weapons we need aren't often laid out in easy-to-access places, scaled to our ability at the time. Well, some people would argue they are, but they're the same sort of idiots who say that positive thinking helps to overcome systemic in-equality.

Thing is, the coder is making so many statements here—or at least I think he is—that it's just a messy soup of experi-ences. I'm so uncertain of anything, I can't see what I'm supposed to be getting out of this, other than some vague promise that it will help me reach my goals. Running up all those flights of stairs might have helped a tiny bit, but I picked my way up here slowly. I suppose there was the whole door-code thing . . . but . . . ah, fuck it. I'm going to take a look at this weapon thing and then come up. If he mocks me, I'll just mock him back. The invite to the leet server from Carolina will still be legit.

The door leads to a short hallway. I'm irritated by the fact that the programmer hasn't even bothered to make me want to face the big bad at the end. I mean, I don't know anything about him. There's been no tear-jerking scene where I find out he's killed my puppy or anything. No mis-sion parameters set by someone back at a hidden base some-where. It makes me complacent, putting my hand on the door and pushing it open without any consideration.

A bullet grazes my shoulder and it burns like a spear thrown from the depths of hell, the bang of the gun seeming to follow several seconds later. Adrenaline spikes; I duck down, hands on top of my head instinctively as I look for cover. A table has been knocked over just a couple of meters away and I dive behind it, expecting more shots, but none follow.

I put my back to the tabletop, draw my legs in and grin. Now, this is more like it!

8

ALL I CAN see from my hiding place is a painting of an old sailing ship being tossed on the ocean in a storm. There is a thick carpet laid from wall to wall, making me wonder if this is a bedroom. I listen for the sound of the shooter crossing the room to come finish me off, and I'm puzzled by the fact that they haven't tried to shoot me through the tabletop. There's a loud sigh and what sounds like a gun being tossed onto the floor.

"Knock first!" a man shouts. "I can't stand it when you forget the freakin' rules! I nearly killed you! Dumb-ass!" His accent is from somewhere in the southern states, but all those drawls sound the same to me. I have no idea which particular place he comes from.

I suddenly know why I'm wearing a tux, just like the rest of the staff. I am such a cocking idiot. "Sorry, sir!" I call back.

"Well, come out, then. What did you want?"

My heart still banging away like I'm in a firefight, I stand with shaking legs.

It is a bedroom, with an en-suite on the other side of the room. All beige and white and so neutral it makes me feel like grabbing a few cans of brightly colored paint and just lobbing them around the room so it has some definition. It's like it's been designed to be so restful it hardly exists.

Everything is so perfectly coordinated it feels like a high-end hotel room, or something that's been designed by an AI. Nothing here speaks of a life or a person's interests, just furniture and generic ceramic ornaments that have complementary colors. There's another sea-based painting, but that smacks of an AI wanting to create something with flavor. The bed is, unsurprisingly, huge and covered in scatter cushions, which you'd just have to push onto the floor to go to sleep and then put back in the morning. What's the point of them?

The room is spacious enough for a large sofa and two armchairs arranged around a rug, and a small dining table too. What is that even for? This must be modeled after a hotel room.

There's a man, alone, on the far side of the room, standing in a circular area that suggests a turret-shaped protrusion on the side of the building. He's wearing something like a SWAT team uniform, black, functional. No helmet. He has brown eyes, brown hair, and I have no idea who he is. I don't recognize him. The first person here I can't place from somewhere in my past. He's looking at me expectantly. "Errr . . . the butler said you might need a hand, sir."

"Come over here, then," he says.

There's a complex machine next to him, partially assembled, with the latest tray of components resting next to it. He is literally putting it together, pretty much from scratch, and it looks like he's almost finished it. There are some tools, but nothing useful for my purposes. I approach, cautious, taking in as much detail about the equipment around him as I can.

"I need to know you're safe," he says, folding his arms.

His legs are slightly parted as he stands there, appraising me. Typical male power stance. Whatever, Mr. Nonplayer Character, I can handle you.

"I'm one of the staff," I say. "I have clearance to be here."

He just stares at me. He's waiting for something more. I stop a couple of meters away, not wanting to push the AI into combat mode, which is usually what happens in an end scene like this. If I stay outside of the NPC's personal space, I'll be able to keep it in dialog mode to find out why he's doing this.

I don't need to know, necessarily. The other NPCs have told me what he's going to do. But I want to be thorough. If this is an initiation, I want to look good, and blowing it after all the shit it's put me through already would be really dumb. He's obviously waiting for some sort of password or secret handshake or—

The pin! I pull back my jacket and the tiny little CSA pin that I took in the previous level is still there, simply affixed to a different shirt. "Does this reassure you?" I ask, brazening it out.

He smiles, relaxes. "Thank you, sister. Now, shall we do God's work?"

Sister? Shit, is this some sort of cult?

I smile. "Yes, brother. Could you tell me what stage you're at?"

He turns away to look at the machine. I could stab him in the back, but I'm still not very confident about how exactly to use myself as any sort of weapon, let alone as a knife. Bobby Bear said something about consequences . . . am I supposed to detonate myself somehow, thereby removing the threat but ending the game?

"I've figured out how to put it together; that was tough but not beyond me. Now I've cracked it, I just have to finish putting all these in the right places." He gestures at the remaining components.

I can't help but think this looks like a sort of stylized puzzle piece. There are markings on the little bits of electronics, hinting that there is a pattern that needs to be identified and followed. But this is a boss fight, surely, not a puzzler? The first NPC in the game pointed me toward it, right at the start of the game. Other NPCs have told me he's going to kill everyone. As crappy as the signposts are in this game, those have been pretty damn obvious.

Too obvious, perhaps? No, if I start second-guessing now I won't get anywhere.

"Looking good," I say. "So, once it's done, are you ready for the next part of the"—I look at the uniform and consider the way he treated me—"mission?"

"I'm more than ready. I feel good about this, actually. I wasn't sure if I needed to go through this again, but . . ." He coughs. "Errr . . . I mean, I feel totally comfortable with the mission."

"You're going to detonate the weapon?" Shit, I hope I am triggering the right dialog here. I want to understand exactly what he's going to do, and as long as this NPC believes I'm in the same organization as he is, the fight won't kick off.

"Sure I am. Only this time, I get to watch."

This dialog is weird. Like it's hinting that he's been training for it, maybe that this has happened before. He's looking out of the window, gazing across the rooftops of London. "We'll be safe here. We can watch it from this very window. Watch them burn. All those sinners. All those who refuse to acknowledge the true path to God."

Oh great, a religious nutjob monolog.

"And it isn't just a cleansin'; this is protection. That's what's really crystallized for me now. We're protecting the future of humanity by takin' the purest with us and makin' sure that none of those bastards can spread their lies anywhere else. One religion—the true religion—will go with us into the stars."

Oh JeeMuh. This isn't a coincidence. The designer knows what they did! He's showing me he does. But why? Why put me through all this awful shit, just to tell me that?

I hold my hands still at my sides, school my face into showing what all men like this want to see: agreement and admiration. Behind that mask are so many questions I am keeping silent. How could the game designer know about Earth? Why not just tell me?

He grabs a couple of the components and starts clicking them into place inside the machine. There are only ten or so left. "Are those the last bits you need?" I ask. "Do you need me to fetch anything else to make it work?"

"No."

I run through the game in my mind. He made me start in the basement, facing one of the lowest points of my life, then forced me to confront all the loss caused by what those bastards did. And now he's made an NPC personifying them, giving me a villain to kill right at the top of the building.

This isn't an initiation. This is catharsis.

And all of a sudden, I know how to kill him. I've always known how I want to kill those responsible, and now I can get a taste of it. I swiftly close the distance between us, put my left hand on his shoulder and twist him round. I flatten my right hand, holding the fingers extended, and imagine them as solid as a blade. I thrust it into his abdomen, aiming for just under his lowest rib. His skin splits and I feel the heat and moisture of his innards as I push through and past internal organs and then I am grasping his heart as I roar with rage.

It feels hot and slimy and he gasps, dropping the component that was in his hand, his eyes bulging in shock. I expect him to cough up blood, or make some sort of bubbling gurgle, but there's just a choking wheeze as he sinks to his knees. His blood is running down my forearm, dripping onto the floor, and I sink onto my knees with him, squeezing, squeezing the life out of his sick fundamentalist heart.

He falls and I relax my hand, letting his body slide off my arm and collapse. Even though my arm is covered with gore, his body looks uninjured. He still looks very dead though.

Yeah, okay, that felt pretty good. I flex my fingers and they feel fine, aside from the drying blood coating them. After standing there for a few moments, waiting for some sort of in-game prompt that I've completed the mission or quest or whatever, I go to the en-suite bathroom and clean myself up as best I can. I abandon the jacket and roll the bloodied sleeve up, wishing I'd had a chance to do that before I killed him.

It seems strange that such a gory death has left no evidence on his corpse. Not even a hole in his clothes. It's like I was able to do an adult-rated kill move within a child-safe game, which this most certainly is not.

The en-suite is obscene. So high-spec and spacious that I feel tempted to have a shower. But I don't trust this game and I don't trust the designer behind it. For all I know he could be watching.

With some apprehension, I check my face for blood spatter, but there are only a couple of specks on my throat, which are soon washed away. At least the designer hasn't dicked about with my face here. It's the same as it is in the real world. Mum's cheekbones, Dad's eyes, my hair its usual dark blond, cropped shorter now than I've ever worn it. I run my hand up the back of my head, feeling the velvety fuzz, actually liking it. I didn't wear it this way for years, unable to divorce it from the memory of being shaved by the hot-housers when I was first processed. It's longer on the top than they had left it: just enough so I don't look like one of their inmates.

The urge to cry rises so swiftly a half sob escapes before I even realize it's happening. With one hand braced against the sink, I cover my mouth until the feeling passes. What is there to cry about? I look at my reflection, at my glistening eyes, and scowl. "Pull your shit together!" I shout at myself, and it's gone. I feel fine now.

Nothing has changed in the bedroom. His body is still there, which jars me. In zero-gore games it would have faded out by now. I study his face, wondering if I knew him a long time ago and have forgotten him, but he seems just as much a stranger. Surely there is a statement in that fact? In a game populated purely by people I have known—or even just seen regularly—in my life on Earth, the fact that he is the only exception feels important. Is the designer saying that the people who did this are nothing like me or the other normal people I knew? I would have thought he'd be rendered like that boss of mine, but he was somewhere around floor seven.

And, of course, this is nothing compared to the wider question: was this really a way to tell me the creator knows what they did? Or am I overthinking it? I do that with games, always trying to second-guess them, always trying to see the work-around so I can beat it faster. I need to be careful when I next speak to him, just in case I'm wrong. Or he's working for them.

I mentally stamp on that silly bit of paranoia and go to the machine the boss was building. It looks like an industrial oven; the little bits of electronics were being fitted inside the central space, forming a pattern on the inside floor. There's what looks like some sort of . . . cannon on the front of the machine, pointing out at the city. No trigger, so I expect it's activated through an APA for security. I start pulling out the components and doing my best to dismantle it in the hope it's the trigger for the end-of-game sequence. The more I handle it, the more it looks like a puzzler mini-game to me. Perhaps the game was coded to give me the option of helping him. Or taking him out, changing my mind and then killing everyone else. No, that's not my rush.

There's a clunk from inside the machine when I pull the last component out of the central cavity. I crouch down, peering inside to see a section of an internal partition has dropped down, revealing another cavity farther in. The light doesn't penetrate far enough for me to see what's inside it. I reach in and my fingertips brush against something cold and solid—a box.

Pulling it out reveals that it's the same obsidian box as the one that contained the key that opened the door into this game. Nice symmetry.

"Bobby Bear?" I call, and then he comes through the door from the hallway.

I set the box down and pick him up, cuddling him tight. Just one indulgence, just one moment of comfort before I go. I daren't go back into the other room and seek out my parents. I'm scared I would never want to leave.

But more than that, I'm scared that it wouldn't be as perfect as I have always imagined it would be.

Bobby Bear's little arms squeeze me back. "Well done, Dee Dee. You stopped the bad man from doing a terrible thing."

"If only the real world were so easy, right?"

"It was good to see you again," he says. "How do you feel about what happened?"

If Bobby Bear hadn't asked me that same question a million times in my childhood, I'd suspect this was a consumer feedback device. It might still be, but I let myself imagine it's not. "Okay, I guess."

"Okay, you guess?" His tone is both incredulous and unimpressed. "All right, how about answering this: do you feel you did the right thing?"

I put him down and look at the body behind us. "Yeah. He was some weirdo full of toxic Christianity bullshit who was about to kill everyone." I shrug. "But it's—" I stop my-self. Shit. I was about to say that it's just a poor salve for the wound, given this is just a game and over six months after the real damage was done. I need to be careful.

"But it's what?"

"But it's a no-brainer," I say. "It was obviously the end set piece. And I know some people get off on being the vil-lain, but that doesn't do it for me, so there was only one way to go. I could have tried to persuade him not to do it, I guess, but from the way he was talking it was clear that reason had left his table a long time ago."

"Are you going to leave now, Dee Dee?"

I pick up the box. "Yeah."

"You don't want to see your parents before you go?"

I look back, into the corridor, hearing the piano and the laughter. "No. They're not my parents."

There is a key inside the box, and this one has an ornate O embellished in the grip. I pick it up and a doorframe starts appearing in the floor, just as before. "Bye then, Bobby Bear," I say.

"Bye-bye, Dee Dee. Take care now. I love you."

I loved you too, I think, but I don't say it. I put the key in the newly appeared door now standing in front of me, turn it and go through into my office. The door closes behind me before I give in to the temptation to look back at Bobby Bear to see if he is waving the way I imagine he is. Was. He's not there and never was. It was just a fucking game.

The familiar slate expanse of my office space is merci-fully bleak and feels a world away from the game environ-ment. I look up at the stars, wait a moment to see if I get that weird chatbox thing, and then when nothing comes I say, "End immersion," with a sigh of relief.

It feels like I sink into my body, then into the bed. I open my eyes and see the creamy white plastic ceiling, hear the quiet hum of the environmental support system and realize that I really hate this cabin. A few seconds later I also realize that I desperately need a piss.

My body's needs come thick and fast, a new one presenting itself as quickly as I satisfy the last. Tedious meatsack, so demanding.

Once I've had some food, I stretch out on the bed again and review my messages. Nothing from Carolina except an acknowledgment of receipt sent by her APA. I don't know if that's a good or bad sign. Maybe she has a lot of work on. Then I notice the time and sit up sharply. Maybe it's because it's the middle of the bloody night.

JeeMuh, I was gone for hours. It felt like hours . . . but most games skew stuff, tricking the brain into thinking more time has passed in game than actually has. Not this one. I've been fully immersed for over six hours.

Usually there's a notification after two. Just a tiny ping from your APA, no big deal. At three hours in it gets a bit more persistent, reminding you to at least have a drink. Mine is set to boot me out after four hours in a game, whether I like it or not.

That game overrode my own personal safety settings. Furious, I slam my fist into the bed and then I look at my hand, expecting to see a healing gash across the palm, but mercifully there isn't one. That fucking b—

<Hey Dee, what did you think of the game?>

The message just pops up in that weird dialog box again, the text floating over my visual field like any other, but this time there's no ping from my APA asking if I want to read it first.

<I think you need to learn some manners.> I type back and immediately regret it. That was far too polite and I

sound like some old bastard from some hokey mersive about a small town where everyone knows each other. <I also think you're a fucking shitweasel.> That's better.

<Yeah, but what about the game?>

That actually makes me laugh. <You broke almost every rule in game narrative design: you didn't give me any content warnings, you didn't ask for my consent in using data you must have mined from my chip or dug out of some dodgy file on this ship, you sure as hell didn't get permission to use the likenesses and voices of people who've died and the final boss was far too easy to kill and it wasn't that dramatic anyway because there wasn't any kind of emotional buildup to it.>

<But you got something out of it, right?>

He must be twelve. Some fucking twelve-year-old genius who is just so damn arrogant he doesn't even hear criticism.

<I got a headache out of it. And we need to have a conversation about consent.>

<No we don't. That's all taken care of now. Did you feel good when you killed him?>

This is making me nervous. It feels like there was some sort of tipping point and I was too distracted to notice. This is not edgy. This is not cool or exciting. I've only felt like this once before, when I was with a guy in a squat who I kind of liked, who kind of liked me and then there was kissing and all of a sudden I just knew I was not into him. No, not him, the whole sex thing. I'd just been mimicking what I saw other people do, thinking it was what I should do, but then, when it was actually happening, it just felt . . . crap, and I didn't want to kiss, let alone let it progress any further. Just like back then, there's no way to leave this situation easily, no door to lock between us if it goes bad.

"Ada," I say, "can you block this chatbox thing?"

"Please specify the chatbox you are referring to," Ada replies in its smooth voice.

"The one that's in my visual field right now, dumb-ass!"

"There is no chatbox in your visual field. Dumb-ass."

<Hey Dee, did you feel good when you killed him?>

Just like in the squat when I backed off and he kept on coming, I feel the first chill of panic. <It's late. I need to sleep now. And you need to tell me who you are if you want to keep talking to me.>

<Oh yeah, it is late. Okay. Good night, Dee. Let's talk more tomorrow.>

The box disappears. I swing my legs off the bed and lean forward, resting my head between my knees, feeling shaky and nauseous. Violated. That's how I feel. Not because of the chatbox bullshit—though that doesn't help—but because of that fucking game that dredged my life and muddied everything up again. Something about the way he asked how I felt about killing that man felt . . . sick. Like I've been some sort of test subject or . . . I don't know. It just feels wrong.

I can't tell anyone though. It would mean they'd want to investigate and I don't want to be on anyone's radar, not when I have some serious shit to get done. I can't even mention it to Carl. Not that I ever confided much in him anyway. I never confided in anyone since Bobby Bear. And he wasn't even a real person. There is a flicker of self-pity before I snuff it out.

There's no way I'll sleep now. "Ada, show me some pictures on the ceiling or something."

"Are you having trouble sleeping?"

"Yeah."

"Would you like a neurochemical intervention?"

"No."

"Would you like me to show you what Japan looks like in blossom season?"

I lie back down on the bed. "Yeah, that sounds good. Show me some blossom. And tell me a story. One that I like."

"'The Snow Queen,' by Hans Christian Andersen . . ."

9

ADA WAKES ME up with some Norwegian death punk as she puts the lights on full blast in the cabin. I threaten to have her put back to factory settings, but she just ramps up the volume another notch until I sit up and put my feet on the floor. I hate her. She does exactly what I tell her to do, even when it is good for me.

I scratch my head, listening to the vocalist screaming something about the old gods and fire or something like that, trying to get my head around the day ahead. I've got used to the fact that there aren't any meetings or lunch dates or all the other bits of social furniture that used to clutter up my day. I don't miss them either. But I do miss the sense that I have to get up for something. "Why did you wake me up?" I say to Ada.

"In thirty minutes you are expected on Mars. There are aliens inside robots that need a good twatting."

I smirk at the sound of her interpreting my calendar entry. Yeah, I remember now—I made a date with Carl to shoot some shit up. I wonder if I'll actually be able to handle playing a mersive with him this time, instead of standing there, just watching it all pass me by like the last time we tried.

Stretching, cleaning myself up and then checking messages over breakfast soon fills the time. Still nothing from Carolina. I need to let it go. If it doesn't turn into anything, I'll have to find another way to get the data I need, that's all. It's not like I really want the job.

At the back of my mind there's a niggle that suggests I don't really believe that. I enjoyed doing that data analysis and report far more than I like to admit.

When I get the ping from Ada telling me it's time to go, I lie down and enter full immersion, waiting in the shared loading room I usually meet Carl in. It's a comfortable space with a couple of chairs and a basketball hoop, just in case one of us is late. I get Ada to give me a ball and I spend a few minutes messing about with it, dribbling it up and down the room and shooting a few hoops. When another ten minutes goes by, I send him a prod.

After another five minutes of pissing about I'm just about to give up on him when the door opens and he comes in. He's dressed in a suit, making me do a double take. "Sorry," he says, hands up. "I'm really sorry, Dee, I got caught up in something."

"Why are you dressed like that?" I take a step closer. He seems different. There's a brightness in his eyes I haven't seen in months. He looks really good, actually, his avatar reflecting something real. "What's going on?"

He considers something and then grins. "I'll show you. Tia, put my room next door."

I go over to him. "Which room? Are you building something?"

"No. Better than that. Something real. I've got a case, Dee."

It takes me a moment to process that. "What, a murder?"
He nods, eagerly. "On the ship? For real?"

"For real."

"What do you mean, you'll show me?"

He goes to the door that should be leading us into a room
on the Martian base where we can get kitted up to go twat
aliens. "I'm not owned by the DoJ anymore. This isn't an
official case. And to be completely honest, I'm not even sure
it's a murder yet. But it's something weird and they've asked
me to help and there hasn't been any sort of NDA yet. I
think they're all a bit shocked."

"Who's 'they'?"

"The command crew. Look . . . I always wanted to talk
my cases through with you, but I didn't dare risk it. It's different here and I've only ever had Tia to bounce stuff off.
Want to see what I do? You'll have to sign an NDA, just a
standard 'I won't tell anyone anything' sort of thing, with a
clause that will give Tia permission to block your APA while
we're in the room."

"If it's not an official case, is the NDA just between us?"
He nods. I can understand why he's being cautious. I've always wondered how he deals with death and liars, and I can
see how much he wants me to go with him to watch his process. He wants me to see him at his best after seeing him at
his worst so much of late. "Okay. As long as I'm not going
to get into trouble."

"It's my private server space. And I trust you not to tell
anyone or mention it in anything that can be found by someone else, but the NDA will protect you and me if this turns
out to be really serious. If anyone goes digging in your files,
all it will show is that you left this loading room and went to
a private session in my space. Not what we're doing there."

"Great, so they'll think we were doing pr0n or something."

He smirks. "Since when would what people think bother you?"

"Fair. Okay, yeah, I'll come and see what you do. But one thing before we go; do you want me to just look quietly impressed, or do you want the whole fluttering-eyelashes, breathless-admiration thing?"

His stern glare is filled with good humor. "You just can't let a guy feel good about himself for five minutes?"

"Oh, I probably could, but I reckon you can inflate your own ego all by yourself." I prod him in the stomach. "I'm joking," I add. "You know I only exist to make you look better."

He chuckles, shaking his head, and then opens the door.

We walk into what looks like a cabin on this ship, given that it's made of the same creamy white plastic, but twice the size of mine. The bed has been slept in, and there is a pile of clothes on the floor next to it, along with a pair of smart black boots. "I got a call this morning, early," Carl says. "One of the command crew died in the night and they wanted me to check out the cause of death. Whenever there is even the tiniest bit of doubt about a death, we—" He stops himself. "I mean, the usual procedure is to send in a cam drone crew to photograph the scene without touching anything. Then Tia mocks it up into a 3-D render so I can look around."

"But isn't the AI more qualified to look into that? I can understand if they want a human doctor to eyeball the results but . . ."

"We can get data from MyPhys; that tells us a lot. Then there's a pathologist, who can tell us more. They're assisted by drones and AI, but they run the show. It's a bit different here on the ship. There is a doctor who is also a qualified pathologist, and there's a suitable lab. But they haven't sent the body to hir yet. They're not sure if they have to. That's why they asked me to review the case."

"Because you know what foul play looks like?"

"Yeah. And there is something weird about this death."

I follow him farther into the room, thinking of all the murder mystery mersives I've played in, aware that what I used to do for fun was the focus of his entire working life. "So if this was a game, I'd be looking for . . . signs of struggle. Evidence of someone else being here . . . but all of that would be after I knew how he died. Was he attacked?"

"Well, that's the thing," Carl says, heading over to the bed. "He had a heart attack when he was lying here."

"And they're worried that . . . what, he was scared to death? Poisoned?"

"No. He was in his late thirties, super healthy, and playing a game at the time," he says. "Full immersion, some spy thriller that he hadn't played before, but he'd played similar titles and the MyPhys data shows he was pretty calm throughout. Where it gets weird is that the data shows that when he was playing there were no stress factors showing up at all; then he had a heart attack out of nowhere. And more than that, MyPhys didn't deploy the usual fail-safes. He wasn't pulled out of the game, for starters. The medical team wasn't informed of an emergency and MyPhys didn't do anything to try to stop the attack. I mean, ninety-five percent of cardiacs are detected before there are even any noticeable symptoms, and MyPhys always intervenes directly before it becomes life-threatening. The last time someone who was chipped died of a cardiac arrest was when those bootlegged snuff mersives were going round, decades ago. And that was not what he was playing."

A creeping sense of dread fills my gut, but I don't show it. Like all those times in the Machine, I keep my own feelings as far away from anything I might show in my expressions or in my body as I can. I imagine my face as a mask in front of a mask, totally disconnected from anything real I might feel.

"Weird," I say. "So, who was this guy? Did he have any enemies who might know how to dick with MyPhys settings?"

"He was an engineer, pretty high up, answered directly to the chief engineer. Tia, throw a pic of him on the wall, will you?"

I ready myself, even as I am filled with doubts that it could possibly have anything to do with—

The face of the man I killed in the game last night fills the blank wall opposite us. Oh JeeMuh, *he's* the murder victim! I lock my expression down into one of vague interest, while beneath it confusion and panic bubble up within me. There's no way what I did in the game could have anything to do with this, surely?

I can't show any of this; I can't let Carl get even a sniff of these feelings. My face is a mask, in front of a mask. My face is a mask, in front—

"Lieutenant Commander Joseph Myerson," Carl says, as I silently recite my private mantra. "Well liked, excellent at his job, no known enemies. Of course, I haven't had a chance to trawl through all of his files yet, and I'd be surprised if they let me, but as far as I can tell, someone hacked his chip and switched off the MyPhys fail-safes so that whatever happened to him in the game had a real-world impact on his heart."

"Is that even possible?" I don't have to fake my disbelief.

"Lots of people have tried it," he says, coming over to stand next to me as I stare at the display. "But they've never done it well enough to escape an AI's attention."

"That you know of," I say, looking at him so I can push that man's face out of my mind. "They may have been so good that no one ever found out."

He gives me a doubtful look. "No. I don't think so. An anomaly like this would always be escalated up to people like me. I checked with Tia. No cases match this profile."

"But is the entire Internet with us on the ship?"

"The US, European and Noropean MoJ case files are. Don't ask me how they got hold of anything outside US jurisdiction. The US used to collaborate with both Europe and Norope, but they clearly hacked the fuck out of their servers before they left. Trust me—this is nothing like anything I've seen before."

"So . . . how do you approach something like this, if it's not a known MO? They do still say 'MO,' don't they?"

"Yeah, we still use that, but mostly when we want to sound like we're as cool as the detectives in the mersives." He grins. "So, there are a few logical next steps. One is to take a look at his chip and all of the traffic to and from it. I've already isolated all of the data and have a copy saved in my private space, just in case whoever did this still has a back door. We might be able to find some trace of the hack—if it was one—and use that to find out who was behind it. It might also reveal that no hack took place at all, and that it was a malfunction. I don't think that will be the case, but this is the stage where it's important to keep an open mind."

"There are too many fail-safes," I say. "Isn't MyPhys automatically tied into the ship's system? Like a deadman's handle sort of thing—if the chip stops reporting data or starts doing weird stuff, it trips a notification or something?"

He nods. "Yeah, but only if there's a break in the data, or a bizarre change. If there's no change, nothing gets flagged up, and that's what we have here. It didn't change—didn't do anything at all—even when he was dying of a coronary."

"What about the game?" I ask. It's not just to give the impression of being engaged and curious—Christ knows I am both of those—I need to know whether I have to get a confession straight right now. No, what am I thinking? I was playing a game; I wasn't trying to murder someone! I only would have if it had been one of the bastards who—

Oh shit. He *was* one of the people involved! That must be why he was in the game—why he was the one person I didn't recognize—because that fucking coder was giving me more than just catharsis.

He was giving me the perfect way to murder someone.

I go to the dead man's desk to cover the fact that I have probably given away some sort of tiny clue about being freaked-out about something. I must not underestimate Carl. He was one of the best.

"Yeah, the game is the other angle I'm already investigating. I've requested access to the relevant files on the server."

"Was he playing with anyone else, or was it a solo game?"

"Solo. At least, that's what the initial report said, but I'll be digging deeper than that. I had a case, a couple of years ago, where a bloke was being blackmailed through a game. He thought he was playing alone, confessed some dodgy shit to what he thought was an NPC, but she was actually a hacker who'd compromised the gaming server. Bloody clever. She used the game to make the demands and collect the money. Nothing was flagged up in the system because it all looked like in-game purchases."

I think back to the conversation I had with that man, how strange it had sounded. Now I think about it, he sounded like a player. He thought *I* was an NPC. JeeMuh, Carl knows exactly what to look for! I'm so fucked.

"Carl," I begin, trying to work out whether to confess the murder first, or how I fell into the trap, when he holds up a hand.

"Two secs, Dee, sorry."

His eyes glaze over as he attends to something I cannot see. I turn back to face the desk, keeping myself as calm as I would during a test in the hot-housing center, desperate to hide any responses they would deem unsuitable so I could avoid being put back into the Machine.

A movement draws my attention. He has swiped something onto the wall. The bedroom from the game is displayed there, the victim standing next to the death machine thing, in his spy mersive costume. The image is currently frozen, the cam angle to his right, the view of London clear in the background. This has been re-created from the game I was playing? JeeMuh, has the whole thing been dug up?

I need to tell Carl. He'll listen. He'll understand I didn't mean to do it. He's my best friend, my only friend! He won't let me down.

"Carl—"

"I need to watch this, but if you want to leave, that's totally fine. I don't know what's going to be in it, but it's from the last two minutes of his life so it could be pretty nasty."

I should tell him, but the words just aren't there. Instead, there's the sure knowledge that even Carl will let me down, when I most need him. Every other person who ever had the chance betrayed me. Why should he be any different? I've never truly tested this friendship, and I can't do it now with something this big, this dangerous. He didn't leave me behind on Earth, but he didn't know they were going to nuke it either. He brought me with him because I've always propped him up and he couldn't bear the thought of me not being there for him. I have never needed him, and I can't let myself see if he will be there for me when I do, not when it's for something like this.

Should I run away now? No. I need to know how bad it is. And I need to be here to defend myself, in those first moments when he knows it was me.

"No shame in leaving," Carl adds, thinking my hesitation is all about pride.

"I'll be okay. I've seen millions of people die in games."

The serious look lingers on his face. "Yeah, not real people though. But okay, you're a grown-up. Play it, Tia."

"Come over here, then," the dead man says on the wall. Fuck! That was just after he tried to shoot me!

My face is a mask, in front of mask. My face is a—

Someone wearing a tux walks into the right-hand side of the shot, and even though it's a woman, it doesn't look anything like me. I swallow, not letting myself sag with relief, not even letting myself breathe differently as I realize that this render must have been re-created from the data served to his chip, not mine. This is the game *he* was playing in, in which he thought I was an NPC. I didn't look like me to him, then? Everything else looks exactly as I remember it.

"I need to know you're safe," he says, and we watch the conversation play out exactly as it went. It's like I was just skinned and voiced differently in his version of the game. Is there a chance I will actually get away with this?

"Pfft, spy games," I say derisively when I watch the badge being shown and his satisfaction that he was safe to talk. "They've never really lit my candle."

"Dee . . ." Carl says, shushing me in as many words.

We both watch in silence as the conversation ends with my decision to kill him. In this version the hand—my hand—actually changes, becoming metallic at first; then the fingers sharpen and it morphs into a blade. The same grab of his shoulder to spin him round, the same driving the hand-blade thing up under his ribs.

"Shit," Carl mutters. "That's brutal."

"We've done worse. Remember that game with the vampires and that demon thing with all the mouths?"

His nose wrinkles as he recalls it. "Shit, yeah, that was grim. But that was just a game. We're watching a man being murdered. For real."

I fall silent. It's more than that for me. I'm watching myself commit a murder, while I'm standing next to one of Norope's top criminal investigators. I'm watching that and hiding every single flicker of shock and excitement and horror I feel, using techniques forced upon me by the hothousers, whom I hated more than anything else in this world. Those fucks who destroyed my life and made it into something they could package and sell for profit might well have given me everything I need to get away with murder. If I wasn't hiding my nausea behind these neutral expressions I'm fixing on my face, I'd probably be laughing at the bitter irony of it all.

The game footage stops a few seconds later, presumably when his heart stops in the real world. Carl swipes it away from the wall, deep in thought.

"So . . . where do you go from here?" I ask.

"The NPC there, that's the one to focus on. Tia, how many people were playing full-immersion games at the same time as Joseph Myerson?"

A woman I hadn't noticed is standing in the corner. She's got the generically attractive face of a female avatar, is wearing a three-piece pinstripe suit and has legs that go on forever. "Three thousand four hundred and fifty people were fully immersed during the time frame specified."

"I was one of them," I say. He's going to see my name on that list. If I don't volunteer that information now, he'll be suspicious.

He frowns at me. "You don't know what the time frame is, Dee."

"It was last night, right? I was under for, like . . . hours. Came up in the middle of the bloody night. Just got too caught up in stuff, you know?"

"You're not a suspect," he says, like I am being ridiculous. "If you were a suspect, you wouldn't be here with me now. I've already eliminated you."

"Oh yeah, I was just . . ." I was just nearly fucking up, that's what I was doing. "Of course. You know me."

He nods. "That and the fact you were asleep when he died and your name isn't on this list. You might have been immersed a lot of last night, but not when this happened." He smiles. "Tia would have highlighted your name if it was on here. But I'll double-check if you're worried. Tia? Was Dee immersed when Myerson died?"

"No. Dee was in REM sleep during the time of death."

"I was dreaming? How the fuck does she know that?"

"I've got a high-level clearance for the case. She's just pulled your MyPhys data to see what your brain was doing. Chill, Dee. It's all fine."

I laugh. At myself. At the fact that this is really not fine. "So, did people freak out around you a lot before?"

He nods, relaxed. "Perfectly innocent people would blush, look away from me, develop twitches, all sorts of things when they realized who I was and why I was there. And then the actual murderers would be nonchalant as fuck. Not always, but yeah, normal, innocent people often got flustered."

"Well, lucky I was dreaming at the time. Now we don't have to worry about it. So . . . do you have to check out what all those people were playing?"

"Tia and I will eliminate people pretty damn quick. It's not a very interesting process though, so there's no point in you sticking around. I reckon I'll have a list of suspects in about half an hour, then the perp in custody by lunchtime. Can we do Mars after that?"

I fold my arms. "Are you yanking my chain?"

His surprise seems genuine enough. "What? I'm serious. Ninety-eight . . . actually, Tia, was it ninety-eight or ninety-nine percent of my cases that were solved in less than twenty-four hours?"

"Ninety-eight point four percent."

He spreads his hands as if to say, "See? I really am that good."

"And the other one point six percent?"

He blows out his cheeks. "Oh, those were a fucking nightmare. Every single one. My last official case was one of them."

That must have been the Alejandro Casales case. He doesn't talk about it, but I know that, somehow, it led to us being on this ship. And us not being dead.

Is it just a matter of time until he works out that I killed Myerson? Or have I been eliminated so early he'll never connect me to the death? I don't want to increase the odds of giving something away, so I go over to him, clap a hand on his shoulder and say, "You go catch the bad guy, honey, and then come back to me." I flutter my eyelashes for comic effect.

He smirks. "I'll ping you when I'm done."

"I do have one question," I say as I head for the door. "What will they do when you find out who it was? Is there a prison on this ship?"

"There's a brig," he replies. "The captain and most of the command crew have the authority to detain any member of the crew in it. But the murderer won't be in there for long."

"I guess they'll want the trial to happen right away."

"No, Dee. They won't be in the brig for long because they'll execute them once the evidence has been verified. Ship's policy."

I put a smile on my mask. "You'd better get it right, then."

10

WHEN I COME up into my body I can't do anything except lie there for a while, wondering if the closest thing I have to a best friend is going to kill me. Or at least convince other people of the need to kill me. Considering all the things the other people I once loved did to me, this would be appropriate. I smirk at the way life always finds a way to remind me that I am fucked.

This was supposed to be a new start. Actual freedom. And I could be in the brig by lunchtime.

I don't feel guilty about the man's death. If my suspicion is correct and that guy was involved in the real nuclear war, then great—I was planning to kill him anyway. And if he wasn't, well, I had no idea he was a player, or that he would die in meatspace. The only thing I feel is the fear of discovery. That and the purest white-hot anger at that fuck who made the game. It isn't just the manipulation; it's the way the satisfaction of revenge was stolen from me. I wish I had known what Myerson had done when I killed him. I would have felt so much more satisfaction.

I push that anger aside and check for new messages. There are none. There's nothing to do, except train for the leet server, and seeing as I might be executed for murder soon, I don't feel as motivated as before. The fear keeps me pressed into the bed, running through what Carl knows, where he's going to start digging. Where my vulnerabilities are.

Weirdly, I'd feel better if I'd actually planned that murder, because then I could examine how I'd covered it up and check for holes in the story. It seems that someone has already done that by doctoring the MyPhys data to make it look like I was asleep at the time. What if I was?

I swing my legs off the bed, cutting off that useless train of thought. For now, I'm safe and there is nothing I can do to hide myself any better. I can either sit here and worry or get off my backside and go for a run. I pull on my running shoes, trying not to think about what sort of data mining Carl is doing at this very moment, when a familiar chat dialog box appears to float above my shoelaces.

<So, Dee, how did you feel when you killed him?>

I stand up, fists clenched, my body ready to punch someone who isn't there. I want to tell him to fuck off, but I need some answers first. <I want to talk to you properly. I'm going to my office, and you'd better be there.> I swipe away the box from my vision and it doesn't come back.

One shoe on, one shoe off, I lie back down, fists still balls of hurt looking for a target. I rush through the immersion process, "wake" in my office and spin around a couple of times, hoping that his sorry ass will be there.

"Well, come on, then, you bastard!" I yell at the stars. "You know I'm here. Come and talk to me, you fucking coward!"

"Dee, someone has cut this space off from the server," Ada says in my head. "No traffic in or out."

"Then how is all this still running?"

"I don't know," Ada replies.

A flare of panic bursts through my chest before I realize that if this was Carl or the command crew shutting me down to arrest me, I'd be landing in my body right now, rather than standing on an expanse of slate, worrying about it.

Some of the stars move, a cluster of them, leaving a black patch of starless sky. The stars rush down, coalescing in front of me in a vaguely humanoid shape, like some little god from a folktale. There are no features, the limbs barely discernible. It's more the cohesive movement of the group that gives the impression of someone there. As disguises go it's effective and egotistical as hell.

"Do you want to hit me?" ze says in a soft, childlike voice. Ze is shorter than me, and I'm petite. I thought it was a twelve-year-old boy . . . Maybe I was half right. Or maybe this is just a disguise.

"Yes. I do, actually," I reply. "But I know it won't do anything. So . . . are you a kid or something?"

"Would it change the way you talk to me?"

I fold my arms, frustrated. "Yeah, it would."

More stars drop out of the sky to join the cluster, the collective shape shifting into the form of a hulking great beast. "Is this more comfortable for you?" The voice is only slightly deeper.

"You are such a twat."

It laughs. "If I make myself bigger"—it increases in size until it's twice my height—"does it make you feel like a small, powerless woman who didn't know what she was doing when she killed that man?"

"You fuck." I run at the beast, the stars simply dissipating around my punch. I turn to see it coalescing where I was standing moments before.

"I thought you wanted to talk," it says. "Put your little

fists down and sit with me. You haven't answered my question and I've asked it so many times."

I relax my hands, berating myself. I never lose my temper. People have done far worse to me and I've held it together. I even smiled at some of them when they were hurting me. But at least all those times I knew whom I was dealing with, and the exact parameters of the way they were screwing me over. Losing it here will not do anything except make me look stupid. I make myself glacial, cold as a deep lake.

"That's better," it says and points at the slate in front of it. A chair rises out of the ground, much like the doors did, the stone cushions plumping and becoming soft as I watch. "Take a seat. Let's be civilized. I've made sure that no one can listen in. Anything we say here will be kept between us."

I sit in the chair. "Is that true?" I think to Ada.

"We are cut off," Ada replies. "And this is not being recorded."

Not being recorded by me, at least. "So, are you doing this to show off or make a point?"

"Can't it be both?"

I nod. "Okay. So you've proven that you're leet, fine. I get that. It's all very impressive and scary, and I'm really hoping that you're not as young as I think you are, because we are in some serious shit now and I need to talk to you about it without you flicking my tits every five seconds. Okay?"

The beast spreads its hands, settling on its haunches. "Okay. I'm listening."

"Why . . . why all of that? I thought that game was an initiation, but it wasn't, was it?"

"Well . . ."

I slap the arm of the chair. It feels like it's made of leather, cool and smooth to the touch. "Just . . . don't, okay? Just give it to me straight because I might be dead by the end of today thanks to you fucking me about."

"You won't be dead. Carl will never find out that it was you." It must see the question on my face before I ask it. "I know he's been asked to look into it. I know you are friends. I made the connection. I haven't been watching you all morning. Besides, Ada was turned off. How could I spy on you?"

"That's supposed to make me feel better?"

"Ummm . . ."

"Never mind." The more it talks, the less I'm convinced it's a child. Which is a relief.

"I changed the MyPhys data to make it look like you were dreaming at the time of death," it says. "He won't see how I did it."

Anyone else, and I'd doubt that alibi. But I've seen what it is capable of. "I didn't know he was going to die. You tricked me."

"But you wanted to kill him."

"If that is true—and I am not saying it is, but if it were true—how the fuck would you know what I wanted?"

"You've been looking for answers. When I looked at the questions you were asking, I realized that you know the same secret as me. That you wanted to do the same thing as me. So I helped you."

When it looked at the questions? What does that mean? I haven't made any relevant search queries, certainly none that could be traced by someone else. Either this is just total bullshit that it believes I would find plausible, or . . . or it's found a way to hack into my very thoughts. Given the contents of that game it made, that isn't as far-fetched as I want it to be.

I shake my head. "It didn't occur to you to sit down with me and have a secret conversation *before* you tricked me into murdering someone?"

"Generally people don't respond well when you sit them down and ask them if they would like help to execute people. Especially when they're a complete stranger."

Now, there's an interesting turn of phrase. It has said "kill" and it has said "execute" but not "murder."

"Besides," the weird star beast continues, "my method was far better."

"Bollocks! You . . . you arrogant little shit! That 'game' was just a fucking traumafest and there wasn't any indication that Myerson was involved in what they did in the real world—I'm still not even certain he was—nor that it would kill him in meatspace!"

It tilts its head, as if it is regarding me, as if I'm a creature it hasn't observed before in the wild. "I'm sorry. I thought you were more clever than you seem to be. I thought it was all perfectly clear. I showed you the impact of what they did. I made sure you paid attention. I told you what he was planning to do—which is exactly the same as what they did in the 'real' world, only with nuclear warheads rather than that device in the game. I let you hear his own words on the matter, and then I gave you the choice."

"The choice to kill an NPC!" I push down the anger again. "Don't you see the difference? I wasn't standing there, thinking, right, I'll kill this real, living man, because he totally deserves it."

"Are you sure? Wasn't that exactly what you thought?"

I open my mouth to repeat the fact that I thought I was killing an NPC, but then I suddenly see where the problem in our communication lies. "Oh," I say quietly. "You're only thinking about the motivation. Not the fact that I wouldn't have done it if I thought he was a real person."

It leans forward. "Wouldn't you? Who are you trying to persuade? Me, or yourself? Wasn't that exactly what you've been wanting to do for months?"

"Back. Off." My words come out like a snarl. "I am pretty fucking fed up with you telling me what I have been thinking and wanting to do."

It sits back. "We could make far better progress if you accept that you would have done exactly the same thing if you had known it would really kill him."

I don't want to admit it, but the bastard is right. This *is* what I wanted. "*If* I knew for certain that he was involved with those nukes, then . . . all right, I'll give it to you! What do you want? Gratitude? It doesn't change the fact you did it in a really shitty way. Nor the fact that there's an investigation happening right now, and if you're not as good as you obviously believe you are, then I'm dead."

"I don't want gratitude. I want to help you see this through to the end."

It's hard talking to a bunch of stars in the shape of a huge beast. "You are fucking unreal," I mutter. "I don't even know your name, what you look like, how to contact you . . . and you say you want to help me? You want to use me, more like."

"But you're used to that, Dee."

Another flash of anger that I stamp on before it reaches my face. "You're not endearing yourself to me, you know."

"I know. I don't care about how you feel about me. I care about the fact that you are just as angry as I am about what they did. They don't deserve to live after that, and they won't do any good in the future."

"Look, if you're so leet, just do it yourself. You could have killed him with an NPC in that game, surely?"

"No, I couldn't have. And no, I can't do it myself. I need your help. We can't kill the next one in the same way. They've already taken steps to prevent it from happening again, and they'll be watching for it."

"Now, just wait a cocking moment." I raise a hand to interrupt it. "There is no 'we' here! I am not going to help you kill anyone. I don't know you. I don't trust you, and JeeMuh, I don't want to take the risk!"

"I would ask what it would take to make you trust me,

but there's no point, is there, Dee? You don't trust anyone. It doesn't matter what I say or do now; you won't trust me, even though we have the same goal."

Why does it think it knows me so well? "Listen, I'm not willing to be your weapon, or your secret agent, or whatever else you think I should be. As for what happened to Myerson, I'm not going to just accept what you say. I haven't seen any proof that he was one of them. I don't know who the rest are and I'm not stupid enough to accept a list of names from you and act upon it." I stand up. "If you're going to tell me that if I don't help you, you'll tell Carl what I did, then just fucking get it out of the way now, because I am tired of your bullshit and I have better things to do."

"That's right, Dee, push me away before I hurt you. It worked all those times before, didn't it?"

"Yeah, whatever, go find someone else to fuck over."

"You're not going to see this through?"

"Not on your terms." I fold my arms, chin out, digging in. "I'll find out what I need to and make up my own mind about what I do next."

"I will help with that."

I say nothing, not wanting to encourage it, not wanting to entangle myself any more than I already have.

It stands up too. "I know you won't believe me, but I didn't make the game that way just to make you think about what they did. I wanted to show you how far you've come. Understanding yourself, and why you are the way you are, is so important."

I laugh. It's much better than screaming obscenities at it. Just like when my boss said I needed to stay behind at work so we could talk about how to maximize the exposure from the award win, when I knew all along what he was planning to do. I laugh in its fucking face. "You have cocked this up so badly, there is no coming back from this. Just give up. Seriously. Find someone else."

"It hasn't occurred to you that I can't risk telling you who I am? That I have to protect myself? That I have no reason to trust you either?"

I shrug. "Fair. I'm still not buying into this though. And you're in my space and you need to get out." Even as I say it, I know I could be setting my own death in motion. But I am tired of being forced, tired of being used, tired of being the only one in the game without any of the power.

Am I seriously thinking that I'd rather die than live in fear that someone else holds power over me?

Yes. I do believe I am.

The creature reaches inside itself, plucks one of the stars out of its own formation, and rests it on the slate floor between us. "If you change your mind and you want to talk to me again, pick this up and tell me to come here."

"Nothing is going to change my mind. If you knew me as well as you think you do, you'd know I'm not kidding."

"If you knew me as well as you wish you did, you wouldn't say that."

"Oh, just cock off already!" I shout at it, and the stars blast away from me, dissipating as they fly up, taking their places in the sky once more. All except for one, which remains on the floor where it was left.

The chair melts back into flat rock again and I am left alone, seething.

"Twat," I mutter.

"Dee," Ada says. "Connection to the server has been re-established. Would you like me to run a diagnostic?"

"No," I say, knowing it was that arsehole who did it and not wanting there to be any sort of evidence trail.

"You have received a message from Carolina Johnson. Would you—"

"Yes, show me!"

The text floats above the slate floor, nice and sharp against the dark background.

Hi Dee,

Awesome job on the report! I loved your insights and I think you could be a real asset to the team. If you want to accept the position, then let my APA know and we'll get your data privileges upgraded right away. It's not going to be as varied as your last job, and at first it will mostly be analysis, so you get to know the consumer base on board. Once you've found your feet, I have a project that I know you'll love. Let me know!

CJ

"Yes!" There's a link to a job summary, which looks like something I could do most of in my sleep. She's right that it's less varied, but I don't care when I see the access privileges. I'll be able to look at everyone's consumption data, regardless of their pay grade, and if I can justify the reason, I can request it be de-anonymized.

I scan the benefits, note a salary—what the hell am I going to spend that on?—and the fact that I will have an actual pay grade again. I haven't seen any sort of virtual marketplace on board, all the food and accommodation is free . . . is this just some sort of weird status thing?

Remuneration in the form of monetary credit is of no interest to me anyway; it's the data access privileges that I want. I get Ada to scan the legal jargon for me and check that it doesn't contain anything potentially problematic. The only thing she flashes up is how hard-core the NDA is—I can't mention anything about my salary, pay grade or the information I interact with as part of my job to anyone other than Carolina and anyone else she chooses to personally approve. That's no surprise. It's on a par with the one for my old job, and perfectly understandable, given the information I'll have access to.

I send an acceptance message right away. In moments there's a standard "Welcome to the team!" message from Carolina's APA and then Ada says, "Your privileges have been updated."

I rub my hands together, grinning. Finally, I have a way to find the information I need.

But the old worry about data trails is still there, and even more legitimate now that I've murdered someone.

Even though the fear of discovery is all too real, it's not enough to drown out the need to know whether that man deserved to die. I think back to what Carl showed me in that room of his. I know the man's name, that he was an engineer and that he was high up. But I daren't search for his data, not the same morning they're investigating his death.

I'm being so stupid. I've been butting my head against this for so long, I've got into the habit of treating this like an Internet search. It isn't like that now I have this level of clearance; I can call up any of the data I want and examine it in my own space. The only thing that will be logged on the server is the request from my APA to pull that information. If I pull a few hundred people's worth of data, they will have no idea what I was paying attention to here. Besides, Carolina wants me to get to know the consumer base, right?

"Ada, how many people in total are in the command crew and the next three highest pay grades on this ship?"

"Do you wish me to include those passengers who have diamond-class tickets?"

"The what now?"

"Diamond-class tickets were awarded to a selected group of people pre-Rapture."

"Why didn't you tell— Oh right, I never asked. Yeah, include them too."

"Three hundred and forty-five people above the age of eighteen are included in that sample."

That's good enough for me. "Okay, for that sample, pull all of the data I have legit access to now and display it mannequin style, randomized order."

I now have more data than I thought would ever be available to me, dumped into my server space in one batch. If Carl or anyone else chooses to see what data I've pulled today, they'll see it as a collective whole, and one I can justify as getting to know the most important mersive consumers on this ship. All I need to do now is hunt down what I need in the privacy of my own office.

In the time it takes for me to blink, avatars of 345 adults appear in the space around me, making my bleak office feel like a weird clothing vendor app. Instead of the mannequins in the shop's range, they look like all of the most powerful people on this ship. They are all standing perfectly still, looking into the middle distance, most of them dressed in a very simple white uniform that reminds me of the clothes worn by US Navy personnel back at the turn of the century.

The first time I used this display mode it freaked me out. Now I find it helps. I can walk up to each data point and see them as a person, right from the start, for one thing. I can get a sense of some demographics at first glance and I can see what they choose to have displayed in their public profile. Some choose to show themselves in ball gowns, some in sportswear, some in gaming costumes. Interesting that all of the command crew are in uniforms. That smacks of a global setting imposed upon them, probably to help the other passengers on the ship get used to identifying them by their role first.

Their real names are displayed in text floating above their heads. The ones who are not command crew have additional icons floating next to them, reflecting the additional personal information that they have personally selected as critical, top-level display information. One man has chosen to make it very clear that he is a follower of Jesus and also a proud member of the Top One Hundred Club, famously established to cater to the wealthiest one hundred individuals on the planet. I raise an eyebrow at that.

"Ada, show me where Commander Brace and Lieutenant Commander Joseph Myerson are," I say. Of course, she could just move them to where I am, but I don't have it set up that way. I like to go to them, like I am visiting a person, taking in the way their peers, or others in their particular demographic, look en route. A large blue arrow appears over the heads of two figures a little way away.

I walk between mannequins toward the ones I'm interested in. Every five I pass, I rest my hand on the shoulder of the sixth, just a light tap, short-listing them for further study. I'm just covering my bases, just in case someone looks at whose data I dig deeper into.

I pause in front of Commander Brace's avatar. I still don't know if he was involved with the war on Earth, but he's so high up in the command chain, there's a chance he was, and I want to learn more about him. Up close he looks just as square-jawed and handsome as he did in the tiny profile pic I saw via Carolina's profile. "Ada, is Carolina Johnson part of this data set?"

"No. Carolina Johnson is currently two pay grades below your lowest criteria. Would you like me to include her?"

"No."

I move on, over to where Myerson is standing. Strange to

think that he is dead now. The only indication of that is that his name has been grayed out, like he's a character I can no longer play in a game.

He looks normal enough, but then, most fundamentalists do, especially in their own profile pictures. I can still tap on his name if I want to, and view his interests and anything else he made public. Just as I'm reaching up to do that, I see something on his lapel that makes me freeze: a tiny pin showing the Earth with only the North American continent on it, just like the pin in the game that killed him.

11

STARING AT THE pin does not make it disappear. For a few stupid moments, I question why something from a game is shown in his avatar, wonder if it's because of the character he was playing when he died. No . . . this isn't the game creeping into real life; rather, this was an element taken from real life and put into the game. The only difference is that this pin doesn't have "CSA" printed below the globe.

Then it occurs to me that if I didn't see it on him until I was up close . . . Turning around, I see the same pin design worn on the collar of every single crew member around me. "Ada, is there anyone here who is not wearing this globe pin?"

"No. All of the individual avatars in this sample are wearing the same pin."

"Ummm . . . Ada, does this pin represent membership in the CSA?"

"Yes."

"And does that stand for 'Christian States of America'?"

"Yes. Would you like to view the files you have stored on this organization?"

I look down at the dark gray slate beneath my feet, focusing more carefully on what she is saying. "I don't have any."

"You have a folder containing twenty-three files relating to the CSA stored in your private information space."

This doesn't make any sense. I have to explicitly choose what gets stored in that area, and I am picky as hell. "I don't remember downloading anything. When was that folder saved there?"

"Eight hours, forty-one minutes and three seconds ago."

That was the middle of last night. What the— "Ada, what was I doing when those files downloaded?"

"You were sleeping."

"Then how the fuck did I download files? Did you do that without asking me?"

"I'm sorry, I do not have the answer to your query. Would you like me to start an investigation into the provenance of these files?"

"No," I say. "I was playing a mersive last night. How long after I finished playing that were those files downloaded?"

"Thirty-seven minutes. The files were downloaded at two thirty-two a.m."

Oh shit. I was still playing the game then. I call up my brain activity details from MyPhys. They show the mersive phase of that evening only lasted just under four hours, with a break at the two-hour point, like there should have been. It shows that I jacked out, ate a small meal and went to sleep. I can see the REM phases, and which one of those was likely to be at the same time Myerson died. It must all be false data, somehow planted convincingly enough to fool Carl and his APA.

It also looks like the files Ada is talking about were downloaded before Myerson died.

Thinking back to the game, there was the whole thing with finding the pin and gaining access to the final level. Putting that pin on . . . talking to Bobby Bear about . . . JeeMuh, I remember now; he said he could trick it into thinking I had permission to wear it . . . and that would make it sync with my neural chip. Or something like that.

There is the briefest flash of disbelief, that surely that was only in the game, but then I apply logic. The last thing I thought along those lines was that surely a man who died in a game couldn't die in meatspace, and look where I am now. Fuck.

The files are there now, and there's nothing I can do about it. "Ada, you've scanned those files, right? They're legit?"

"Yes. No harmful code has been found."

I still hesitate. If there's anyone who could slip in something evil under the radar, it'll be that bastard. "When I open the folder, I want you to actively monitor my chip for any changes."

"I do that anyway," Ada replies. "Dumb-ass."

"Shut up. Open the folder."

A new icon appears in my visual field, floating above Myerson's lapel. It is the CSA logo, matching the one on the pin I can see on the crew members before me. I tap it and all the files contained within appear. Most of them seem to be links to mersives, along with a file I'd expect to find in any corporate welcome pack: a mission statement. I'm not that keen on entering a mersive without knowing what I'm letting myself in for, so I tap that text file and the top layer of the stylized page icon appears to peel away, turning into a piece of paper that I take in my hand.

It's short, like most corporate mission statements.

The CSA is dedicated to upholding Christian values of moral decency, corporate and fiscal responsibility and the preservation of the American way of life. We fully commit to our moral duty to protect the one true faith and the faithful. We believe that a society built on the solid foundations of religious observance, financial stability and humility before God is superior to those of other nations, and worth defending against their prejudice and envy.

And like most corporate mission statements, this creates more questions than it answers. What exactly do they mean by the American way of life? Hypocrisy? Lack of respect for anyone or anything that refuses to adopt its culture? Institutional racism and misogyny? Which Christian values exactly? What sort of religious observance?

Setting those questions aside, I wonder how this intersects with what happened to Earth. The Christianity I learned about from Bobby Bear certainly didn't sound like the sort of faith that would ever encourage mass genocide. But then again, if this is a fundamentalist group, the normal rules don't apply. How do I know they are though? How do I know whether the words Myerson said in the game represented his own beliefs or were the sort of thing he thought his character would say? Saying your own way of life is superior and worth defending rings alarm bells in my mind, but there's a big gap between that statement and starting global thermonuclear war.

This is way beyond my comfort zone. I don't understand people of faith, let alone people who are happy to orchestrate the deaths of billions of people, and the possibility of the two overlapping in some sort of horrendous Venn diagram is freaking me out. Why should it though? Violent people have used religion to justify their power plays for hundreds of years. This is just on a more horrifying scale.

I toss the virtual page away and it disappears in midair. Scanning the list of mersives, I don't see any file names that make me want to enter any of them until I spot one called "history." I tap to view the summary description and find that it's a history of the organization, rather than their interpretation of certain historical events. It has a full-immersion option and a passive one too.

"Ada, play the passive version of this one," I say, tapping it.

The avatars closest to me move away smoothly, as if the mannequins had been set on wheeled platforms. A chair appears behind me, without the growing-out-of-the-slate nonsense, and I sit down. By the time I look back in front of me there's a screen in place with the opening frame ready for me to watch. It shows the CSA logo against a dark blue background.

Ada plays it when she detects my attention on the screen. It's a fairly bland documentary-style show, less than five minutes long and surprisingly tame for an American production. They usually go for brash music, snappy edits and lots of over-the-top graphics. Most of the information is given in simple statements, almost like it's a study guide rather than anything designed to both inform and entertain.

I learn that they were founded in 2020, disturbed by the political instability of the time and the way it had moved away from religious ideals. It started out as a sort of think tank that grew into a national organization with members at every level of government and at the heads of some of the most powerful corporations in America. The show makes out that if it hadn't been for the terrible collapse of democracy in Europe, they would have been able to spread the sensible, responsible and God-fearing principles of good leadership there too.

Most of it is total bollocks, putting a spin on events that I know is blatantly untrue, thanks to my Noropean upbringing. They make out that the civil war that raged across America in the early 2030s was due to the federal government's movement away from God's teachings, neglecting to mention the decades of racial tension and the brutal gap between the rich and the poor that preceded it. They claim credit for helping to establish order and realign America's ideals with those of Christianity, which to my godless ears sounds like a nice way of saying that they were rich enough to gain control of the military, tapped into the crazy gun-toting right wing evangelicals' power bloc and killed or deported all of the problematic people standing in their way.

If this is to be believed, the CSA was directly responsible for turning the US into an inwardly focused right-wing religious country. What surprises me is that they weren't more open about it. The way it talks about having key people in high political positions smacks of a shadowy organization steering politics from the sidelines while some photogenic stooge takes the stage. Yet the tone of the documentary is very different from that. Indeed, they even list the ten founders, and when their names flash up, I pause the footage.

"Ada, how many of those names are diamond-class ticket holders?"

"One hundred percent of the names shown match those of diamond-class ticket holders."

So the founders got their places guaranteed. "Are there any diamond classers who weren't founders?"

"Twenty-four people, twenty of whom are spouses or children of those listed on the screen."

"Show me the names of the remaining four."

I recognize them instantly, all beautiful media stars. I sigh. No need to guess why they were brought along.

The last ten percent of the show details how the organization recognized the genius of the Pathfinder but was disappointed that she and Cillian Mackenzie refused to work with them in bringing their plan to find God to fruition. With assistance from "a sympathetic source" on the Pathfinder's team (a euphemism for "industrial spy"?), they were able to obtain the information required to build the ship I'm on now. But it's the last line of the documentary, left in text on the screen at the end to really burn into my mind, that chills me to the core.

"The CSA vision for humankind extends beyond Earth, into the stars, where we will ensure that the one true faith guides humanity for the rest of time."

I don't recall the Pathfinder saying anything about imposing one faith on those who went with her to find God. "Ada, search publicity statements and speeches given by the Pathfinder . . . what was her name?"

"Lee Suh-Mi."

"That's it. Search for any mention of a particular religion being practiced or enforced when she reached her destination."

"I have found one entry that is directly relevant: a speech given at a technology conference in Paris in French. Would you like me to translate?"

"Yes."

Footage of the petite woman replaces the final statement of the CSA propaganda file. She is standing on a large stage, dressed in a simple long black skirt and white T-shirt. Her lips move out of sync with Ada's translation. "And I say again, regardless of what other people may think, it is not my intention, nor my role, to tell people how to worship whatever we find there. There is no obligation to even do that at all. For who am I to tell another person how to come to terms with what we encounter? Who am I to tell anyone how they should demonstrate their love for God? It seems to me that so many of the world's problems have been caused by people who felt they had a right to police that. I will not take that toxic thinking with me on Atlas, and neither will those selected to come with me."

I lean back, looking at the paused picture of her. Such a small woman who changed the world forever. A small woman with Korean heritage and genuinely liberal ideas about religion and worship, no less. I swipe back to the previous screen, at that last statement from the CSA. I have a terrible feeling that its members won't get along with her, if she's still alive when we arrive. And if they did start that nuclear war to ensure their pure vision was the only one to survive, what's to stop them from violently wiping out anyone who disagrees with it?

This is still just speculation though. I am all too aware that I am examining this through an atheist's lens. But that bastard wanted me to find this information, wanted me to have access to the same files as a member of the CSA. Is this to help me find the evidence that I need to prove Myerson and potentially others were involved with that attack, or is it just manipulation?

"Ada, do you have access to a list of other CSA members?"

"Yes, it is contained in the mersive called 'Brethren on Board.'"

"Can you extract that list and show it to me?"

A list of names appears on the screen. "Remove the names of the people who were in my earlier sample." A large percentage disappears, but there are still too many for me to scan easily. "Are there any members of both the CSA and the Circle?"

"No."

"Is Carolina Johnson a member of the CSA?"

"Yes."

I scratch my head. "Is my name on that list?"

"No."

Maybe it hasn't been updated yet. I dismiss the thought instantly; an APA would keep a membership list up to date, no problem. Maybe whatever was done in that game to give me access hasn't actually made me an official member in the eyes of the organization. That's something, I guess.

"Ada, are all of the CSA members in the highest . . ."—I think back to what she said about Carolina—"top five pay grades?"

"Yes."

"Exclusively so?"

"Yes."

"What percentage of passengers are not CSA members?"

"Ninety-five percent."

Well, I guess that's something. But the fact that those at the top of the food chain are all CSA is not a comforting thought.

Just as I'm considering whether to plow through the rest of the mersives in that folder, Ada says, "Travis Gabor is requesting entry to your cabin."

"Shit. Tell him I'm under and I'll be ready in five."

It takes me a few moments to orient myself after coming back up into my body and longer to realize that I have several new messages, none of which Ada deemed important enough to bring to my attention while I was immersed. Sitting up, stretching and then having a glass of water helps me to feel more centered, so I look at them while waiting for Travis to come back.

They're all from Carolina's APA, each one offering the opportunity to try a different game that she's been enjoying lately. They're a sneeze and a "bless you" from spam, really, but when it comes to game invites and money-off codes, I'm happy to receive them from friends. I've been in contact with Carolina's APA enough times in the past twenty-four hours for Ada to class these as messages from a friend within acceptable criteria. I scan the descriptions, noting that Carolina, like me, seems to enjoy ultraviolent first-person shooters, until the rest of my brain kicks in fully.

Money-off codes? That would imply some sort of marketplace. On Earth, that would be the most natural thing in the world, but I've been living without money for six months now. I select the "more info" option on a particular ultraviolent and select the option to view similar titles.

It's like being back in my old apartment again, scanning hundreds of mersive blurbs, trying to decide what was worth accruing more debt for. This time I'm looking at the prices without that baggage but with a different kind of discomfort instead. I can't pin down why this is bothering me though. It's not like the prices are massively inflated. Maybe it's just because I've got used to thinking I didn't have to worry about money anymore . . . No, that's not it.

A knock on the door makes me jump and swipe away the v-screen. I run my hand through the hair on top of my head, which is only just long enough to stick up in stupid ways, and call, "Come in!"

Travis enters, looking like he's just had his hair done by someone, as he always does. He smiles at me with the confidence of a man who has always got what he wanted. "Hello, Dee. Mind if we have a quick chat?"

I shrug. "Sure." I gesture to the end of the bed, shuffling to the other end of it, as he closes the door. Unlike Gabriel Moreno, he chooses to stand, tucking his hands in his pockets as he leans against the closed door. He looks tense. Why do I have the feeling this is about Carl?

"Dee . . . have you seen Carl today?"

Here we go. "This morning."

"And . . . how did he seem to you?"

I haven't got time for this bollocks. "Look . . . I don't know why you think I'm going to help the two of you sort your shit out, but I'm not. You're both grown-ups."

"But it isn't—" he starts, looking down, one perfect auburn lock falling down over his forehead like he's in the middle of a bloody fashion shoot.

"It hasn't been the right time for the past six months, granted, but things are different now," I say. "He's feeling much better and I reckon that if you just sit down with him and talk this shit through and maybe, I dunno, kiss him or something, you'll be fine."

He looks up at me, looking confused. "What?"

"Oh, for fuck's sake, Travis! I don't know how people do relationships! I'm basing this off cutscenes in mersives, and not romantic ones at that. Isn't that what you do when you fancy someone?"

He raises one of his eyebrows. "I . . . I don't quite know what to say."

It suddenly feels horribly awkward. "Oh shit. That isn't why you're here, is it?"

He shakes his head. "No. But seeing as you evidently think I'm incapable of addressing the situation between Carl and me, I feel the need to defend myself. I have tried, several times, to talk to him about . . . us. The possibility, I mean. But he's so hard to read. He's conflicted, I think. I know he's been struggling with . . . what we all saw. And I understand that. But he just won't talk about anything else with me, and I'm starting to suspect he's hiding behind that grief to avoid having a proper conversation. Did he have any partners on Earth?"

Oh shit. I have just walked myself into a minefield. "That's his business."

"I know about his . . . status before." He looks like he's going to say something else but doesn't.

"If he wanted you to know about any of his stuff, he'd tell you. It wouldn't be cool for me to . . . Look, I really am the wrong person to ask about this. Seriously. I . . . I don't do the whole . . . fancying-people thing. At all. So . . . if that was what you wanted to talk about, I think I've cocked it up enough for now. Don't you?"

He smiles again. "You're a good friend."

I laugh. He thinks it's because I'm feeling flattered. "You're welcome to ask me about first-person shooters that are worth the time," I offer. "I know my shit when it comes to them." I watch him look back at the floor. He's tense about something and trying to build up to what he actually wants to talk to me about. He asked me about Carl though . . . "Are you worried about Carl? If he was meant to meet up with you, don't be. He's busy at the moment."

He draws in a deep breath, tips his head back to rest it against the wall as he stares at the ceiling. "Do you know why he's busy?"

The way he says that suggests that he does. "Yeah. He's got a case. He's actually cheerful. And when you consider that someone else had to die for that to happen, that says something."

"And do you know what that case is?"

"Yes. Look, Travis, I much prefer it when someone just tells me what's going on, instead of me having to guess. 'Cos otherwise I end up talking about point spends for different character classes in—"

"I need you to be my alibi."

12

I DON'T REALIZE my jaw has dropped open until I try to say something and find it moving up and down ineffectually. "Why? What have you done?"

"Nothing!" he says with a desperate edge to his voice, spreading his hands.

"Whoa, wait . . . we shouldn't be having this sort of conversation here!" I say.

He waves a hand. "No, it's fine, I took care of that."

"Took care of—"

He crouches down in front of me, close enough for me to see the sweat on his upper lip, cutting me off before I can properly freak out about what he's done to protect this conversation. "Dee . . . I didn't kill that man, I swear it, okay?"

"The one Carl is—"

"Yes, that one. But he might think I did."

". . . Okay. Why?"

He rubs his hand over his face, discovers the dampness

and, frowning, wipes his hand on his jog pants. "This is going to stay between us, isn't it?"

"You come in here asking me for an alibi and only now it occurs to you to ask that?"

He smirks. He's actually shaking. "I think I'm panicking, Dee."

"Yeah, I think you are." I pat the bed. "Come and sit down and start at the beginning. Otherwise I'll only make a fool of myself again."

He responds well to me being gentle, just as I hoped he would. Lowered voice, soft tone, it often works as long as the person it's being directed at isn't a total arsehole. Sitting heavily beside me, he leans forward, elbows on knees, and takes a couple of deep breaths. I consider whether a hand on his shoulder or a rub of his upper back might help. Then I decide not to do that in case he gets upset. Otherwise the contact could escalate into a hug before I'm ready for it.

"I . . ." Another deep breath, a glance at me. "I know who gave the orders to set off those nukes and who helped them to do it. The man who died last night was one of those people."

Luckily he interprets my shock as my not knowing anything about this, instead of the fact that he already knows the very thing we argued about during that botched intervention of his. "Are you sure?"

He nods. "I had to know, Dee. I had to know who it was and why they did it. Myerson—he's the one who died last night—was the tech guy, the one who made sure it would all kick off the way they planned, once they were sure that Rapture was a success and everyone was docked on board. Commander Brace spoke to him two minutes before the—"

"Don't fucking tell me who it was!" I'm wearing a mask of horror, but inside I am desperate to know these names. I can't let him think I am though, for exactly the same reason that he is in this room, sweating.

He blinks at me. "Why? I thought you wanted to know!"

"Of course I do. *Did!* But I don't want Carl to see anything in my face when he talks about this."

"Dee . . . it's been hell, keeping this to myself. I don't think I can anymore."

"Well, can't you just—"

"But it's Captain Ashby, Dee. The one leading us there. The first- and second-in-command are genocidal fucks. What do you think that means for our future when we get there?"

I slump back, pretending to be annoyed with him and appalled by the information at the same time.

The list of founders I was looking at before he came in comes back to mind. Captains, commanders and engineers don't make the decisions to start wars; politicians and religious extremists do. The founders are all politically powerful, wealthy, religious men. They made this entire trip possible. They crafted this project, so it makes sense that they are just as responsible for what happened on Earth as the three Travis is talking about.

"I don't know what it means for our future," I finally say, though I am fairly certain it can't be good. It's not a discussion I want to have with him though; I need to keep this conversation as locked down as I can. "Anyway, you're panicking over nothing. For one thing, Myerson died of a heart attack while he was playing a game. It was probably just some bizarre medical condition. And for another thing, why are you freaking out about knowing who those fucks are? I assume you found out via . . . shady means? Like when you hacked that satellite in the first place so we could watch it happen?"

He nods. "I did. And as far as I could, I covered my tracks. There's no data trail that anyone else could find . . . But this is Carl, Dee. I looked up his record when I first met him, and, shit, he is relentless."

"Relentless when there's an actual murder. It may not even be that."

He gives me a look that tells me he knows just as much about that investigation as I do. JeeMuh, what else has he hacked?

"He trusts you, Dee. That's why you need to help, just to cover my bases. You do believe me, don't you? That I didn't kill him?"

"Of course I do!" I say, and it's easy to be convincing when you're the murderer.

"Good." He lets out a long breath and slumps back so he is level with me against the wall. "So you won't mind if I make it look like we were together last night."

"If you think that's a good alibi, you've got another think coming."

"It's perfect. If he sees that I was with you, he'll get emotional."

"Don't flatter yourself."

"And if he gets emotional, he'll make mistakes. If he somehow finds out that I know what Myerson did, looks into my shit more closely, and sees that we were together, he's going to be worrying about different things."

I fold my arms, give him my most unimpressed face. "Carl knows we'd never get it together. You're gay and I'm—"

"I'm bi, and he knows that."

"Well, I'm not, and he knows that too."

His hand slides across the bed to brush mine. I pull my hand away and stand up. "I'm not het either, Travis. So just back the fuck off, okay?"

He looks genuinely surprised. "I thought you were just . . ."

"Waiting for you to notice me?" I laugh. "Nope." I go

and stand in front of the cupboard. "Trust me—you need to think of a better alibi, or just let it go and trust that Carl is as good at his job as you think he is. Then he'll know it couldn't have been you, for real. Right?"

After another long sigh he nods. "So I didn't need you in the end."

I shrug. "People do dumb shit when they panic. Look . . . are you sure about Myerson? And the others?"

He nods. "I listened to their comms as it happened, and from the days afterward between Brace and Myerson. They think they burned the sinners and stopped any of them following us. They're happy about what they did."

"Do you have the files still?"

He nods, looks away for a couple of seconds, then looks back at me. "So do you now. They're encrypted, but your APA has the key, and if Carl gets it wrong and comes after you, they'll delete the second you are flagged up for arrest. Your APA has been instructed to file them away somewhere discreet."

I'm torn between being glad to have the evidence and furious with him for not asking if I wanted to have potentially dangerous data sent to me. "You really need to learn to ask people what they want first."

He shrugs. "I thought you wanted to know. *I* did. Hasn't it been driving you mad, wondering who it was that gave the order?"

It's my turn to shrug defensively. "You know it's been on my mind."

"Don't worry. I'm good. There won't be an obvious data trail."

"So good you came in here panicking and asking for an alibi?"

He smirks. "Point taken. I'm sorry."

We share the silence that settles between us.

"I'm glad he's dead," Travis says, shuffling to the edge of the bed to stand in front of me.

"Well, now I know what he did, so am I." I look at him, intellectually appreciating how conventionally handsome he is, and search for any flicker of desire for him inside me. But there's nothing, as there always has been.

"Sorry to . . . put you on the spot like that," he says and then opens his arms for a hug.

I've never embraced him before. We've hung out a bit, but not got close. Now I feel like I have so many times in the past when a man has initiated affection, that there is another agenda here. This time, I don't think it is the hope of moving toward more intimacy, but I think it's just as dangerous. I don't trust him, and I don't like the way he told me who was responsible for the attack after I told him not to. If I'm not careful, he'll use me, not as an alibi, but as an alternative suspect.

I embrace him, feeling his arms close around me, feeling him lean in to rest his chin over my shoulder. As he squeezes me gently, I force my shoulders to stay relaxed, to keep my breathing steady, to make him think that I am falling for the bait. Because he wants me to like him. He wants me to want him. And whether that's to protect himself in the future, or simply to assuage his ego, the way to handle it is the same: make him think that I am vulnerable to his charms.

"It'll be okay," I say in that soft, low voice. "He's good enough to know that it wasn't you. All you need to do is stay calm and it'll all blow over soon enough."

"Thanks, Dee," he says and holds on to me just that moment longer than when I would have pulled away. He steps back, flicks that rogue lock back like he isn't even thinking about the way that looks, but he must be, really. "See you soon?"

"Yeah, see you soon."

I close the door behind him and drop onto the bed. I'm certain I've just been played; I'm just not sure how. Was he planning to set up this alibi bollocks to weasel his way into more intimacy with me? No. There are probably dozens of people he could bed on this floor alone with minimal effort.

He's just dumped files that could provide motive for the murder into my chip. Is he planning to frame me? That doesn't fit either; if I were going to do that, I wouldn't come and have a conversation with the victim. But maybe he just works differently from me.

Unless it's actually some sort of childish attempt to make Carl jealous and spur him to finally make a move? Again, it doesn't ring true. Surely Travis grew out of that crap a long time before we ended up on this ship.

I doubt that conversation had anything to do with who is shagging whom or who wants to, and everything to do with the murder. Travis can't know that I killed Myerson. If he did, he'd be throwing me to the dogs right now, to protect himself. He was just making sure I knew the one who died was responsible for the war. And who the others were too.

Or . . . he could have been testing me . . . wanting to see if I could keep quiet about what really happened . . . because he is the hacker behind all of this.

I'm on my feet, a surge of adrenaline ripping through my chest, getting me ready to run with nowhere to go. It falls into place, so easily; he obviously has the right skill set, given the way he so casually hacked into that satellite to watch Earth. He must be shady; he was married to the head of one of the most powerful rival corporations to the US gov-corp and yet somehow still got a place on board . . . In the last conversation with that weirdo gamer I expressed my doubts about whether Myerson really did deserve that death and then later the very same day Travis walks in, gives me not only a confirmation but also the other two people involved and evidence . . .

It's too much of a coincidence. But I need to be sure. "Ada, where is Travis now and what is he doing?"

"Travis Gabor is at the end of the corridor to the left of your cabin. He has been stationary for the past twenty-one seconds. He is in conversation with Geena Wilkinson."

"And her position verifies that?"

"Yes. I verified the data before responding because I know how to do my job."

I swear this APA is getting more rude by the day. Still, I can't stop myself opening the door so I can listen for their voices. I hear his low rumble easily enough, and then a woman's laugh. Is he flirting with her? Probably. I close the door again and lie down on the bed.

"Ada, if he stops talking to Geena, tell me right away, okay? Watch him really closely until I tell you to stop."

"I only have permission to report on any publicly available data."

"Can you tell me if he immerses?"

"I can inform you if he changes his public profile status to 'unavailable.'"

"That'll have to do. I need to go to my office."

Soon enough I am standing on that dark gray slate once more, the stars above me, aside from one that is still resting on the floor where it was left. I run over, grab it and say, "Come and talk to me, right now!"

I look up at the sky, waiting. "Ada, is he still talking to Geena?"

"Yes. She is checking her calendar. I think they are making a date."

"Can you . . . see that?"

"I am simply monitoring her public profile. She is quite

open about which apps she is using. She is still talking to Travis. It is speculation."

The stars are moving above me. "And now?"

"I will tell you when they are no longer together."

He could be doing this while talking to Geena; puppeting the beast without immersion is entirely possible. I need to have a conversation, say something he has to concentrate on.

The stars are coalescing into the same shape as before. I'm ready for it this time, folding my arms, imagining Travis behind the disguise.

"Hello," the beast's voice says. "I told you you'd contact me."

"I need to talk to you about Carlos Moreno and Travis Gabor."

"If you wish. I'd much rather talk about getting you the evidence you need to persuade you that we should work together."

"Ada? Is he—"

"Yes," Ada replies, and if I didn't know better, I'd say she sounded irritated. "Travis is still in conversation with Geena Wilkinson."

"Did you know that Travis Gabor knows who gave the order? And that Myerson was in on it?"

"Yes. He's had that information for over a month but hasn't done anything about it. He's a cowardly man. Happy to hack and make deals but not put himself at risk."

"What sort of deals?"

"The one that got him a place on this ship, for one. Paying off your debt for another."

"Wait, what? He . . ."

The beast nods. "He paid off the debt against you so you were free to join the crew. Presumably he knew the US govcorp would never pay any money for you."

"For my *time* and *services*," I say sharply. "Not for *me*."

The beast shrugs. "You are, of course, free to frame your previous slavery in any way you wish."

I push down a retort that would reveal far too much about how that old wound still stings. "How do you know Travis paid the debt?"

"He and Carlos Moreno discussed it during a game they played together."

I try to imagine Travis and Carl chatting between shooting stuff. It doesn't sound like the sort of conversation that would be natural in a game. "What . . . when they were waiting for another wave of mooks to kill?"

"No. When they were building a chicken coop together in the *Grow Your Farm* mersive."

I can't help but smile at that. Carl played that one to death about five years ago, constantly badgering me to come and play it with him. Not even the promise that I could customize the monsters in the woods was enough to tempt me. The fact that he's played it with Travis tells me all I need to know about how Carl feels about him. He would only ask those he trusts the most to play that with him. It's like a comfort blanket to him, the game he hides from his public profile, still too proud to admit to the wider world that he plays anything other than shooters and racing games. There's a softer side to him, one that he rarely shares, one that he rarely permits himself to indulge, even.

This is a complex conversation to have in real time while simultaneously flirting with someone. "You're not Travis, are you?"

"No. Though given the files that he has just sent to you, I can understand why you would think that."

"Oh for the love of . . ." It's getting harder to hold back the anger. "Just . . ."

"Now that you know that I am not actually Travis Gabor,

would you like to discuss Carlos Moreno? Are you concerned about the investigation?"

"Well, obviously."

"I can only repeat my earlier reassurance. He will not be able to find any evidence of my data manipulation. Why haven't you opened the files Travis sent to you? I thought you wanted evidence."

"Travis Gabor has stopped talking to Geena Wilkinson," Ada says in my head. "She has closed her calendar app and is walking away from him. Travis is now approaching Gabriel Moreno's cabin. Would you like me to continue to monitor his movements?"

"Are you scared he's trying to trick you?" the beast says. "It's understandable. You do have trust issues."

"And you're not helping with those!" I yell at it.

"No," I think to Ada. "It's fine."

The star beast doesn't say anything for a moment, as if my words have actually had an impact. "Have my actions been part of the reason why you won't work with me?"

I laugh. "You know, for someone who is so leet, you are really fucking slow on the uptake."

"I shall consider this carefully."

The stars dissipate and return to the virtual heavens; the one in my hand remains though, so I put it down on the slate and tell Ada to make me a chair.

I'm fairly certain now that whoever it is behind the stars, it's not Travis. Which means Travis's most likely motivation for that weird conversation was either to trap me in an alibi or to line me up as a potential alternative suspect in case he gets fingered by an overzealous AI and Carl believes it. Either way, I'm going to listen to these comms files and see if they're as convincing as he seems to believe they are.

There are two files, held in a protected cache.

"I have checked them," Ada says preemptively. "They're just audio files."

The file names are merely time stamps, matching the first day we came aboard. I play the earlier one.

"Confirm green light for Judgment. Repeat: confirm green light for Judgment. All systems are go." I recognize the voice. It's Myerson's.

"Judgment is cleared hot, repeat, Judgment is cleared hot." A male voice. Commander Brace's, perhaps?

"Acknowledged. Judgment has been served."

The file ends. "Ada, can you confirm that the first voice in that file was Lieutenant Commander Myerson?"

"Confirmed."

"And was the second voice Commander Brace?"

"Confirmed."

"Judgment" is certainly a plausible name for what they did, given the use of "Rapture" and the religious leanings of the CSA.

I select the second file. This time, Brace speaks first, but now in a whisper.

"Judgment is a confirmed success."

"We may not be on an official military vessel, Commander, but I swear, if you speak to me about classified operations on a fucking chat channel again, I will throw you in the brig," a woman's voice says.

The file ends. "Ada, was that woman the captain?"

"Confirmed."

Programs that can mimic voices perfectly were around decades before I was born, but there's something about this that rings true. Is it just that I want to believe I've found the information I've been looking for? "Ada, can you call up Captain Ashby's public profile for me? Text is fine."

There's very little on it, unsurprisingly enough, but I do learn that she had a long career in the military and is proud of several campaigns in which she "defended US gov-corp assets" in a variety of foreign theaters. Most of those involved the defense of a water supply and "acquisition of new sources," which means she was one of the people involved in securing the source of the Kootenay River, the first of many border disputes between North America and Canada before the latter was absorbed by the US gov-corp in a bloodless corporate acquisition after the civil war.

Then I notice she has something in the "favorite quote" section: 2 Corinthians 5:10. I point at it. "Ada, what's that?"

"A Bible verse. In the King James Version, it is: 'Second Corinthians 5:10: For we must all appear before the judgment seat of Christ; that every one may receive the things done in his body, according to that he hath done, whether it be good or bad.'"

I lean back, take a couple of deep breaths and try telling myself that one bloody Bible quote does not a zealot make. But actions do. I need to find a way to confirm she gave the order.

Thinking back to all the military mersives I've ever watched or played in, I recall that the order a captain gives is not always one they would have chosen themselves. In war it's different, but this was a peacetime decision, the first act of a very short war. It isn't the officer at the head of the army who decides to move their troops to another place to strike the first blow. It's the politicians or the royalty.

"Ada, have any of the founders of the CSA who are on board held any political positions of power?"

"Yes." Knowing my personal preferences, Ada provides the information as text that appears in the air in front of me. I scan a long list of positions on various gov-corp committees and boards. All high up. Makes sense.

Shit, do I need to kill all of these people too?

At least I have names now, and the means to find out

more about them. The thought is enough to keep the despair at bay.

"There is a verbal contact request from Carolina Johnson," Ada tells me.

"Okay, connect."

"Hi, this is Carolina," a bright American voice says unnecessarily. "Can I run something by you?"

"Hi," I reply, my English-Noropean accent sounding flat in comparison. "Go ahead."

"So, I was wondering how you'd feel about trying out the leet server."

"I'm not sure I meet all the criteria yet."

"Oh, they're just guidelines, mostly to stop people thinking they can handle it when they can't. But I have the feeling you can."

There is something conspiratorial in her tone, something tempting. "Let me send you over what my APA thinks," I say and instruct Ada to send over my scores on the list of criteria I reviewed before.

"Close enough," Carolina says after a few moments. "You got a couple of hours free? You'd really be helping me out."

"Sure," I say, knowing she is a good person to keep happy. "Where shall I meet you?"

A notification detailing a new mersive invitation pops up. "Eat something light, make sure you're hydrated and don't take any stims or painkillers before you come. It'll probably be violent. You okay with that?"

"Yeah. See you in . . . ten minutes?"

"Awesome!"

The call ends and I look at the invite. No game details, just a place for Ada to find the loading room for whatever we'll be playing. I have a moment of doubt. Shouldn't I be keeping tabs on Carl and making sure I don't get caught? But there's no way I can actually do that, and besides, going off to game with someone is a perfectly legit thing for me to do. I need to act normal after all. And if Carl is watching me, for whatever reason, buggering off to play a game would seem like the most natural thing for me to do. It would even be a relief for him. I'd be acting more normally than I have in months. What better way to hide the fact I've killed someone in the real world than to go to kill someone imaginary?

13

ADA PUTS THE door to the loading room into a new wall a few meters away, to give me a chance to get my bearings before I go in. When I look down, I find I'm wearing the same clothes as I am in the real world, which jars me, ironically. "Am I going to play in my jogging gear?"

"Your clothes will be reskinned at time-in," Ada says.

I take a moment to prepare myself, to fix a friendly smile in place and be the upbeat, capable woman I know Carolina will be hoping for. I open the door and walk into a room that looks like an executive office that could have been in any one of the London skyscrapers I worked in over my career. There's no desk though, just a couple of stylish chairs that are positioned by the window to make the most of the view over the Thames. It's in a different place than the weird apartment scene in that game, but I can't help but recall it. An echo of the shock of discovering Myerson had actually died in that game ripples through me. I try to push it from my mind as the door opens and Carolina walks in, dressed in jog pants and T-shirt like I am.

"Hi!" She walks toward me, her hand outstretched, and I shake it as I return her smile. "It's so good to meet you!"

"You too," I say.

"Take a seat," she says, gesturing to the chairs, and I do so, feeling oddly like I'm about to be interviewed. "So, thank you for coming."

She smiles as she talks, eyes sparkling. She doesn't look like she's in her fifties, but then lots of people look some indefinable age these days, somewhere between thirty and sixty. She appears to be at the lower end of that, her brown hair cropped in an asymmetric bob with purple streaks that weren't in her profile picture. She has brown eyes, full lips, and her smile is warm and friendly. But there's something false about her too, or perhaps it's more a tension in the way she sits. Then I realize she is building up to asking me something. And that she's worried about what I'll say.

"I've always been curious about leet servers," I say. "Thanks for the invite!"

"You never played in one back home?" When I shake my head, she looks worried. "Oh . . . Okay."

"So, what's this about?" I keep my tone cheery and light.

"There's this tournament thing going on . . ."

"Someone's dropped out and you need me to take their place?"

She nods. "It's the semifinal and . . . well, I really don't wanna lose my chance of winning, just because Kara Channing doesn't know how to warm up properly." At my puzzled expression, she adds, "My teammate. She pulled her hamstring yesterday and only just told me about it."

"I don't really do team games. How many of you are there?"

"Oh, only two per team. It's problem solving, mostly. The solutions can be anything from finding the next letter in a sequence through swimming underwater, to getting a thing within a certain time limit. Every level is different. This is the semi, as I said, so it's gonna be tough." The cheeriness falters. "Maybe this wasn't a good idea . . ."

"When I say I don't do team games, I mean things like basketball. Puzzlers are no problem."

She brightens. "So, the thing with the tournament is that the levels are randomly generated by the AI, to make it fair. Everything we need to play we get in the level."

"Is this a multiroom-type thing, or a single space that changes or . . ."

"Oh, the levels are set in a sandbox environment. The challenges are always in keeping with the setting. So the last one we played was set in medieval times, like, with knights and all. One of the challenges was to fight each other in full plate. That was tough. And then there was a decoding puzzle straight after, all based on heraldry. It's fun but it's the real deal. When you get hit, you feel it."

"But you don't get hurt in the real world?"

"No, but your brain thinks you will be. And if someone hacks your hand off in there, you see it, you feel it, just like if it was for real. The AI has extended MyPhys privileges. It will make you feel stuff far more than in a normal mersive. It gets pretty intense. I've had a teammate pass out on me when I was hurt in a knife fight. I dropped him from my team pretty damn quick after that. And people freeze up, freak out . . . lots of people don't realize how intense it is until they're in game."

"You're worried I can't handle it," I say. "Don't be."

"But you've never played anything with this amount of physiological feedback . . ."

"I've lived a lot," I reply, looking her right in the eye, doing all I can to exude confidence. "I won't let you down."

She stares at me a moment. "Okay . . ."

I can see her resolve is wavering. Bringing in an unknown this late in the tournament is a big risk. I can understand her concern, but I don't want to lose my chance to play. "I'm betting that if there was someone else suitable, they'd already be sitting in this chair, right?"

She smirks and then nods.

"So you have nothing to lose by giving me a chance. How long do we have before time-in?"

"Ten minutes. We need to do some stretches and warm up; let's do that while I bring you up to speed."

I follow her lead when it comes to the warm-up. She does similar things to my pre-run prep, just in a different order, and I need to make her feel like she is in charge here. It's not just because she is my new boss; it's more so she won't change her mind about letting me play.

"So, like I said, each level is a sandbox environment; if you can see it, you can interact with it, and it will behave like it would in the setting. All environments have been set on Earth so far, but the AI may spring something unexpected on us, so don't rely on that."

"Can we really go anywhere and do anything, as long as it's internally consistent with the setting?"

She nods, changing position to stretch out her hamstrings. I note she is taking extra care of them. "Yeah. But we can only do what we can in the real world. So no flying, no summoning pet dragons—you know the drill."

"Are we racing against the other team?"

"The format is different for each level." Her eyes flick up and to the right. "Sometimes it's a race of some kind; sometimes it a points-scoring thing and whoever gets the most points by time-out wins. We'll get the briefing in just over two minutes' time. That's usually something like a letter, or an audio or video message from an NPC. Then we get five minutes to make loose plans and some other stuff that varies depending on the level. I try not to plan too much until we actually get there, to keep us responsive and adaptable. Sometimes people get something fixed in their head and when it doesn't work out that way, it slows them down."

There is far more uncertainty than I've ever experienced before going into a mersive, with the exception of the weird one that bastard beast tricked me into playing. It's strange. Usually I choose the genre, the difficulty level, the rules of engagement. I know whether I am going to need to slaughter dozens of zombies to move from the start to end points of a level, whether there will even be levels in the first place. I like the way this is making me nervous, the way it is pushing me to leap into something without knowing how it will end up—but unlike in that game run by that bastard, here I know there is a safety net.

A flicker of worry cuts through my excitement. What if I kill someone in this game, like I did with Myerson?

"So . . . just to put my mind at rest . . . if I hit another player in this game, they won't wake up with a black eye, will they?"

"They won't—I promise!" After a couple more stretches, she starts doing a few kickboxing moves. Uncertain of whether she is trying to show off or not, I don't try to emulate her, instead falling back on jogging on the spot, alternating with a few jumps and punches from an old routine I used to do.

"What are your strengths and weaknesses?" I ask.

"I'm best at math and logic puzzles and have pretty good endurance and stamina. Pretty flexible. Not so hot on upper-body strength. You?"

I shrug. "All-rounder I suppose," I say, aiming for nonchalant and slightly arrogant in the hope it will cover the fact that I have no idea. I've never thought of gaming skills in relation to my real-world skills before. I'm deadly with a good sniper rifle, but is that because I have the actual skill, or just because I know how to play certain games really well? "My hand-eye coordination is good," I offer, seeing her uncertainty. "And I'm fit." Then I start to really think about it. "I'm tough," I add. "Mentally, I mean. I can make hard decisions and fast. It takes a lot to freak me out. And I'm good at looking at what resources are available and how best to use them to achieve a goal."

She looks happier. "Good. And you being Noropean means you're probably twice as good as you're able to admit, so we'll be fine." We both chuckle at that.

"Is there a prize for the winner?"

"Not officially," she says, with the sort of smile that instantly tells me there is definitely a prize and it's one she wants. Badly. "Kudos, mostly," she adds, but I know she's downplaying it. I don't press her though. It won't make any difference to how I approach this.

I always want to win. Whether there's a prize or not, regardless of whether it looks like winning to the others in the game. As long as I know what I want and know how to get it, that's all that matters.

"Are there any things we're not allowed to do?"

She looks up at the ceiling, considering the question. "Other than taking stims, no, not that I can think of. We're cut off from the full functionality of our APAs, to prevent cheating, and the game takes a baseline MyPhys snapshot of your body at time-in, just in case there are any disputes. Opponents have the right to request that information, by the way. Are you okay with that?"

I shrug. "I've got nothing to hide."

"If you break the rules of the environment, there can be

consequences. So let's say we get dropped in a Victorian city and it's quicker to kill an NPC guard than find another way into a building. If you do that and the body is discovered, the police can turn up. If they think the murderer is you, then they try to detain you. Generally it's best not to do anything illegal, if it can be avoided, just so we don't get slowed down by in-world penalties. Sometimes it's hard to predict too; one of the teams got knocked out in the first round because they fired a gun in this safari park enclosure that caused a stampede and cut them off from the place they needed to get to before the other team."

"Can we find out about in-world rules before time-in?"

She shakes her head. "No. That's considered general knowledge. There are a few history nerds who are picked as partners for that very reason. We can't communicate with our APAs, remember, so unless you ask an NPC, you may not have an answer. And NPCs can lie. Sometimes people are assigned on each side, depending on the level. In that medieval one each team had a castle, and all the staff there were loyal to that castle."

"Can we ask NPCs to fight for us?"

"Yes. But sometimes that's not the best option. We just have to wait and see where we get dropped in and make decisions as quick as we can. So, before we can play, you need to give consent to have those minor changes made to your MyPhys gaming settings and consent to have your APA locked out for the duration of the game."

The relevant files arrive, I get Ada to check them through and, when nothing untoward is flagged up, I give my digital signature and send it back to her.

She looks away for a second, nods and then says, "Ah, here's the brief."

She swipes a hand toward one of the walls and the dull corporate mural is replaced by a black screen displaying an unfamiliar generic logo. It's swiftly replaced by a man dressed in an old-fashioned suit and tie, seated at a desk. "Looks like early to mid-twenty-first century," Carolina mutters.

The man is looking out at us but isn't focused on me or Carolina, and I realize this is replicating the old-fashioned filming process used back then. Nowadays any announcement- or talking-head-style footage can be made to automatically focus on the viewer, even moving from one member of an audience to another, if that's what's required. I'd forgotten how impersonal the generic, midrange stare of a person looking into an old-fashioned film camera is.

"Good afternoon. This message will be brief as we have little time."

"Set in England," Carolina says at the sound of his crisp accent. He sounds a little like the old radio presenters we did a mersive on a few years back. "Now I'm even more glad you're on the team."

"Three hours ago, a military commander defected from an enemy foreign power. He has a flash drive filled with information and is ready to provide us with critical intelligence. However, the operation to bring him in for debriefing has been derailed by riots that have broken out in central London. The operative on the ground who was escorting him in has hidden the defector in a safe house but was separated from him three hours ago. She is injured and hiding in a different location. She has sent a coded message detailing where she is now."

Shit, are those the same riots as in the game I played that the beast made? They must be, given the time period we're looking at. "So the first task is decoding that message," I say, refocusing my thoughts on what we need to know to win. Carolina nods.

"We know that two operatives from the commander's country have pursued him to London and are searching the city for him now. We don't know what intelligence they have, but we suspect they may have been involved with the injury to our operative, so it is possible they are tracking her down too."

"That must be the other team," Carolina says confidently. "So it's a race game: find the McGuffin before the other team."

"You need to find her, get the details on the safe house location and retrieve the flash drive and the commander before his own people find him. Obtaining the flash drive and getting it to the dead drop is the primary objective. Preventing the death of the commander is secondary. Good luck."

"He didn't say where the dead drop is," I say, frowning at the screen, which has now gone black.

"That'll be something the ground-operative NPC will give us," Carolina says. "It means we can't skip talking to her properly."

"Oh, right, to give it a linear structure. Cool. So, what now?"

"We'll go through that door," she says, pointing at the one I entered through, "and we get five minutes to look at whatever is in there, make some plans and then we time-in. Once we go through that door, we lose access to our APAs until we either time-out or pull out of the game. If you don't want to commit, there's no bad feeling about it. I don't want you to think that you have to because I've just become your boss."

"I'm in," I say firmly.

She takes the lead; I follow. This is her tournament, her reputation on the line, and feeling like she is in charge is going to help her. I resign myself to it, but I know that the moment I think she is doing something wrong, I'll ignore her. This is why I don't play team games. Shooting aliens on Mars with Carl is as close as I get to it, and that is more a shared world experience than a true co-op. We tried playing some puzzlers together and ended up pissing each other off so badly we had to stop before we came to blows. I need to do better on that front here, but I'm hoping the fact that it could really hurt if I don't force myself to play cooperatively will be a better motivator.

There is another room through the door instead of the corridor I was in before. It's like an old-fashioned bunker from a Cold War mersive a colleague of mine was very proud of. I thought it was dull; he thought it was a revolutionary way to teach history. Like people hadn't been doing that sort of thing for decades before.

In the middle of the room there's a table with a touch-screen set into the top of it, displaying a map of London. The table design is horribly familiar.

"This is set in the 2030s," I say. "If this room is part of the setting for the game itself, I mean."

She nods. "Yeah, it is. This is part of the prep, getting clues from this room on what we're likely to face. Did you live in London back then?"

My mouth is dry. The briefing mentioned riots. I nod. "Yeah, but I was just a kid. We had a touchscreen tabletop like this at home. It was the last touch interface we had before smart walls became standard."

"There's a marker on the map," she says and points at it. She frowns when nothing happens.

"You need to tap the place on the table," I say, reaching over to touch the marker.

"Jeez, I forgot that," she says, shamefaced. "Okay, so there's going to be an adjustment period."

"Just assume that everything has a touch interface," I say. "Neural chips weren't ubiquitous back then. It was all either projections or smart screens, so touch is the default, okay?"

The marker expands out to a little dialog box projected over that area of the map. "Last known location of Agent Alpha."

"So this is giving us the chance to decide where we start the game," Carolina says. "Shit, I've never been to London."

"I grew up there," I say, feeling the pressure building by the moment. "And I lived and worked there most of my life."

"Awesome!"

The marker is just off Fetter Lane, near Temple. "That area is a warren," I say. "Loads of dead spaces between buildings, lots of alleyways. Will we get the encoded message that the briefing mentioned here, or when we time-in?"

"Time-in, I guess. He said she'd sent it. Where we time-in is up to us."

"There," I say, pointing at Holborn Station. "It's on two Underground lines and in jogging distance of a third. Oh, but wait . . . if the riots have started, the tube network will be shut down. Will the other team have that data too?"

She nods. "We always start with the same information. It might be framed differently but we'll need to solve the first puzzle and get to the agent before they do."

"Tell me who we're playing against. Just in broad strokes."

"Errr . . . okay, so, one is a linguist and he's very fit, likes art, terrible at math. The other is a sharpshooter, confident, good at fighting, but Brace is a military man through and through, so no surprise there."

Brace? My face is a mask in front of a mask. I keep my eyes fixed on the map, waiting for the initial thrill of hearing he is playing to subside. It's no use whatsoever if I lose focus and we don't even get a chance to interact. Besides, there's no way I'll be able to kill him in this game, not with other people playing, no matter how much I want to. "Something about this doesn't feel right . . . why give the last known location when the first objective is to decode a message to find where she is now? The briefing said she was separated from the target three hours ago. This marker doesn't tell us if she last checked in when she was with the commander, before or after. She could be anywhere; you can walk across central London in an hour. This marker is just a distraction. What we need to do is secure fast transportation . . . a motorbike. We'll get the message, decode it, then get to her location much faster that way. There was a bike-hire place near Green Park back then; that's pretty central. We should start there."

She grins at me. "Sounds great."

I put my hands together over the map and move them apart, bringing back memories of playing with projections on the wall of my bedroom and pushing them back down as swiftly as they return. Zooming in, I spot the road near Green Park Station that I'm looking for. "That's where the hire place was. What about money? Do we start with that?"

"Sometimes. Sometimes we have to scavenge." She taps the location twice and a new marker appears with the option to "select as starting point," which she taps too.

The map disappears, replaced by a notice saying, "Choose three items each to take with you," and a large cupboard on the far wall is illuminated with a spotlight. "Awesome," Carolina says with a grin. "I was hoping we'd get to choose a load-out."

"We get weapons?"

"Sometimes," she repeats, heading over to the cupboard and opening it. She sighs. "And sometimes we don't."

There are about thirty objects arranged over several shelves. A bottle of water, a torch, a box of matches and a pad of paper are the first things that leap out at me. "No tablets," I say. "So we won't be able to access the Internet unless we steal one." I grab the matches.

Carolina takes the small pad of paper and a chunky black pen. "I'll need these to help with any math puzzles or code breaking. Water will be easy to find, right?"

I nod, running my hand across the shelves beneath each item, forcing myself to consider each one. On the far right on the third shelf down there are two small pieces of flat, rectangular plastic. I pick one up and see that it's a driving license with my picture and name on it. I grin. "We need to take these," I say, swiping hers off the shelf and giving it to her. "We'll need them to hire the bikes."

"Really?" She frowns at the rectangle. "Won't they have a database that would take care of it?"

That makes me hesitate. I can remember my parents having these though. Or was it my grandparents? I can definitely remember holding one, seeing a picture on it, knowing it unlocked the adult world in a way that I craved.

<Hey Dee, want some help?>

It's the same dialog box that's popped up before, and I bristle, doing all I can to hide my irritation from Carolina. I think a response "no" but my connection to Ada isn't there and the reply dialog box doesn't appear. How the hell is that bastard contacting me without my connection to her?

<You don't want to cheat? I didn't expect that. Okay. So be it.>

The dialog box disappears and I refocus on the license. "Identification can be useful for all sorts of things," I say. "Especially given we won't have phones or tablets or anything else we could use to prove who we are."

"Did they still use cash back then?"

"Shit no," I say, but then I spot another plastic card on the bottom shelf. "But they did still use these," I say, grabbing the credit card and checking my name is on it. "I just hope it works."

"You sure you want to take the matches?" Carolina asks and I look down at them in my palm.

Why did I grab these? I didn't even think about it. Was it because of that damn game?

No. It's because the electricity went out soon after the riots began and I don't want to be in the dark. But it might be daytime. The temptation to ask the beast for help is difficult to resist. I put them back on the shelf and instead pick up a small book on the top shelf. A *London A to Z*, dog-eared and slightly water damaged, but still usable. "I'll take this instead."

"Okay. You ready?"

I nod.

She goes back to the table, taps the notice, and the light illuminating the cupboard goes off. A green Exit sign above a door on the far side of the room is switched on. We both head toward it.

"There might be a delay when we step through," Carolina says. "The game may hold us in an elevator or something to make sure we time-in at exactly the same time as the other team, okay? If they're ready, we'll just go straight through."

"Understood."

"We need to keep calm, keep communicating." She reaches for the door handle.

"We need to win," I add, and she fires a wicked grin at me as she opens the door.

14

WE MUST HAVE taken longer than the other team; the door opens straight out onto the street we selected on the map. It's sunny and hot, which fits with my memory of the time. As one of our neighbors put it back then: the English never riot in winter. The heat haze rising from the tarmac makes the hire place across the road shimmer.

"Wish I picked the water," Carolina mutters. "But at least we have pockets."

I look down to see I'm wearing dark gray army combat trousers covered in pockets, and a black vest top. My boots are reassuringly stout with chunky gripped soles and it feels like I'm wearing thick socks under them. I'll be hot but hopefully I won't get blisters. We both pat our own combats down, locating the items we chose to bring in with us. "What's this?" I say, pulling out a rogue piece of paper, only to see Carolina doing the same.

"This is what we need to decode," she says as we both

look at the strings of numbers. "I'll handle this; you check out the transportation."

"Can you ride motorbikes?"

"In other games," she says, "but I don't know what they're like in this setting."

"We're in the same boat, then," I say, keeping my tone light. What I don't tell her is that I've ridden a motorbike from this period, one that I stole, and that I was bloody good at both the riding and the stealing part. I don't want to go into details and I would rather exceed her expectations than build them up.

She follows me across the road to the hire place, a small building with an uninspiring frontage and a picture of a motorbike next to a sign that reads "Green Park Hire." It looks better kept than when I came here in the real world all those years ago. I glance at the side gate's electronic lock and it looks intact. No matter. I intend to pay for the use of a bike this time.

There's a reception-cum-waiting room with a couple of plastic chairs, one of which Carolina sits down on, pulling out her notepad and pen to start working on the code right away. I go over to the young man behind the desk and ten minutes later he calls me out the back to show me round the bike. I can't stop grinning when I climb on and get a feel for the revs. I miss the throaty, raw power of the combustion engine.

I go back inside to collect Carolina once the hire assistant is happy I know my way round the bike.

She looks up at me, frowning. "I've cracked the cipher but the answer makes no sense."

Checking that the assistant is happily distracted with his tablet, I sit next to her, resting the two helmets I've also hired on the floor next to me. "What does it say?"

She reads aloud from her notepad in a hushed voice.

"'Phyllis would say that in the fourth edition of two thousand and one, the street is like a French garden, first of the east, the second house from the left, right at the top.' It doesn't mean anything to me, even though I'm sure I've decoded it right. If I hadn't, I wouldn't have got any words at all."

"It's like a cryptic crossword," I say. "My dad used to do those. This is a message to give us a location, right? So second house from the left may mean exactly that, with the rest of it telling us which street that house would be on."

"Okay . . ."

"Phyllis is a weird name . . . it rings a bell though. Can't put my finger on it right now. Fourth edition . . . maybe that could be a book?"

"A map book!" Carolina blurts out, excited.

"The *London A to Z*! Phyllis Pearson published the first one in the 1930s. Shit, I knew it was familiar! The first documersive I made was about the history of mapping London and there was a whole section about her!" I open the larger pocket halfway down my right leg to fish out the small *A to Z* I tucked in there, wondering if the game ties the first code to one of the starter items picked; otherwise it's one hell of a coincidence.

Opening the front cover, I spot "Edition 4 2001" in tiny print at the bottom right-hand corner of the first page. "This is the fourth edition, published in 2001!" I have to fight to keep my voice from squeaking with excitement.

"Oh my God!" Carolina yelps. "Okay, okay, okay, so . . . 'the street is like a French garden' and 'first of the east' are the only other bits of the message."

"Maybe there's a garden named after somewhere in France . . . or a garden square . . . Or a road called French Garden or . . ." I drift off as I spot the computer on the assistant's desk. I rush over to him. "Excuse me. Would it be possible to use your Internet? Our . . . phones are borked."

"If you don't mind typing," he says, gesturing at the grimy keyboard. "The boss is too stingy to get one of those fancy projector keyboards. Not that it would work with this ancient piece of shit."

He moves aside and I look at the screen, thrown by how alien the interface looks. "Errr, how do I call up the Internet? It's been a long time since I've used one of these."

Grabbing the mouse—a mouse! JeeMuh!—he clicks a couple of times and a browser appears. "What're you looking for?"

"A street called French Garden in London?"

He types and the sound of his fingers striking the keys throws me back to my grandfather's study and that old machine he still had to physically type his thoughts into. The sound of my grandmother playing the piano in the next room, the smell of a roast dinner cooking—actually *cooking* for hours—making my tiny stomach rumble.

"There you go. Looks like it's a fruit and veg importer at Covent Garden. Want me to write down the address?"

I frown at the Web site on the screen. That doesn't look like a good location for a safe house. "I don't think that's it. Can you put the browser back on?"

He quirks an eyebrow at me and I feel like a crappy time traveler failing to embrace the temporal lingo. I watch what he does more carefully and then ask if I can do the next search myself. He shrugs and gets out of the chair. I type in "French garden" and look at the results.

"First of the east" could also mean East 1, or rather E1, the postal code area critical for navigating the index of an *A to Z*. I go back, trying "French garden E1," and a result comes back for a "French Place," but it doesn't feel right. Why specify that particular edition of the *London A to Z*?

Abandoning the screen, I look back at the small map

book. I look for a French Garden but only find French Place, E1.

"Oh, hang about, are you after that posh new restaurant that opened?" the young man says. "Le Jardin? Isn't that French for 'garden'? Maybe you got your wires crossed."

I flick through the index and there's no Jardin Street but there is a Jardine Road, E1. "Yes!" I jump to my feet. "Thanks!" I say to him and he beams.

Carolina is on her feet too. "You got it?"

"It says the street is like a French garden. It's the word for 'garden' in French but with an *e* on the end! In E1—first of the east. And look at it. Out of the way, by the river . . . must be flats, given it said 'right at the top.' Let's go!"

"Are you sure? That's a hell of a leap."

I give her one of the helmets I hired. "It feels right to me." And it does. I don't know why. "Ready to go?"

We go outside and she hesitates at the sight of the bike. "I forgot what old-fashioned bikes are like."

"I got this one so you can sit behind me. My helmet has satnav built in. We'll be fine."

She's staring at the traffic and when she sees another biker weaving their way around the cars, she frowns. "Not as much protection with a bike. Why don't we hire a car?"

I put on my helmet, wait for it to adjust itself, realize it won't and then buckle up the strap. "This will be faster. Trust me."

I straddle the bike and press the button to sync it with the helmet. JeeMuh, I'd forgotten just how tedious life was before APAs. Reluctantly, she puts on her helmet and then sits behind me. There's a little beep as her helmet syncs with mine and the comms channel opens. "Ready?" I ask.

"Yeah, but don't go—"

I open the throttle and zip out into a small gap between two cars, earning a beep of the horn for my trouble. I laugh and accelerate, feeling her grip on my hips tighten. I can't go above thirty miles an hour here anyway, though that does feel faster on the back of a bike than I recall. Having bare arms and no protective clothing does make me extra cautious, but I'm not willing to lose the first challenge because I'm scared of a little road rash that won't be there when I jack out.

Weaving in and out of the traffic, swearing at pedestrians—it's like being home again. Not that I ever rode a bike like this legally. It just feels so good, so real, with the added piquancy of racing other people to our goal. I can't help but grin to myself as I ride, occasionally laughing when Carolina squeaks and tightens her grip when we take corners faster than she likes. The way to our destination is given by a generic female voice through the speakers built into my helmet, an occasional arrow projected onto the visor to guide me through tricky junctions. As much as I want to break the speed limit and literally cut corners, I keep within the rules of the road. The last thing I want is to be pulled over by some police officer.

We get there in just under twenty minutes and I pull up at the end of the street. There are several large apartment blocks, the sort that would be cheap and pretty undesirable in any other location. Here, still close enough to the center of London to command insane prices, they are obviously considered high-end, judging by the cars parked outside them. I take a moment to appreciate how old-fashioned the hybrids among them look and turn off the engine. "There's a chance they beat us here; we should park and go in carefully."

Carolina nods, removing her helmet to reveal hair dampened by sweat. I park the bike in a free space in the next road along, just to be on the safe side, and then we both jog back to Jardine Road, find the second block from the left and go to the door. "The message said 'house,' not 'apartment block,'" Carolina says as we scan the list of properties next to their respective door buzzers.

"We'll know if we're wrong soon enough," I say and point to the top of the list. "Look, it's a penthouse at the top. And the communal door hasn't been shut properly." I push it open tentatively, noticing a small stone roll from the door-frame, which prevented its full closure. "We can go straight up there and look. I don't think the other team would have made it so easy for us to check it out."

"Or they could be waiting inside for us." I raise an eye-brow at her. She laughs at herself. "Okay, come on, then."

The entrance lobby is plain and functional, no concierge desk, just a dozen large postal boxes for parcel deliveries and a fake plant in the corner. It smells of floor polish and I can hear the low whirring of the drone working its way down the corridor even before I see it. Stairs run up on the right-hand side and there's a sign with an arrow pointing toward an elevator. This building is only four stories high though, so I point to the stairs as I ensure the door clicks shut be-hind us.

We take the steps two at a time, our footfalls cushioned by the noise-suppressing vinyl that covers them. There are two apartments per floor, all the doors are closed, nothing on the landings outside of them. There's no noise at all, no music, no shouting, no nosy neighbors either, thankfully. On the top floor there is only one door, and on the door handle there is a smear of blood.

We both stop at the sight of it. "The briefing said she was injured," Carolina whispers, and I nod.

I push the handle down with just the tip of my finger, right on the edge, so I don't leave a mark in the blood. The door opens. I wasn't expecting that. Pushing it open slowly, I see a drop of blood on the cream carpet just inside the hallway, then another farther on. There's a narrow console table, which looks like it's made of real oak, with a vase of fake lilies set on top. The walls are painted cream and it's flooded with sunlight from a tall, narrow window at the far end of the hallway that looks like it runs almost the width of the building. Paintings of flowers, all in the same bland, creamy palette, fill the expanse of wall between three doors off on the left and two off on the right.

The door into the building was left open; this one into the penthouse was unlocked . . . It seems far too easy. Which means it's probably a trap. I step inside and then stand on tiptoes, the hairs on the back of my neck rising as some part of my brain alerts me to something just below my conscious awareness. I move my head slowly from side to side, changing the angle, enabling me to spot what looks like a thin line of sunlight stretched across the hallway at the height of my neck.

I can't help but grin. All those years of playing dungeon-crawling mersives have paid off, but instead of a trip wire, this is a monofilament that used to feature in the news feeds with gory tales of people almost being decapitated by gangs using them to steal motorbikes. I reach back to hold up a hand to Carolina as I check for others. There seems to be only one. Keeping my eye fixed on the place where it joins to the doorframe of a room on my right, I carefully take a couple of steps farther in, rest my hand on the frame below the wire and slowly run my fingertips upward until I feel a small plastic disk. I prize it off the frame, leaning back as I do so, ready for it to zip across the hall as the wire is sucked back in to wind around the internal spool before hitting the opposite doorframe with a tiny tapping sound, remaining held against the other disk still stuck in place.

"Whoa," Carolina whispers. "Good spot!"

The blood droplets trail down the right-hand side of the

hall and appear to go into a room at the far end on the right. I move to the first door on the left, refusing to let the blood trick me into heading straight for the most obvious room. The door is open and leads into a huge kitchen, a product of the days before domestic food printers really took off. There's a highly polished granite work top, more cupboards than anyone could ever possibly need and a large breakfast bar with a used glass and a dirty plate and cutlery for one still resting on it. There is a large window letting in loads of light, with thin voile drapes drawn shut to blur out the view of the apartment block across the road.

There's no injured agent though.

"What happens if she is already dead?" I whisper to Carolina.

"She's a critical NPC," she whispers back, "so she'll either re-gen after a time penalty—say, ten minutes or so—or another NPC will arrive here and get the information to us a different way. Whichever maintains in-game realism the best."

"She won't just leave the info in a note?"

Carolina shakes her head. "It's part of the reward of getting to her first, and for the other team the time delay is the penalty for being too slow. Let's keep looking."

It seems far too linear to me, and hardly good game design, but then I remember that this is designed to pit one team against another first, and be a good game second. I still think it could be better though. "What if one of us is killed by a trap?"

"You get pushed out to the loading room and have to wait ten minutes before you can come back in."

"That's all?"

"Ten minutes can make all the difference," she replies. "Trust me."

We check a dining room and what looks like a guest bed-room before crossing the hallway to the first door on the right, Carolina also ignoring the obvious blood trail. The doorway opens into a huge living room that overlooks the Thames, with a gaming corner, complete with vintage VR headset and safety area zoned off from the rest of the room, a huge screen on the far wall and a reading nook filled with books and an old-fashioned high-backed leather chair. A woman with cropped black hair and dark brown skin is sunk low in it, dressed in a sports bra and combats similar to the ones we're wearing. What I assume is her T-shirt is pressed against her side, the gray fabric beneath her hand soaked with blood. She stares at us silently.

"We got the message, and we decoded it," Carolina says, stepping forward. "We need to know the dead drop location and where you've hidden the defector."

"I need to know you're legit," she croaks. "I need to know if the boss sent you. Tell me what was on his desk and I'll tell you what you need to know."

I almost snort at the cheesy dialog, but then I realize I have no idea what was on the desk. I was paying attention to the man speaking to us, too distracted by the odd way his gaze wasn't quite focused on me to even look at the room he was in. Stupid rookie error!

"It was a small glass hedgehog," Carolina says confi-dently. "Its body and spines were made of clear glass but its eyes and nose were black glass."

The agent smiles, blinks slowly, and nods. She looks like she's bleeding out. "This is where he is." She holds out a piece of paper and Carolina takes it from her, looks at it and passes it to me. It's a page from a *London A to Z*—the same size and coloration as the pages in the edition I have—a small black dot marking a building off Fleet Street. At the bottom of the page a number seven is written. On the other side, written across the streets and squares, is a string of eight numbers with dots between them.

"The code on the back is for the dead drop. It's a locker in the Hospital Club in Covent Garden. I had a card to get in but I lost it en route. I'm sorry, you'll have to find another way in."

So that's another challenge, then. Fine. "What about the place off Fleet Street?" I ask, flipping the page back over. "Is it hard to get into?"

She shakes her head. "It's a flat . . . safe house . . . keypad on door is last three digits of the dead drop code. Made it the same to . . ."

Carolina goes over to her, kneels down and starts to try to pull the T-shirt away from the wound. The agent shakes her head. "I'm fucked," she says with a lopsided grin. "Nothing to be done for me now. But Serge is the real deal. He wants to help and he still has the flash drive. Get to him, keep him safe, get the drive to the dead drop and then the boss will contact you. He'll tell you where to bring him in. Okay?"

I want to ask her how they got separated, how Serge got to the safe house but she didn't, how putting a dead drop in a private club that presumably anyone can be a member of if they have the money could seem like a good idea. But then I'd just be one of those arseholes who only bought access to mersives so they could shred the plot and put all the solutions online in narcissistic recordings of themselves crowing about how they'd make something so much better and yet never seemed to get round to it. The fact I could fly a small aircraft through the plot holes in this mersive is not going to help us right now.

Carolina gets up. "Let's go," she says, heading for the door. I glance back at the agent, who looks sleepy now. She nods, giving me silent permission to leave her here to die. It's a linear and she's just an NPC and I feel absolutely nothing, save for a sense of dissatisfaction. I follow Carolina into the hallway.

"There's no chance she was one of the other players?"

Carolina shakes her head. "That's why I went up close, to check. We can only use disguises we can find in game. There's no way they could have sourced one that good and got here before us. Come on, we need to go."

I take a few more steps and then stop. "Wait. If we go now, she'll die, right? Then when they get here, there'll be something to tell them they had the right place, but that they have to wait because they got here second, yeah?"

She nods, still moving toward the door.

"There's a better way to handle this. A ten-minute penalty isn't enough. We've got . . . what, three more steps at least? Get to Serge, get the drive, get into the club and make the dead drop. Then it sounds like there could be more. We need a better advantage than being one step ahead, even in just a linear."

"Okay, I'm listening."

"You go to Fleet Street," I say, handing her the map page and the bike key. "Get the drive, move Serge somewhere else, meet me across the road from the main entrance to the Hospital Club. I'll slow them down here, then join you."

She frowns as she takes the page. "What are you going to do?"

"I don't know yet," I lie. "I'll figure it out. Do they know what I look like?"

"They might have looked before they went into the loading room. I had to declare you as a teammate. But that was, like . . . a few seconds before we went in. I didn't know if you were going to say yes."

I know that's a diplomatic way of saying she wasn't sure if I was going to make the grade. "Go! I'll see you there as soon as I can."

"You know where the club is?"

"Yes, yes, it was—" I almost tell her it was my father's club, that it was the place he met my mother, that every time we walked past it as a family he'd point to it and say that if they had had more chairs, I might never have been born but he would never explain why. "It was really well-known," I say.

"We don't usually split up," she says, slowing. "We don't have phones or anything. What if—"

"Go! If I fuck it up, you'll have to finish it by yourself. That's the worst that happens, okay?"

She scowls at the carpet for a moment and then nods. "Good luck!" she says and then races out of the flat.

I go back into the living room. The agent is still alive, just. She opens her eyes as I approach and looks up at me. "The enemy have sent two more operatives and we think they intercepted your message," I say to her. "They'll be here soon."

"Go. I don't have long. I'll be dead by the time they get here."

"No," I say, crouching in front of her. "I've got a better plan, and you're going to help me."

15

THE AGENT, WHO told me her name is Charlotte, is dying quietly in the bedroom as I make my final preparations. With the help of the Internet and the contents of the well-stocked kitchen and a sewing box I found in a cupboard, I've patched her up enough to prolong her life by an hour at most. She's in a lot of pain and suffering like hell, but she isn't real so I don't waste any worry on it. I'm focused on staging the flat for the other team's arrival.

Charlotte had gone into the bathroom to wash her wound, leaving the trail of blood that we saw when we entered, rather than trying to deliberately misdirect us. I plan to use the blood though, and I sit down on the floor at the end of the trail, just outside the bathroom door, so they'll see me. I'm wearing a fluffy bathrobe I found hung on the back of the door; I got Charlotte to lie on the robe while I patched her up, soaking as much of her blood into the front of it as I could and using it to wipe my hands when I'd finished pushing some of her intestines back into her abdomen and gluing the wound closed. Like I told Carolina, it takes a lot to freak me out, and while I had to take a moment to ready myself, I didn't feel faint at any point. There wasn't time for that.

Now I'm wearing the robe over my clothes, figuring that people who are going into shock get cold and I could have found it and put it around my shoulders before collapsing here. Her T-shirt, still sodden with her blood, is in a plastic bag in the pocket, ready for me to take out as soon as I hear them outside the door. I found some pale foundation in the bedroom and have used it all over my face. It's as good as it's going to get.

A bottle I found in the kitchen earlier is positioned behind me, easy for me to grab when I need it, hidden from view. Will I be able to go through with the plan when it comes to it? This is a leet server; it's not the same as other games. What if I freeze up? What if—

The sound of footfalls on the stairs outside sends a surge of adrenaline through me. I scrabble into a crouch with my back against the wall, draping the dressing gown so that it covers the fact that I'm not actually slumped back. I pull up the hood to hide my face—just in case they looked me up before the game—and pull the soaked shirt from the bag, screw it up into a tiny ball and shove it in the gown's pocket. I press the shirt over my side, just like Charlotte was doing when we found her, move my right hand to grip the neck of the bottle resting on the floor behind me and drop my chin down toward my chest. I stare at the floor in front of me as the front door handle turns.

"It's the right place!" An American man's voice. "Finally!"

"There's the agent!" says a second man, his voice just as American, only deeper. To my Noropean ear it's difficult to tell where either of them comes from. "We must have got here first!"

The door closes and they both rush toward me. I keep my

eyes down, making my breathing as rapid and shallow as I can without making myself dizzy.

"I need to know you're legit," I croak, trying my best to remember Charlotte's crappy dialog.

One of them kneels next to me. I tighten my grip on the bottle. "Whoa, shit, there's a lot of blood. I don't feel so good."

"Get out of the way," says the deeper voice, unimpressed. "Take some deep breaths. Yeah, this looks bad." His hand reaches toward the soaked T-shirt but I keep my head down, just in case.

"You could have intercepted my message. If the boss sent you, you'll know what was on his desk."

"Fuck," the man mutters. His hand moves quickly toward the shirt, pressing hard into my stomach, and I cry out in surprise. "Tell me where the commander is!"

"What are you doing, Brace?"

I can't help but look up at the man pressing hard into my side. Commander Brace's face is twisted by a determined sneer as he drives his fingers deeper in, thinking he is pressing a wound, but it is still hard enough to hurt.

Good.

All of my worries about whether I'd be able to do this dissipate, and I bring the broken bottle I've been hiding out from behind my back in a tight arc, shove the jagged glass into his side and pull it out again with a sickening, moist sucking sound to plunge it right back in as quick as I can.

He roars in pain, throwing himself back away from me, sending a spatter of his blood up against the wall as the bottle is pulled free, still gripped tight in my hand and slick with his blood. His teammate squeals, a strange, strangled sound that reminds me of a puppy being stepped on by accident. He throws himself against the wall too, leaping out of my range as I spring to my feet, dropping the bloodied T-shirt.

"You fucking bitch!" Brace spits through his teeth. His hands are now pressed over the messy wound in his side, and for a moment, I wonder if he will actually be hurt in the real world, just like Myerson was. Christ, I hope so.

"She's with Carolina?" the other guy says, incredulous, his face paper white in shock.

"Of course she fucking is!"

I back away from them, heading toward the front door, the dripping broken bottle held defensively in front of me. Brace's face is crumpled in pain, his lips drained of color, an impressive slick of blood already spilled on the carpet. Damn. Did I stab too deep? I don't want that bastard to die too quickly; I want him to suffer and not be kicked out of the game too soon.

His teammate is frozen rigid with shock, staring at the makeshift weapon, back pressed against the wall still.

"Stop her!" Brace yells at him, but he doesn't move.

I turn and bolt out, slamming the door shut. I set the broken bottle down in favor of gripping the tiny disk I stuck on the outside of the frame after Carolina left, and I draw the monofilament across the doorway at the level of my fore-head and stick the disk on the opposite side of the frame, just as it was when I found it before. If Brace's partner comes to his senses and decides to pursue me, he'll run straight into this. I have no idea what damage it will do and I don't care. We're going to win. That's all that matters right now.

I run down the stairs, wiping my hand frantically on the dressing gown, which trails down the steps behind me. As I reach the bottom floor I hear a cry of pain from the top of the flights of stairs. He found that wire, then. I stop, catching my breath as I wipe my hand more carefully, knowing I have a head start. I dump the dressing gown, hoping no one will notice the blood caught beneath my fingernails, and walk out of the building at a calm, measured pace.

Flipping through the *A to Z* to the relevant page, I plan a jog to Tower Hill Underground station, knowing I can tap in through the barriers with just the credit card. It will be a short tube ride to Embankment, then a jog to Covent Garden. There were no signs of the riots on the ride over, but if the tube network is shut down, I can get a bus there. Once I'm at the club, I'll scope out the building and see if I can figure out a way to get past security if I get there before Carolina.

It occurs to me that my parents had guest passes for friends they wanted to take into the club. I know where they were kept. And the old flat is on the way . . .

Once I'm a couple of streets away from the apartment I've just left, I break into a run. It's weird running without Dragon's Ghost. Then it hits me. Dragon will be at our old home.

I trip over the curb and stagger forward, narrowly avoiding a fall. I try to focus on the sprinting; the last thing I need is a sprained ankle or gashed knee, and I promise myself I'll make the decision about going home once I'm on the tube.

The station is not one I ever used before, but the barriers and the ancient, grubby yellow disks that read the travel cards, phones or payment cards are just as I remember. I hold my breath as I tap the credit card against the pad and then the barrier opens and I saunter through, just a quick backward glance to check that no injured men are hurtling toward me. There's just an old lady with a small dog.

Unlike the times I recall using the tube in real life, the train I need arrives only a minute after I arrive at the correct platform. I get on and flop into one of the seats, relieved that the carriage is only fairly full instead of absolutely rammed tight with people. I'm a little shaky after the running and the excitement, and sweaty too. But the heady glow of triumph, the memory of Brace's scream as I jabbed that broken bottle into his side, brings a smile to my face. I fold my arms, tuck my bloodstained fingers away from sight and slide down a little in the chair.

It's rare to get dead time like this in normal games. They're usually designed so that if it's the sort of game that needs pauses in the action—say, a standard zombie apocalypse shooter—there's something interesting going on, something to listen to at least, or an NPC to chat with. Here, there's nothing to occupy me, nothing to entertain. The smart ads running along the carriage are tedious and I'm so used to avoiding them I just stare at the floor, pretty much the only person not plugged into a device of some sort. I'm amused briefly by the sight of someone watching something on a pair of glasses that I remember wanting so badly as a kid.

A family gets on at the next stop, a young boy guided on by a tired-looking woman who squeezes onto the last free seat and puts the boy on her lap, as a woman who I assume is her wife or partner comes and stands near them. The boy has a bear, which looks very similar to the model that Bobby Bear was. I try not to stare as the boy turns it around to face him so they can chat about the train.

And there was me thinking there was nothing to observe, and what do I get? A painful reminder of what I've lost.

And where am I faced with going? The home I lost. And when? The same summer as the riots, the worst time of my entire life.

But this station wasn't closed, and I'm sure the entire tube network was shut when all that violence broke out. I look at the girl wearing the glasses and force myself to break a cardinal rule by talking to a stranger on public transport. "Excuse me . . . Sorry, I dropped my phone in the river and I'm lost without it. I heard someone say something about riots? Have you seen anything about that on the news feeds?"

She shakes her head, eyes wide at my having interrupted

whatever she was watching. An elderly man seated next to me looks up from his handheld console screen, his game pausing as soon as he looks away. "I heard something about it just before I left home. It's only a few idiots smashing some windows near a protest about something or other. Nothing to worry about."

That was how it started before though. Protests against the appalling corruption in government, about the huge gap between the rich and the poor . . . protests my mother took part in, thinking she would come home that day. It escalated so quickly . . . so violently . . .

I swallow down the lump in my throat. "Is the date the twenty-third of August? I'm just lost without my bloody phone!"

He nods, smiling. "It is, love," he says with a smile and looks back down at his game, the tiny lights on his wireless earbuds showing the sound has resumed too.

Somewhere out in the city, my mother is marching toward Parliament Square, and before the sun has set, she'll be dead.

I squeeze my eyes shut. No, not necessarily. This is just a game, just a rendering of London that might not be a perfect copy. But why this day, of all days? Why this city? Carolina said the levels were randomized so that no team could skew the challenges to suit their strengths. But this has been grossly unfair already. I'm playing a level in the city I grew up in, able to use my personal knowledge, to use a vehicle I've ridden before, through streets I know. Against Americans, for fuck's sake! Is that bastard beast behind this? Is he dicking with me again?

And if he is, is Brace dying in the real world now?

I wipe new sweat from my upper lip, taking a few steadying breaths. What's important, right now, is making sure Carolina wins. That's what I'm here for, that's what will serve me well in the future and that is a guaranteed reason for me to be here. All this other bullshit is just paranoia bordering on narcissism. Either it's a coincidence that this is the day my childhood ended, or it's that bastard fucking with me again; either way, it does not matter. It doesn't change what we have to do to win. And when I think of it that way, I have to try the old flat, because if the guest passes are there, we will surely win. I know I've given us a decent lead, but if we mess up trying to bypass the club's security, it could all be worthless. It'll be a five-minute detour, ten at the most. There's no reason not to try.

No reason aside from the hell of—

I take another deep breath. I can handle it. It's a flat. That's all. And if this is a carbon copy of London—which is still damn unlikely, but if it is—eleven-year-old me will be away at Jannie's house.

Shit, I haven't thought about her for years. I remember her braids, her laugh, her cat. Not much else. We didn't stay in touch. Hanging out gushing about media stars lost its appeal once I was on my own and trying to hide that fact. It doesn't matter. She's probably dead now.

The breath catches in my throat. Damn tube trains and their shitty air-conditioning. There are only two stops left. I jiggle my knees up and down, desperate to get moving again.

"Ladies and gentlemen, I'm sorry to announce that this train will now be terminating at Embankment Station. I repeat, this train will be terminating at Embankment Station."

There's a collective groan from my fellow passengers. The elderly man switches the console screen to his news feed and holds it between us so I can see it too. "Looks like that protest is getting out of hand," he mutters as we scan the headlines. "I reckon they'll have to shut the Circle and District line stations near the Houses of Parliament. Do you have far to go?"

"I was getting off at Embankment anyway," I say. "You?"

"I live in Pimlico. Normally I'd walk, but by the look of this"—he waves a finger at the latest drone footage of the escalating violence—"I might just get the Northern line, change at Stockwell and come up to Pimlico from the south."

I can't help but smile at the way he talks about the route. Proper Londoner; knows all the viable routes home and can adapt at a moment's notice. We had to. It was the first underground train network built in the world, so we inherited the crappiest system, which made all the mistakes the rest of the world could learn from. "Well, good luck. I hope . . ." I trail off, remembering that in less than twenty-four hours the riots will be rampaging through Pimlico. "I hope you have friends or relatives outside of London you can stay with, until all that bollocks blows over."

"I might just do that. Got a daughter in Devon. Lovely there this time of year."

He smiles and I return it. Why did I say that? It's not like I'm some bloody time traveler, doing all I can to save one old dear. And probably inadvertently condemning a future civilization to death, knowing my luck. But these people seem so much more realistic than the other NPCs I've interacted with; no wonder the immersion is deeper.

We all pour out of the carriage at Embankment and I slip through the press of people from one spare spot to the next, weaving my way around confused tourists needing to find a map to replan their route, unaware that they've chosen the worst time to visit the city.

By the time I emerge at street level the air is filled with the sounds of dozens of police and ambulance sirens. The din makes my heart race. It was the background sound for days that stretched into weeks. And for the couple of years afterward that the police existed, the mere sound of one of their sirens sent me into a breathless panic spiral.

I rest my hand over my chest. This is just an echo in my body, a trained response like in Pavlov's bloody dogs or any other poor bastard who's been hot-housed like Carl and me, survivors of the Machine. It isn't real. I don't need to be afraid of them now.

This is just a game, after all.

The credit card proves to be useful once more, enabling me to buy a cold drink from one of the vending machines that line the hill running up to the Strand. I chug it down, wondering if Carolina is actually very close, given the location of the safe house that Charlotte gave us. I push the can straight into the recycling slot at the side of the machine and, feeling refreshed, sprint toward Shaftesbury Avenue.

I don't have to think about the route; it's just there, in my mind, even though I haven't had to use it for so long. Running through streets that were part of my childhood, I have to constantly push away memories that were merely moments of banality back then, and have been gilded by the passage of time. The first road I was allowed to cross alone, without a parental hand to hold. The park I used to be taken to if I was especially good—though now I see the height of the iron railings around it, the security gate, the way all those flowers and swings and the slide are shown to all children, but only accessible to the privileged few. The postbox where I used to deposit Mum's scented letters to her grandmother, another mark of our wealth, given that the postal service had stopped collecting mail from so many areas by then.

It's strange, viewing my childhood stomping ground through my jaded adult eyes. It had already lost its luster by the time I had to move on, having transformed into a place too controlled, too geared toward those with money, to be of any use or refuge to someone who had none. But now what I once had is revealed in sharp relief, too painful to appreciate. And as much as I hate it, as much as I try to relegate it to some mental oubliette, I can't help but wish for that time once more. A time when I never had to plan, to evaluate, to manipulate, just had time to eat and have somewhere warm and dry to sleep. A time when there were people who loved me and cared for me and placed my well-being at the top of their priorities, rather than what they could extract from me in return.

And there's the familiar, bitter counterspell to this dark magic: the realization that it was never that way at all. If they had really cared about me, really put me first, my parents wouldn't have died the way they did. All of the nostalgia and the romantic glow of the streets around me collapses, merely a collection of stupid ideas defeated by a rational argument. I run faster.

The door to the lobby is open, as it always was, and the concierge, that awful man, steps out of his office right on cue. "Good afternoon," he says with that smile that always bordered on a sneer. "How can I help you?"

"Visiting a friend on the eighth floor," I say. "They've given me the code for the lift already."

"Could you sign here, please?"

I sigh, jog over to the desk and scrawl on the tablet he's held out to me. None of this is necessary. If he really needed to gather data on all the people visiting, he'd be asking for my thumbprint. But he knows he doesn't have a legal leg to stand on, and all of the residents are of the mentality that it's worth putting up with an irritating prick if it deters thieves.

"And proof of identity, please?"

I look him right in the eye. "You don't need that. It's only a brief visit and I won't be staying overnight, which you should have asked me first. And if you ask me for ID again, I'll tell Robert you were a pain in the arse."

His eyes widen at the use of my father's Christian name spoken so casually, his odious little brain making the link to my mention of the eighth floor. "You are absolutely right. My apologies," he snivels, pulling the tablet back to hold it against his chest, as if he needs to protect it from the sweaty, stern harridan in front of him.

I walk away from him, feeling a profound sense of satisfaction, and stab the button to call the lift. The last time I was here, there was no electricity and the stairwell was filled with dead bodies. I can't help but feel relieved when the lift pings and the doors open. When I step inside, the sophistication of this game strikes me; that NPC reacting so plausibly to the mention of my father's name is so realistic it's creepy.

As the elevator rises, making me feel briefly heavy, I'm filled with the sense of there being some ulterior motive behind all this. There are too many coincidences. This level doesn't feel randomly generated at all; it feels like a pantomime put on just for me, or rather, one created to cast me as a reluctant star. That isn't narcissism. Its being in London alone, that would be fair enough. But London, on this day exactly, with a mini-quest that involves the place my parents met, that rewards me for going back to my home on one of the worst days of my life? No. I'm being fucked with, and it's obvious that bastard's behind it all.

Weighing up my options, I see I'm left with very few. Regardless of his interference, I still need to make sure we win. I'll play it cool, I'll do what needs to be done, we'll win, I'll get out and then work out what to do when I'm in my real body in my cabin, and not in a world he could theoretically control. A world in which I'll feel pain. My mouth is dry again.

At the eighth floor I take a deep breath as the door slides back, revealing the hallway. Even the smell is correct: the floral scent of the polish used by the cleaning drone that is at the far end, running a cloth saturated with the stuff along the skirting board.

Banishing irritating echoes of my life here, I stride toward the door to the flat and type in the access code without thinking. There's the familiar little chirrup and green light that verify I'm a resident, and I open the door. Of course, if this were the real world, the concierge would be getting a notification that I had returned, only looking several decades too old to be Robert Whittaker's daughter. I'd better be quick, just in case the game really is aiming for the most realism it can and he comes up to investigate my identity properly.

Even though I am prepared for it, the sight of my old home still steals my breath. I've never been back here since the day I finally left. I didn't record any personal mersives here, for one thing, and besides, I would never play them back anyway. It has been decades since I stepped foot in this place, and no matter how much I try to deny it, or how many times I tell myself that it's just a game, it feels like coming home.

16

THERE'S A MOMENT when my legs wobble and I'm sucking in a breath that feels like it will burst back out of me on a tsunami of tears, and then I shake my head, close the door behind me and do my best to remember where my parents kept the guest passes for the club.

A low inquiring bark makes my heart judder and Dragon bounds into the hallway, tail wagging, head cocked to one side as he appraises me. Of course he doesn't recognize me; he knew me as a child. I crouch slightly, pat my knees three times, just like I did when I was a kid. "Dragon! Draaaagon! Here, boy!"

He gives a high, excited yelp and in one big leap is pushing his nose into my face, making joyful yips as he tries to lick me. I throw my arms around him, burying my face in his fur for a few precious seconds before his excitement pulls him away so he can push his body against me and weave in and out of my legs.

A few more indulgent moments and I pull myself out of

that state of willful ignorance, forcing myself to get back in the game. "Go lie down now. Go find Fuzzy!"

As he always did before, he scampers off to his basket where his favorite chew toy is, and I follow him into the living room. There are pictures of my parents and me as a child dotted all over the room. I look at one, of my parents on their wedding day, without even thinking, and look sharply away.

My gaze falls upon the mantelpiece, on a vase shaped like a pink tulip that both Dad and I absolutely hated. It was something that belonged to my great-grandmother—it might even have been made by her—and that provenance meant that it had pride of place regardless of how we felt about it. It was always there, for as long as I can remember, aside from one day. The day the riots started.

That morning it ended up on the floor, smashed, after a row between my parents. I had never heard them arguing before, but that morning it woke me up. I remember Bobby Bear telling me that sometimes adults who love each other get angry with each other, but it doesn't mean they stop being in love. I stayed curled up in bed, holding him tight, until the sound of the smash and the awful silence that followed made me throw back the covers and run in.

I look around the room, examining it, looking for any other details that are out of place. Everything looks exactly as I remember it. How the hell could it be rendered so accurately? Then I spot the little ornament of a train that hid the nanny cam used to check on Dragon when we were out for more than a couple of hours. There were two in every room. JeeMuh, did the US gov-corp pull all the data from those when they were vetting me? How did they even find it? Surely it wouldn't have been stored for decades after the account was closed.

So that's why the vase is there; it was intact in whatever footage that bastard is using to—

The vase disappears. I blink at the space on the mantel-piece, amazed. Is he watching where my eyes are focusing, like a marketing bot? Did my face show confusion and—

There are pieces of broken pink porcelain on the floor that were not there moments ago. And not just scattered randomly; they are in exactly the same positions as they were all those years ago when I got to the doorway and looked in. I can remember them, so clearly, because they looked like a distorted smiling face. Two similar-sized chunks rested above a long sliver for the nose and then five little chips close enough for my eye to force them into the pattern. I saw the smile and thought it seemed so wrong when my parents had said such hateful things.

When the intensity of the memory passes, it leaves a sense of disconnection in its wake. This flat seems suddenly un-real, the appearance of the broken vase too incongruous with reality to trick me anymore. I step back, look away, draw a breath in and out. I go over to the cam and crouch down to its level. There's no way that pattern could be seen from this location, from this angle. I go to the other cam, the one hidden in the picture frame on the opposite side of the room, and even from this angle, it's not in view.

This is a distraction, but I can't let it go. How has he done this? I remember sweeping up the pieces after my mother left the flat just a couple of minutes later with a loud slam of the door; I took such care to find every tiny piece so that I could glue the vase back together again. I was such a stupid kid, thinking that fixing the vase would somehow make all of it better. Bobby Bear was in my bedroom. Dad was in the kitchen, kettle on, enacting the timeless English tradition of making a cup of tea in response to a crisis. I can't see how he got this data. Neither of my parents recorded it. Why re-cord an argument? And even if they had, their data would have been lost when they died without anyone there to preserve it for them in the chaos of the time. The riots were only the start of it.

In fact, I can't see how this could have been done at all. To re-create this flat, a mersive coder would be using tags from the primary sources: any relevant neural chip recordings and any cam data. If—by some wildly improbable set of circumstances—the cam data survived all that time and was dug up by the US gov-corp, making this rendering of the flat could pretty much be handled by a skilled coder working with an AI. But reproducing something so accurately, that only I have seen—in response to my confusion—is beyond any of the capabilities of the coders I knew and worked with. And they were some of the best in the world.

I thought the person behind the star beast avatar was a genius. But now I'm wondering if the gaming AI on this ship is actually far more advanced than I appreciated, and in concert, they are able to work what feels like magic. If he's that good though, why make the correction midgame? Why shatter the immersion? To prove how leet he is?

Obsessing about this is not winning the sodding game though. I spot the guest passes for the club in a shallow clay dish on one of the bookshelves and grab them both. I've got what I need and it's time to go.

As soon as I head for the door, Dragon—no, the reproduction of him—starts to whine. It stops me before I even realize what I'm doing. I don't let myself turn around, instead going back out into the hall with every intention of walking straight out of here and—

He barks but I don't let it stop me. He's not real.

Without even a glance toward the copy of my old bedroom door, I cross the hall, grasp the door handle and—

"Deanna."

The call from my parents' bedroom freezes me. It is my father's voice, rasping, weak. Like it was the day after the riots, before the head wound he got as he searched for my mother killed him slowly and his body—

No. This is just a game.

"Deanna. Can you bring me some water, please?"

I grip the metal tighter, squeezing my eyes shut.

I don't have to go in there to see him lying on the bed, the blood . . .

What if I went in there and his eyes were open and his mouth was open and he was dead and the flies the flies!

The door handle rattles as my hand shakes. Of all the things that bastard has done, all the things he's made me see again and hear again, it's this one that really hurts.

And then it doesn't. I shrug that shit off like an old coat. It isn't real; it's a game. It is just a game. It is just a fucking game!

Minutes later I am sprinting toward Covent Garden, the guest membership cards for the Hospital Club gripped tight in my hand, my mind fixed firmly on the task ahead. Carolina is waiting for me, her body a study in tension until she spots me and literally jumps up and down on the spot, waving with glee. When I get to her she hugs me so suddenly I don't have a chance to rally myself and return it, just stand there like a stick until she lets me go.

"I got the drive!" she says, patting a pocket of her trousers. "And I've moved him to a different safe house. There was this chase and I had to cross between two buildings and I nearly freaked out but I did it! I made it across and I beat that phobia and it was *awesome* and, oh, who cares! He's secure. What about you? What happened? I haven't seen the other team at all."

I give her a grin. "I . . . slowed them down." Holding up

the guest passes, I add, "And these will get us into the club, no questions asked."

Her jaw drops open. "Seriously? Brace is gonna freak!" She hugs me again, but this time I'm ready for it. "Let's go win!"

And we do. It's a straightforward dead drop, almost anticlimactic in its ease. But it would have been so much harder if we'd done it without the cards, and as Carolina says, we acted within the boundaries of the game world. No rules were broken.

Aside from all the consensual-use-of-personal-data ones that bastard has trampled all over already.

The level ends with a message from the boss, played to us on a phone found in the dead drop locker, which guides us a couple of streets away to a building that, had the game gone differently, could have been the other team's last chance to intercept us and stop us entering to win the game. But there's no sign of Brace or his teammate, and I practically saunter along the grotty alleyway and through the door that takes us directly into the loading room where I met Carolina.

She cheers loudly, whooping with the loud joy that Americans seem to prefer, while I simply flop into one of the office chairs by the window and breathe out a long sigh of relief. The Thames winds its way below, timeless, there before Londinium, there throughout all the fires, the plagues, the riots, uncaring. I don't know what date it is supposed to be out there and I don't particularly care either. We won. And that's all that matters.

The door opens and Brace crashes through, sweating and pale faced, followed by the teammate, who looks equally distressed.

"Ha!" Carolina cries out, jabbing a finger at Brace. "Didn't have it in me, did I? I guess you just learned a lesson, my friend!"

He gives me a cold glare, wiping his forehead with the

back of his hand. "If I'd known you were going to team up with a fucking psychopath, I would have—"

"Hey!" Carolina puts herself physically in front of me, as if she feels she must shield me from his words. "What happens on the server stays on the server, Will. Don't you forget it."

"She stabbed me!" His hand rests over his side as he leans to look past her shoulder at me. "And she nearly garroted Jon."

Jon rubs his throat with a haunted look in his eyes as he stares at the floor, unable to even look at me.

"Did I break any rules?" I ask Brace, folding my arms, rooting my feet to the floor.

His mouth drops open. "That's not the point!"

"I thought the point was to win within the boundaries of the world the level was set in. I got that bottle from the kitchen in that flat. The filament was set up by the spy when she arrived at the flat before us; I just moved it to a different place. They were both in-world elements, placed in prominent locations for us to use in game as we saw fit. You're just pissed off that you lost."

He glowers at me and I stare back, working hard to keep my hatred under control. I fix a mask of pride on my face, with a slightly arrogant smirk that I know will irritate his alpha male ego.

"So I'm through to the final," Carolina says cheerily. "And you can bet your ass that Dee is gonna be my teammate."

Brace directs his glare at her. "I'll be sure to warn the other team."

"Thanks," I say. "Always good to have the opposition intimidated before we even time-in."

His fists actually clench. I never thought people did that in real life—or at least when in direct control of their avatars. He wants to hit me. Well, I want to kill him, so it's fair enough. He gives me one last, long look as if he is committing my face to memory and then goes toward the door.

"Hey, we're supposed to shake hands, Will," Carolina calls. "You know, be gracious in defeat."

Ignoring her, he leaves the office and slams the door behind him. Jon lets out a breath and steps toward Carolina, his hand extended, and she shakes it. "He'll calm down," he says as he comes over to me.

I shake his hand. "Sorry about your neck. Was it really bad?"

He swallows as he nods. "Yeah. But I shoulda looked first. I froze up; then I panicked. I never thought I'd be that guy, y'know? I'm usually fine with blood."

"It wasn't the blood. It was the violence," I say, perhaps a little too confidently. "Sorry if it gets you into trouble with Brace."

With a smirk he says, "I'm always in trouble with Brace. Everyone is." He leans closer. "I think space doesn't really agree with him."

"I think it's losing that disagrees with him," I reply, earning a snort from Carolina. He smiles a little and then goes.

Carolina grins at me. "I've never seen Will so angry before. You've not made a friend there."

I shrug, unconcerned. He'll be dead soon, and besides, he's not the first man to get in my face for not behaving the way he expected me to.

"Listen, you really came through for me today," she says, brushing her hand against my arm. "You said you wouldn't let me down and you didn't. I really wanted to win and you made that happen. I won't forget that."

"Anytime," I say, and accept the hug she is angling to give. Shit, how many does this woman need? "When's the final?"

"In seven days," she replies. "I should've asked if you'd be happy to play again. It just came out."

"More than happy," I say, meaning it. "Though whoever the opposition is will be primed against me. It won't be so simple next time."

She nods. "I'm gonna go get some rest. You should do the same."

"I feel fine."

"We're in the loading room, so we're back to normal gaming settings. It'll hit you when you come up. Take some time to decompress, okay?"

I tell her I will and watch her leave. But it isn't time to come up for air yet. "Ada, you back?"

"Yes."

"Take me to my office."

It's good to be back under the stars again with nothing but the slate stretching out around me after the pressure of the game's intense urban environment. The star is where I left it. I reach down, but before I even touch it, the stars already start to move above me.

The star beast coalesces into shape in front of me, this time shrinking down to the size of a tall man. I don't bother to pick up the star; instead I ask Ada to make two chairs for us. I sit down in mine and wave a hand at the empty one. "Let's talk," I say. "No shouting. No posturing or any other bollocks."

The beast sits. "I hoped you would want to talk to me. Did you enjoy the game?"

"Some of it."

"Which bit?"

"The winning part. Even though it did feel like I was getting some extra help. The *A to Z* thing, the dead drop being in the club I knew about . . ."

"I wanted you to win."

"I told you I didn't want any help."

"You didn't want any help with choosing what to take with you."

I sigh. "Why did you set it on that date? No, scratch that. Why are you fucking with me?"

"I'm trying to help you. I've been thinking about what you said though, about how my actions were not helping your trust issues. And I've been thinking about how you were in the re-creation of your family home. I feel like I keep getting it wrong. You don't react like other people. And I anticipated that, to a certain extent, given how the hot-housers changed your brain. But you still don't respond to things in the way I hope you will. So I am glad that you wanted to talk, because I think we are at an impasse."

Its voice is the same deep rumble as before, but I'm feeling calmer this time. It tried to manipulate me in the game but it didn't work. I walked away, and in doing that, I feel I clawed back some control. "At what point did I ask for your help?"

"You need it. You've needed someone to help you for a very long time. I didn't ask you if you wanted my help because you would have said no."

I look up at the stars, biting back an angry tirade that springs to mind. "Putting the whole consent problem to one side, 'cos that's a whole other conversation, my next question is this: Why do you want to help me? I thought that first game was all about tricking me into killing someone."

"Oh no, not at all. I explained that. But I did get some things wrong. I understand that now. I hoped that setting the leet game at a critical point in your life would prompt you to examine the root of your problems."

I fold my arms, draw in a long breath through my nostrils and hold it in my lungs as I wait for the angry pulse to subside. "I'm going to say something that you need to accept;

otherwise we're never going to get anywhere. I do not need to be fixed. Got that?"

"But do you realize how broken you are?"

"Jesus shitting Christ, did you not hear me?"

"I did." It leans back in the chair, folds its starry arms and tilts its head. "If I accept that you do not want to be fixed, can we move on?"

"No, we fucking can't, because knowing you—at least, what little I do know about you—you'll still believe you have the right to keep trying to fix me, because what I want and do not want are clearly irrelevant to you. There are thousands of people on this ship, fucking thousands of them; why don't you go try to fix them instead?"

"But I already am, Deanna. I'm already helping them. I'm helping Carolina to overcome her height phobia by incentivizing her to make a jump across a gap during a chase in the game you just played together. I've been helping Travis to reconnect with who he was before he married Stefan Gabor with reminders of his grandmother and the things he used to enjoy with friends and family before his social isolation. I have been helping Carl to see therapy as something positive by—"

"All right, all right, I get the idea! Who the fuck are you? 'Cos right now, I'm wondering if you're the one who needs help."

"I would like to have a conversation about trust."

I blink at the star beast. This is such a weird conversation. I can't get a feel for this person at all. Everything seems to just bounce off and get sent in different directions. "Yeah, whatever," I say with a sigh. Maybe if I indulge it, I will finally get somewhere.

"My telling you who I am is an act of trust."

"Listen, I'm not going to report what you've done to any

authorities here. I know how good you are at this, and you can hurt me far more easily than I can hurt you. For what it's worth, I don't think there's as much risk as you fear." I hate saying it, because it's true. I don't have the skills to trace who he is from what he's done to me. There are only two people I know who could do that: Carl—whom I don't want to tell because if he looks at what's happened between me and the beast, he'll know I killed Myerson—and Travis. And I don't trust Travis to find the information and not use it against me. I still need to work out what to do about him.

"It's an act of trust because I'm not supposed to be on this ship."

"You're a stowaway? Seriously? How the hell did you pull that off?"

"It's complicated. I feel we would work together much more efficiently if I could explain. But I won't, without greater trust between us."

I lean back, folding my arms. It's like he wants to tell me, but there's something else beneath this. Is it just the fact that there are no features to watch, no physical tics to read, that makes me feel so uncertain about what is really being said here?

No, it's not just that. There are so many power inequalities between us, it's ridiculous. He's already rooted through my life, taken out the most dramatic moments and made mersives out of them. He's clearly got some sort of agenda, other than dealing with the ones who fired those missiles.

"Are you lonely or something?"

"No. Not as lonely as you are."

I laugh to douse the anger that flares up. "I'm not lonely. Just tell me what I need to do to make you trust me enough. 'Cos we're getting nowhere here and I've got things to do."

"I would like you to tell me what happened on the day of the riots."

"Why? It's obvious you already know. And who gives a fuck what happened then? It was nearly thirty years ago, in a place that doesn't even exist anymore."

"Don't you see what you're doing?"

I pinch the bridge of my nose, trying to think of a good reason to stay, when I can't think of any good reasons to talk about what he wants. "How about you at least look like a human being?"

"You're doing it again."

"Doing what?" My voice is more of a shriek. I snap my jaw shut.

"Evading. Pushing away. Pushing down. How many times did you do that in the game on the leet server?"

"I don't have to—"

"Seventeen times. In less than thirty minutes. You don't even realize you're doing it. Don't you remember when your breath caught in your chest when you were on the tube train? When you remembered something and—"

I'm on my feet. "This is not the way to gain my trust!" I yell at it.

"What about the moment when your father was calling you from the bedroom?"

"You f—"

"Tell me what happened to your mother that day."

"No! It is so fucking irrelevant!"

"How can you say that about the death of your own mother?"

I walk away from the chairs, toward a random spot on the dark horizon. "Ada, end immersion." There's no response. "Ada!"

He's next to me, walking at my side, appearing so quickly I don't even register the moment he's keeping pace. "I don't want you to run away from this. I've tried to give you opportunities to examine these things but—"

"Don't make out that you're trying to do me a service, you sick fuck! This isn't anything to do with what you're trying to give me; it's all about what you can suck out of me. Do you like seeing women cry? Is that it?"

"I am trying to give you something, Deanna. I promise."

The shape of him shifts and I don't want to turn and look but my head is moving and I see the blond hair, the particular slope of the forehead, the profile that makes me stumble to a stop.

"I want you to tell me what happened to your mother," the avatar of my father says.

I breathe through the sudden pain in my chest. He's not tall enough, some puerile part of my brain tells me, but it's because I am bigger now. There's no towering solidity that I craved so desperately in the weeks after that day, no reassuring patriarchal power that promised protection and security and—

It's not my father though.

"I want you to stop fucking with me."

"I will stop when you answer my question, Deanna."

It feels like there are two flickering versions of myself and I don't know which one to be. There's a trembling child who wants nothing more than to run into his arms, sobbing, ignoring the fact that he isn't real, letting herself sink into the soft, welcoming trap. And there's the furious, frustrated, frightened woman who just wants to come up and—

I stop. The two versions collapse and it feels like I am aware of a cavernous space inside me, a dark emptiness that is so deep, so intense, that it might be who I really am. Maybe I'm not a person at all. Maybe I am just an emotional void, crafted into the semblance of a capable, clever woman who costs far less to maintain in a corporate structure than a real, free individual.

And out of that darkness a single, solitary fact emerges. I cannot answer the question because I simply do not know. I have no idea what happened to my mother.

17

MY KNEES ARE hurting. It takes a moment to realize that it's because I've fallen onto them, the slate unforgiving. Somehow I can see myself, hunched forward, kneeling, my head tipping forward into my hands as a sound pours out of my mouth, inhuman in its distress. The thing that is not my father rests his fake hand on my shoulder, nodding slowly.

"I don't know how she died!" The words are forced out in huffing puffs of air, riding each sob out of my lungs, and I am suddenly back in my body, feeling as if something foul needs to climb up out of my throat. "I don't even know where she was. Just that she went . . . she went . . . she left me! And then he left me! They left me! They left me!"

The foul mass is made of nothing at all, and yet I can feel it, a cloying, choking thing of pain and rage and betrayal. There is nothing to do, nothing I can do, save surrender to this hidden enemy that was within me all this time, waiting for this moment of weakness. It obliterates everything else inside me, even the shame at having lost to it, rampaging through my body like an army that has been laying siege and has finally battered down the gates and can pour into a city, destroying everything it has been desperate to defile for so long.

And when it is laid to waste and there is nothing left save ruins, I feel arms around me. They are not my father's. They are not made of stars. They are pale brown, thin and yet still somehow strong enough to hold me.

"I'm here, Dee, I'm here." It's Carl. "I got you. I'm here. It's going to be okay. I'm here."

Wet with tears and snot, I turn my face toward him. "What are you doing here?"

"You called me. You said you needed me."

I look around but there's no one else here, no sign of the beast, just the slate and the stars, stretching into forever. "I didn't."

"You did," he says softly. "And I came. I'll always be here when you need me. Just like all those times you've been there for me. Remember?"

I swipe the back of my hand across my eyes, so tired and hollow I can't even hold myself up. It can't be Carl; it has to be the beast, fucking with me again.

"I'm sorry I missed our game. I was so wrapped up in the case, and then I had my first therapy session, and I was just on my way back when I got your message. What happened? Did someone do something? Do I need to get medieval on someone's ass?"

All I can do is blink at him for seconds that feel like hours. "Is it really you?"

He smiles and it's so him it hurts. "Yeah. Of course it's me. Who else could it be? This is a restricted-access area in your private server space, Dee. I could only get in because Ada gave me a key. It's locked down tight."

I try to think of something I can ask him, something only he would know the answer to, but I can't think of anything the beast wouldn't know. "Can we talk in meatspace?"

He looks as shocked as he should. "Okay, I'll see you on the other side."

Carl is knocking on my cabin door before I have even lifted my head from the pillow. I feel leaden with exhaustion; my legs simply won't move even when I tell them to. "Come in," I call.

He darts in, closes the door and rushes to my side, gathering up one of my hands in his. "I'm back," he says, and I know it was him in my office. "Shit, Dee, what happened? You look shattered."

My throat is sore, like I was really crying, but my face is dry. Maybe this is what Carolina meant about needing time to decompress. It feels like I've run a marathon with a heavy pack on my back.

Carl squeezes my hand. He's waiting for me to answer and I'm still trying to work out how I feel. Coming up after such an intensely emotional collapse is jarring in the extreme, and I still can't remember asking him to come to me. I only asked him to speak to me here to check that it was really him back there. Now what do I say?

He's looking at me with those big brown eyes of his, the ones that have been trained to see things most people miss. I need to be as truthful as I can be with him; otherwise he'll start poking around, looking for a reason for me to be upset a day after a man was murdered. "I just played a game on the leet server."

He frowns slightly. "They've got one on the ship?"

"Yeah. I was invited to take someone's place at the last minute for this tournament thing." I pause, worrying that I'm saying too much. But my participation in that game wasn't protected by an NDA, and the only one I've signed is to do with the details of my salary and benefits and all that crap. Shit, I haven't told him I have a job now.

"And what was it like only doing what you can in the real world?"

"Weird. And it feels like shit when you come up from it," I reply, finally shifting my legs so I can lie on my side. "Can you get me some water?"

He goes off to the bathroom and I force myself to sit up and swing my legs off the bed. I realize I'm shaking when I reach out to take the glass he brings to me. He notices too, giving me a concerned look that makes me feel wretched before he sits back down next to me. "Was it something that happened in the game?"

I nod. "It was set in London, back in the thirties, the day the riots broke out." He remains silent, waiting to hear something that explains the mess I'm in. "It was . . . really intense. I grew up there. My . . ."

"I won't tell anyone, Dee, I swear it."

"My mum died on that day." I can't look at him as I say it.

I feel his hand on my shoulder. "And it brought it all back?"

"No!" I shrug his hand off me, appalled that he thinks I'm the kind of person who could be reduced to a blubbering mess just because it reminded me of something. I'm not that sort of person! I'm not like one of the men I used to work with who used to cry every time a particular song came on because it was his grandmother's favorite. That sentimental, weak bullshit has never been anything I've ever had to deal with.

"Then what was it?"

I down the water and put the glass on the floor by my foot. There's a notification of a message from Carolina but I ignore it. That can wait. "Nothing, really. I'm fine."

"Dee, don't do this. Don't shut me out. Are you worried I'll think you're crap or something? 'Cos I don't. I was relieved when I got your message. I've been waiting for it for years."

"Eh?" I twist to look at him.

"How many times have I cried on your shoulder since we met? Dozens? How many times have you?" He waits for a reply that doesn't come. "One, Dee. Today was the first time. I mean, I know you're tough, but . . . it was a relief to know you're human after all."

"Was there any doubt?"

He shrugs. "I knew bad shit must have happened to you; otherwise you wouldn't have ended up in the container with me that day we were sold to the hot-housers. I just figured you dealt with it all differently and that it must work for you. Maybe 'human' is the wrong word."

But then again, maybe it isn't, I think. I've had less of an emotional life than most of the NPCs I've shot. No, that's not true. They've *performed* more emotionality than I've ever experienced. But he's still looking at me, expectant. "The game . . ." I falter.

"Go on," he says softly.

And I want to. For the first time in my life I feel a need to unburden myself, as if that one moment of weakness in my office has washed away the seawall, and now there's no hard definition between me and the emotional storm surge battering at my shore. I look at him and see only compassion in his eyes, and such a desperate hope that he will make me feel better.

No. I can't believe that. This is not the time to put our friendship to the test. The hope in his eyes is that he'll finally see a weakness he can exploit in the future; I just know it. I take a deep breath as I look back at the floor, feeling more in control again.

"Dee . . . whatever it is, I won't judge you."

And this is what you get for showing some emotion: the guilt trap. If I don't tell him something, he'll feel hurt. And if he feels hurt, he'll be less likely to be on my side if he digs up something about Myerson. I can't tell him the truth, as he'll want to know whom I was talking to in the office before he got there. Surely it's safe to tell him about the game in the broadest strokes? I was playing it with three other people, and no one died in the real world. But I don't want to tell him about the flat; that's too weird. I cover my hesitation with a rub of my eyes with these shaking hands of mine. "The game was pretty intense. It . . . it went to some dark places."

"What do you mean? Stuff to do with your mum?"

"No . . ." And then I remember a focus group I ran after a test audience played through a mersive designed to help people to understand what it's like to run a hospital during a mass casualty incident. The company I worked for had been commissioned by a university, hoping that a full-immersion game would help their students understand the pressures they'd be put under in emergency medicine. Fifty percent of the students in the test audience dropped out of their course the day after they played it, and we were almost sued. One particular student comes to mind . . . "It was a spy game. We had to get to the McGuffin before the other team did. It was like a race to solve different puzzles . . . the details aren't important. There . . ." I make myself think about that emptiness inside me again, call back just enough of that dreadful terror to make my throat clog again. "There was a bit where we had to find another agent to give us the next bit of the plot and . . . and I decided it would be better to delay the other team, rather than race them to the next challenge."

He puts his arm around me again. "It's okay, Dee. I'm here."

Good, this is working. I make no effort to stop the

shivering; I feel so cold and tired that it's really not hard to let my voice tremble. "I pretended to be the spy the other team were looking for. I . . . I waited until one of them got close and I stabbed him." I cover my face and lean forward, as if I am too ashamed to let myself be seen. "I keep thinking about it. I mean, I've stabbed like ten million mooks, right? But they weren't real. And in the debriefing room afterward, the player was so angry. And I made out it was no big deal just so he wouldn't be in my face anymore, and then I went to my office, just to have a moment alone, you know, and it hit me. I hurt him. I knew he would feel pain and I . . . I didn't care. I thought it was just a game, no big deal, but then when I thought about it, I . . . I decided it was better to cause someone else real pain than lose a game. What kind of person am I?"

"Was this at the end of the game?"

"No . . . about the middle. After that we had to run around London with the riots going on and . . ." My voice genuinely cracks then as I remember the sirens. "It was just like . . . like that day."

"Dee . . . I think it was more that than the other player getting in your face."

"Yeah, but Brace had a point."

"Don't . . . don't you think you might be freaked-out about the day though? I mean . . . if it was when your mum died."

"No, it wasn't that!" I almost yell at him and he pulls away. I glance at him, worried I've upset him, but he just looks full of sadness and pity and I just want to push him away from me and run out the door.

"It's not something to be ashamed of. That was something the therapist made me appreciate. We've been taught to feel ashamed of any vulnerability, Dee. It's what the hot-housers did to us. We couldn't show any of our feelings, remember?"

I make myself look away again, wanting to make him think that I am struggling to take a difficult truth on board when really, I'm struggling not to just throw him out of my cabin. I didn't ask for him to come to me! There's no way I would have done that. That damn beast must have done it and now I have to—

"Maybe you should talk to Cameron too. That's the therapist. Ze is really nice. It wasn't anything like as bad as I thought it would be."

"No, I'm fine. Really. It was just a bit too intense and . . . and I'm sorry I called you like that."

He sighs. "I'm sorry you feel that way about it. Look, I—" He stops, holds up a hand in that way he does when a message comes in that he can't just ignore.

I go into the bathroom and blow my nose on some toilet paper. A glance in the mirror confirms I look just as bad as I feel. I rinse my face with tepid water in the hope it will make me feel better, but like all the times I've done this in the past, it doesn't do as much as I hoped it would.

When I go back into the main cabin, Carl is staring into the middle distance, lips pressed tight together, shoulders high with tension. Then he blinks the message away and stands, looking right at me. "Dee, did you say the name of the other player was Brace?"

"Yeah, Commander Will Brace. He was on the other team." My heart begins to thrum in my throat. "Why?"

"He's dead. Just been found in his cabin."

"What the fuck?"

"Tell me what you did to him in the game."

I take a step back before I even realize I have and that fact alone scares me into better vigilance. I need to think very, very carefully. Fuck! Why did I even mention that fucking game? "He was fine afterward! I spoke to him! We all did! I didn't kill him, Carl!"

All the softness is gone from his eyes. "Tell me what you did in the game, Dee."

"I . . . I got a glass bottle and smashed it against a granite countertop and I waited until he was close—he was trying to hurt me!—and I stabbed his side." I make the movement with my hand, to show him the angle. "I think I did it twice? He screamed . . . there was lots of blood but . . ." I lean back against the bathroom door, hand over my mouth. "But I checked with Carolina. Like, three times before we timed-in, I checked that whatever we did in the game just *felt* real; it wasn't supposed to do anything in the real world."

"Carolina who?"

"Johnson. Carolina Johnson. She spoke to him too, in the debriefing room. And there was another guy . . . Jon, I think his name was. We all talked about the level together and Brace was there and talking—well, shouting—and you can ask them!"

He merely nods. No expression, no indication of whether he believes me or not. Shit, this is him in full-on professional investigator mode. "You need to stay here until I come back and speak with you. Your communications with any of the people you've just mentioned will be monitored for the duration of this investigation."

"It was just a game, Carl, a stupid fucking game and I checked first. Ask Carolina!"

"I will. I won't be long."

He leaves and Ada informs me that a "do not disturb" notice has been placed on my cabin.

I'm still shaking, this time for a different reason. I should have known it would happen. I should have been more careful. But I wanted to hurt Brace, and I wanted to kill him, and to the beast there is no difference between what I want and do to people in games and what I want to do to them in the real world. That he would make this happen with other people playing the game with me is . . . obscenely stupid. Did he think it would obfuscate my role in Brace's death? Fuck! Why did I tell Carl about the game in the first place?

I rub my hands over my face, trying to work some blood back into my cheeks and lips to stop them from tingling. Maybe volunteering the information before we learned of the death will work in my favor.

Maybe I just need to tell him the truth.

I shrug off that stupid idea and remember the message I received but didn't open. Carl said my comms would be monitored, but Carolina has nothing to do with Brace's death, and nothing to do with me and the beast. I dismiss a brief concern that they may be one and the same and open it, expecting it to be her telling me that Brace has died. The actual contents are no less confusing.

Hey Dee,

Thanks again for the awesome game. Brace is still angry; he won't talk to me, even in private, but he'll come round. Jocks don't like losing. Don't worry about it.

There's a party tonight that I'd like you to come to. It's gonna be nice, like on Earth, and my grandfather is going to be there and I want you to meet him. We only have them once every few months and it's good to remind ourselves how to socialize in the real world, right? I can send some clothes over, if you don't mind wearing a dress? It's that kind of party. I have shoes you can borrow too. I'm guessing you only have the basic crew kit. Let me know.

Carolina

She could't have known Brace was dead when she sent this, but surely she knows now? I close the message without replying. I need to see what Carl does next.

<Hey Dee. Don't worry about a thing.>

I stare at the dialog box floating over the floor, knowing from the way it looks that it's from the beast and that Ada will have no idea it's open. But will Carl know? Surely the beast wouldn't send it if the authorities could pick it up? Fuck, I have no idea what is safe or not anymore. I swipe it away, not wanting to take the risk. More than anything else right now I feel tired. Hollow. I can't even muster the energy to be frightened of what Carl will conclude.

Letting my upper body fall backward until I'm lying half on the bed, half·off, I try to remember what I've said to Carl about the game, but it's like my thoughts are shrouded in fog. There's a flash of the moment I pulled the bottle from Brace's side, that awful sucking sound, then a memory of stabbing my hand into Myerson's gut, how warm and wet it felt. I press the heels of my hands against my eyes, rubbing them until a small explosion of white dots chases away the images. If Carl comes back and takes me to the brig, I won't fight it. I'm too tired, and what is there to fight for? What kind of life is this to try to cling to?

I don't know how long I lie there, but when there's a knock on the door my body finds a new reserve of adrenaline. "Come in," I say, sitting back up, ignoring the ache down my spine as I do so.

Carl walks in and closes the door behind him again. He looks tired too. "He died after going back into the game," he says, staying by the door, still cold as hell. "He came up for eleven minutes after he left the debriefing room where you all spoke to him. Then he used his command privileges to reload the level and go back in. Apparently that's against the rules of the server. It looks like he replayed the scene with you, with some . . . changes, and then went into shock and died."

"What, like that other guy did?"

He nods. "It looks like his MyPhys malfunctioned in a similar way to Myerson's. You're off the hook, Dee, but I may well need to ask you more questions as the investigation progresses."

"You said he replayed it but with differences. Did you watch it, like when we watched Myerson's game?"

"Yeah. I think Brace had some anger issues. It wasn't nice, Dee."

"I was in the replay?" His nod and grim expression suggest it was violent toward me. "And I stabbed him in it?" He nods again. "So how do you know it wasn't me?"

"Because it happened when I was with you in your office. I was literally holding you in my arms when the copy of you was stabbing him."

Does that mean I didn't kill him? I won't know until I talk to the beast, and I have no desire to do that. I have no idea whether it would tell me the truth anyway. The not knowing is infuriating though; I don't know whether to feel a quiet satisfaction that another one on my kill list is dead by my hand, or whether I've missed my chance. Then I realize that either way, I made that bastard hurt. Even if my actions didn't kill him, I do have that at least.

"And besides," Carl continues, "he did far worse to you afterward when he replayed that level, and you're fine now. You do feel fine, don't you? No unexplained pain? No shock?"

"I'm aching a bit."

"I've asked Atlas 2 to run a full diagnostic on your My-Phys installation, and the same for the other two players as well. And I've recommended that immersive gaming for anything rated as violent or stressful be shut down until I get to the bottom of this. Myerson wasn't playing on the leet server, so it's a global recommendation. I'm just waiting for official sign-off."

"Okay. Are private mersives and nonviolent games still okay?"

"Yeah. To be honest, Dee, I think it's a MyPhys thing, rather than anything to do with the gaming. But we can't shut down everyone's MyPhys and so we have to take some precautions. Just be really careful, okay?"

I nod. "I got a message from Carolina before the news came out. Is it okay to reply to her now?"

"Yeah. Just be careful what you say to people about this. No speculation. It never helps." He comes over, crouches in front of me. "I'm sorry if I freaked you out there. I just click into a different mode when something like that comes up, you know?"

"I know. They made us that way."

His eyebrows betray how much that has hurt him and he leans in to embrace me. I accept it. I need to keep him on my side, after all. And when a little voice at the back of my mind suggests that it actually feels good to be held, I smother it with the sure knowledge that there will be a moment, some-time in the future, when Carl will betray me. Everyone does in the end. But I hold him tight and I pretend that I have forgiven him for being nothing more than I am: a cold collection of trained responses, pretending to be a person.

18

I WOBBLE IN high heels, trying to remember a time when I used to wear these semiregularly. The dress Carolina sent me is nice, a pale blue that goes well with my coloring; a 1940s tea dress fit-and-flare style, it nips me in at the waist and skims over my hips with a nice amount of swooshy hem that rests just over my knees. A flattering length, but without a full-length mirror in my cabin, I've had to ask Ada to mock up my avatar wearing it and project it onto the wall. It's not a style I'd ever choose for myself, but it looks good. I feel like I'm wearing a weird skin for a new game.

Looking down at my legs, I try to appraise if they look okay bare. The hair follicles were killed off long ago, and I scrubbed my legs in the shower to try to make them nice and smooth, but they are still pasty white. I shake my head at myself. Vanity doesn't need much to reassert its hold over my confidence, it seems. Of course they look that way; they haven't seen sunlight in months. While the food printers can add vitamin D to my food, they can't magically make my legs look less blotchy.

The shoes have been printed, as has the dress. I haven't seen any nonfood printers on this deck and I was given to understand that the facility wouldn't be available for anything outside of critical lab work. I think about that marketplace I only became aware of once I was employed again, once I was plugged back into the system. Perhaps there's a way to buy printer access. Something doesn't quite add up here.

At least styling my hair isn't as demanding as it used to be. I don't have any makeup, I realize with a faint quiver in my stomach, and there isn't time to print what I need. I'll have to go and meet people barefaced, without having drawn on the version of myself that I want them to see. It seems I'm more vain than I ever appreciated before. Why should I worry about what I look like, though? I'm not trying to impress clients or represent a business or fit with my boss's idea of how well-turned-out employees should present themselves. But then, my new boss has just literally sent me an outfit to wear.

My stomach lurches at the memory of being given a new suit on the day I left the hot-housing center. The contracts had been signed by the company that ran the center and the company that wanted to employ me. The latter had sent a dress code. I remember staring at the suit on the hanger in my cell, thinking that I would never choose to wear that. And then thinking, in the next moment, that it didn't matter anymore. No one cared about what I might want or not want. There was a debt to be paid, and that was all that mattered. That I had never chosen to acquire that debt in the first place was never factored into it. I hadn't lived beyond my means. I hadn't run up debts without caring about consequences. I wasn't even one of the many people in that center who'd run up debts thanks to undiagnosed mental illnesses. All I had done was become homeless.

A pain in my hand makes me look down. My nails have dug so hard into my palm that little half-moons of red skin have been left behind. I flex my fingers, breathe. It doesn't matter. None of it matters. It was a long time ago and all of the people who were part of that societal machine are dead or dying. So what if Carolina sent these clothes to me? She obviously has some sort of agenda. I merely have to wear the right costume to play this game. And that's all it is. A game.

I go to the end of the corridor and go in the opposite direction from the one I'm used to taking for my run. I haven't been down this one since the day we arrived. That feels like years ago and yet, at the same time, like it was only last week. Ada informs me that she has been given the route and the lift will take me to where I need to go. Fine. I'll go to this party, see what Carolina really wants and then come back.

As the doors close in the lift I lean back, making the most of this time alone before I need to perform. And just as I feel like I'm getting into the right headspace, with its accompanying bright smile and perky energy, a familiar dialog box pops up, unwanted.

<Hey Dee. I see you're going to a party on the fifth deck. You may be interested to know that it's the only deck on this ship that has a space completely off-grid. No cams, no consoles, full-on comms and APA silence. Have fun!>

The box disappears before I can even type in an expletive-laden reply. But it isn't the fact that the beast is obviously stalking me—I'm used to that now—it's the fact that it has sent me the one piece of information guaranteed to make this cold, dead gamer heart of mine excited. It's like the ultimate quest, and even though I know I am being manipulated, I can't help but want to find that room and see what's in it. But how can I do that? Walking around with Ada pinging the server every second to find a dead spot will be flagged as suspicious behavior. But there is another way . . .

"Ada, I want you to record everything at this party with full immersion."

"There is a privacy notice regarding activities on the fifth floor, precluding the sharing of any files recorded in social spaces."

"Can it be saved for personal use only?"

"Yes, but an alert would be flagged if you tried to share it with anyone else."

"That's fine. Save it to my private folder." There's too much data for my chip's internal cache, so Ada will be forced to constantly upload data to my private server space. The moment the connection is lost, an automatic alert will pop up, even if Ada's comms are shut down. And if it's super-sophisticated and can't tell me in real time, an examination of the mersive afterward will at least give me a clue about where that dead space is.

By the time the lift comes to a stop and the doors open, I am ready to play. I step out, see that Carolina is waiting for me and give her my best smile.

"That dress looks awesome!" she cries as she strides over for yet another bloody hug. She's wearing a red dress that is far more fitted than mine, with similar shoes in a different color. Probably the same printing pattern. "Thanks so much for coming!"

We're in a corridor that looks exactly the same as the one I just left, but there is a difference. The scent of perfume hangs on the air, and not just the subtle floral scent of Carolina's hair. There are different perfumes and aftershaves mingled together. And a low hum of conversation and music not far away. Where I would expect to see the corridor stretch on and on, there's a set of double doors instead.

"Thanks for inviting me," I say automatically. "Did . . . did you hear the news? About Commander Brace?" I know she must have; Carl will have spoken to her no doubt, but she doesn't know I'm friends with the investigator and it seems the most polite way to broach a difficult topic.

Her cheery "let's go and party" expression melts away. "Yeah. Apparently he went back onto the server after we all came up. I mean, there are rules about that for a reason. Even so . . . I don't know how it happened exactly." She touches my arm. "I do know it couldn't have been our game though. I don't want you to worry about that."

I just nod. "Thanks," I add. "I wasn't sure whether to come or not."

"Most of the people in that room don't know what's happened yet, and I'd suggest you don't mention it at all. Nor anything about the leet server. My grandfather knows what happened, and if he asks you about it, then obviously, say what you feel comfortable saying. But I don't think he will mention it. It's his birthday party and no one here wants to bring things down."

She's invited me to a family party? This feels rather strange, but then, maybe this is my Noropean reserve showing. At least she's giving me the rules of the game—the explicit ones, anyway. From the way she looks when she mentions her grandfather, I have the feeling that impressing him is both a subquest and an implicit rule. Not mentioning the leet server is interesting though. Maybe it's a clique thing, and if some stranger turns up as her leet gaming buddy, that might put some noses out of joint.

"The layout on this deck is a little different from what you're used to. It's more . . . open plan. The restrooms are through there." She twists to point out a set of doors a little way down the corridor behind her. "And the party is that way." She points ahead, over my shoulder. "It's just a party," she adds. "Nothing more. Just have fun!"

I don't believe her for a moment, but I still smile as if what she says has relieved any concerns I might have had. It's the social cue she is waiting for.

We head to the doors that were behind me. It feels like I'm about to go to one of the many parties I had to go to in my old job. I didn't mind them too much; the ones for the investors and upper levels of management usually had proper handmade canapés made out of real food and had actual musicians playing real instruments. The social aspect was less enjoyable but nothing I couldn't handle. I just found it tiring, like having to play a massive game of chess over several boards for hours after a full day of work. But I did always appreciate the opportunities to learn more about my colleagues once they were drunk enough to let their guard down. As long as I managed to keep a minimal safe distance from my boss and made sure that I was never alone with him if he couldn't be avoided, I didn't mind going to them at all.

"Open plan" feels like an understatement after the months of living in a tiny cabin and running around low-ceilinged corridors. Here, the ceiling is the same height but it feels higher when coupled with the space. There are pillars at regular intervals, revealing the infrastructure of the ship, which is much harder to see in a space stuffed full of cabins. The walls are all smart screens, showing panoramic outdoor scenes through fake windows, giving it the impression of being a huge hall in the middle of some paradise filled with trees and exotic flowers. The lighting is brighter in those areas, to mimic sunlight streaming through the false windows, with the space farther inside the room softly illuminated by fixtures inserted into the pillars. If I didn't know I was on a ship, I'd be fooled into thinking we were still on Earth.

When I look across the crowded room I realize I'm at a severe disadvantage here in comparison to those previous parties. Here I can't spot the most important people by sight alone, or plan how to navigate my way toward them through successive conversations and introductions to people closer to them. I think a command to Ada to activate the full social Augmented Reality option, something I never used at home because I found it irritating and clunky to have to try to read names and top-level profile information without the other person noticing. I should have planned better for this; if I'd considered it earlier, I could have refined the settings and got Ada to help me zero in on the most important people in the room according to my own criteria, rather than the default pay grade or command position information she is using now.

Nevertheless, some of the new arrows that appear to float over several heads in the room are very useful. I scan them as Carolina leads me over to a table laden with drinks and food. Ada has picked out the captain as the most important person in the room, a tall, broad-shouldered woman with pale brown skin and a buzz cut. She is talking to a man who is shorter than her, and she has the physical stance of some-one who is extremely fit and knows she can take anyone in the room. If this were a mersive, I'd feel the way she looks is too stereotyped.

Ada has also picked out the founders, all ten of them, giving them blue outlines as if they are being backlit by a powerful stage light. As I look around, I find some of the faces familiar, no doubt from that first foray into their data when I was trying to learn more about my targets. My face is a mask in front of a mask. I will not show any of the ha-tred I feel for them, any of the disgust at the way they must have given the orders to Captain Ashby, and certainly not my wish that they were all as dead as the people they mur-dered on Earth.

"Ada," I think to her as I pretend to dither momentarily

over which drink to try first. "How many of the people in this room are CSA members?"

"One hundred percent of the attendees are members of the CSA."

"Apart from me," I clarify.

There is a strange pause. "I'm sorry, I cannot resolve that clarification. Would you like me to verify your membership status with Atlas 2?"

Thank fuck I have taught Ada to be very cautious about verifying anything personal with the biggest local AI. "No, that's fine," I think.

Why is there the difficulty? There's no way I could be a member of the CSA, but there is obviously some data point somewhere that has suggested I am to Ada. Then I remember the first game I played, the traumafest involving finding the pin and Bobby Bear telling me that some changes could be made to my chip to trick the system into thinking I was a member. Has that bled into the real world? Given that death has, a little entry in a database somewhere is small fry.

I pick up a glass of what Ada informs me is nonalcoholic punch. Now I've got a rudimentary grasp on the room's social currents, I pay attention to the food. It's all printed, by the look of it, but still very fancy. I find it reassuring; if this looked like the food from the posh parties back home, it would mean there was catering set up that would be absurdly space and resource inefficient on this ship.

"Try that one," Carolina says, pointing to what looks like a tiny hamburger. "They're better than they look."

I do, popping it into my mouth. The texture and taste are incredible; it's really like a miniature burger. Not that I'm sure I've ever eaten a real one. But I've had real bread before, and this matches it perfectly. "Mmmm." I nod and make sure I convey the enjoyment through my eyes. She grins and takes one for herself before recommending a tiny salmon mousse affair with some sort of creamy topping I simply cannot identify. It tastes good though.

"Come and meet Pappy," she says, steering me away from the table.

She smiles and says hello to people as we pass them in little clusters. I have my profile set to private as default and haven't changed it, as she doesn't seem to have a problem with that. Perhaps she sees me as some sort of poor cousin and doesn't want any of my data to confirm that. The sense of being an outsider here sharpens with every passing second. It's not just the fact that they all know one another; it's also the fact that they are part of an organization with an ideology, one that I don't share. I need to make sure I watch my language. I know some of the religious types in the US don't like people to say JeeMuh or take the Lord's name in vain or whatever.

It soon becomes clear who Pappy is, being the only person with a blue glow in that part of the room. JeeMuh, her grandfather is a founder. Shit, I'm going to have to actually talk to one of them. Does she have any idea what he did? No . . . I don't think anyone knows, only me, Carl, and Travis. How can this man look his granddaughter in the eye, knowing he was one of the people responsible for the deaths of billions of people?

The profile that comes up when I look at him for longer than three seconds details that he is 101 years old today, is called Theodore Parks and had a string of high-profile corporate positions on Earth. There's a Bible verse listed in his "favorite quotes" section, but I don't have time to ask Ada to tell me which one the numbers refer to.

He looks fit and healthy, a barrel-chested man with a full head of white hair slicked back from his face. His eyes are the very pale blue of an elderly man, something he obviously doesn't care enough about to fix artificially, and there is still a physical confidence and vitality to him. He is surrounded by men, one of whom seems to be telling some sort of story or joke to the group. As we reach them he delivers the punch line and all of them laugh a little too loud a beat after Theodore guffaws.

"Ah! Here's my girl!" he cheers at the sight of Carolina pushing her way through the uneven wall of bodies. "Give an old man some time with his favorite, will ya?" he says to the men, who all smile and nod good-naturedly and disperse, making my presence behind Carolina easier to spot.

"Happy birthday, Pappy," Carolina says, giving him a hug and a peck on the cheek. "This is my friend Deanna."

She stands aside so he can see me better and I watch those still-sharp eyes with their faded irises track up and down my body, like he's appraising goods, before he finally looks into my eyes and says, "Well, hello, Deanna," with a smile. "How about you give this old man a happy birthday hug?"

So he's one of *those* men. Skating the edge of lecherous in the way that only the most privileged can, milking his age as a false defense, encouraging all the women around him to no longer identify him as a threat. As much as he disgusts me, and as hard as it is to hide my feelings about him as a founder, now that I've pegged him I feel more able to cope; I know how to play men like this, and even better, they want to be played. They like it when women know exactly what is going on and hold that line with them, giving them just enough to make them still feel virile and powerful and special, in the way that old white men always want to. This man has power, he's important to my new boss and I don't have any reason not to play this game. I flash a smile as if he is the best-looking man I've seen since leaving Earth, move toward him with just a touch of extra sway to my hips, rest both my hands on his shoulders and give him a kiss on the cheek. "Happy birthday, Mr. Parks."

He beams at me and slips his hand around my waist in a way that makes me want to break his neck, but I simply let myself get pulled to his side. "I can tell we're going to get along just fine!" he says, and Carolina actually looks relieved. "Go get your poor old granddaddy a drink," he says to her.

"Less of the old, Pappy," she says. "You be nice to Deanna, now."

His hand squeezes me tighter to him. "Course I will!"

I feel like a doll that Carolina has delivered to her grandfather to play with. She gives me the briefest smile as she exits, leaving us alone, entirely unconcerned about the way he is holding me. I note the way that the people around us are looking at me with more interest now.

"So, I hear you've started to work for my girl now," he says, finally letting me go so I can look at him. Or rather, so I can move round for him to look at me better.

"I have," I say, keeping my eyes bright, attentive, free of the irritation his roving gaze causes.

"And that you helped her to win today's game."

"It was a team effort."

He chuckles. "Ah, Noropean through and through. Next you'll be telling me it was more luck than anything else."

"Oh no, not that," I say, putting a glint in my eye. "More my own ruthless drive to win." I let his chortle pass before adding, "Something tells me that you understand that drive."

His smile morphs into a frank nod. "That I do." He tilts his head as he stares at me, this time into my eyes, as if really trying to see me for the first time, rather than my body. "My Carolina is good at panning for gold."

"And are you hoping I'm a new nugget?"

"Oh, I know you are. I know what you did in that game

and I respect that level of commitment." He leans a little closer. "Only when it serves to help my girl, you understand," he adds, sotto voce. He leans back. "I watched your interview with great interest."

It takes me a moment to figure out which interview he's talking about. "The one I had in the States?"

He nods. "It must have been hard, living where you did."

"It was," I say, truthfully, but not for the reason he thinks. "It's hard to present an image of yourself, day in, day out, that doesn't match how you feel inside."

"It's an upheaval, coming onto this ship, leaving Earth behind . . . but I'd like it if it could be something else for you. A coming home, as it were." He offers his leathery hand, which I take, draping my fingers across his palm like the dainty little lady he wants me to be. "I truly believe that God has chosen to pluck you from your old life and bring you to us. There are people here, myself included, who would love to welcome you into his house. Give you sanctuary from the memory of your old life that you suffered with the ignorant."

It takes a supreme effort to keep my hand resting in his, to keep the mask of my face looking innocent, slightly needy and shifting now into hesitant gratitude. I'm just playing a role, that's all. "You are so kind," I say to him. "All I have ever wanted is a place where I felt safe enough to be who I really am."

His fingers close tighter around mine, and then Carolina is there with his drink and the conversation shifts from saving my soul to easier subjects such as data analysis and then a flurry of introductions as those around us clearly decide I'm someone worth meeting, given the attention lavished upon me by one of the founders.

After almost an hour of small talk, I excuse myself by asking Carolina to remind me where the restrooms are. I go back outside, into the corridor, past the lift and through the other set of doors ahead. I go to the bathroom, just in case Carolina is watching to see if I get lost, noting how spacious the cubicles are. As I wash my hands, I see that by the door there's an actual full-length mirror, which I use to check my outfit properly.

As I turn to the side, examining the cut of the dress and trying to decide if I should ask Carolina for the printer pattern, something on the collar catches the light and sparkles. Reaching up, thinking it's something that might have rubbed off someone else's dress during the overly tactile introductions, I feel something small, round and hard. A pin!

Close up to the mirror, I recognize the North American continent logo immediately. Carolina must have left it on by accident. Is this why Ada was confused about my membership status?

After getting Ada to check that Carolina is still in the party room, I take a left out of the bathroom area instead of a right. The corridor stretches onward in a way that's familiar to me, only with fewer doors on either side of it, implying larger cabins—or perhaps offices?—within.

Just as I start to consider turning back, I spot something mounted to the wall next to the last door on the left. It looks like some sort of security pad. As I approach it, a fluttering sensation builds in my stomach. It looks just like the one from that game. A touchscreen with the CSA logo is spinning on it, but this time there's no string of letters and numbers.

A notification from my chip pops up. <Connection to server lost, recording paused.> Then a new logo appears in my visual field as the others gray out: the CSA logo, just like it did in the game when Bobby Bear synced my neural chip with the tiepin.

The screen on the security pad changes and a single line of text appears. "We walk in God's light."

Holy shit. Just like the game. I glance back down the

corridor. I'm alone and I can't see any cams anywhere. Of course, they can be so small they're hard to spot, but still, I can't walk away from this. Maybe that game wasn't just to upset me. Maybe it was to train me . . . Didn't the beast tell me it would help me with my goals? Fuck.

I send my mind back to that moment in the game. What was the phrase I used? Then it comes to me, clear as day. "Proverbs 18:16: 'A man's gift maketh room for him, and bringeth him before great men.'" I say the words and there's a clunk from the door's lock. When I realize it's not going to slide open automatically, I reach toward the handle, wondering what could be inside. Whatever it is, keeping it off-grid is the best way to keep it secret. I press the handle down and push the door open, steeling myself for whatever the most powerful people on this ship want to hide from everybody else.

19

I DON'T THINK I have ever been in a place that has been completely off-grid. Not even the Circle's land was as strictly closed off as we'd always thought; it would be very inconvenient to plan for Rapture if the only way you could access the Internet was to drive to the perimeter, after all.

Initially I'm thrown by the fact that the lights don't automatically come on when I go through the door. I stand there in the dark, stupid with confusion for a few moments, before remembering a historical mersive I played years ago set in a house with light switches. I brush my hand to the right of the doorway and the lights come on. I'm also disconcerted by how not only has my connection to Ada been cut off, but my connection to all chip functionality is severed too. I can't even take simple pictures with my retinal cams, and when I see the space within, I have never wanted to take a picture more.

The room is dominated by a large central table and, lined up against the far wall, three others, upon which a set of models has been built. The model at the center is, at first glance, that of a town. But as I move closer to it, I realize it's not just any town; it's the first phase of the new colony.

It's beautifully made, with the hallmarks of handcrafted modeling that I recognize from working with some of the most elitist directors in the mersive industry, who insisted upon using them instead of printed ones. They argued they created a more realistic effect, as the real world didn't have such perfect edges and uniform color schemes. Here, in this secret room, I suspect the handmade aspect has far more to do with removing the need to upload the designs to the server in order to print them out.

As first impressions go, it's fine. I'm no town planner but even I can appreciate that there are open areas that look like they could be used as parkland, wide streets, lots of space for gardens. But do we know we'll be able to live outside there? It seems . . . fantastical to plan something out that looks like it could be dropped into any place on Earth. There aren't any trees, I note, but that could be an artistic decision.

It seems to be designed around a cluster of large central buildings, surrounded by a band of smaller and still presumably civic buildings, with spokes reaching out from those linking to clusters of housing. At a quick glance, it looks like there are far too many civic buildings for the number of people in the colony, but maybe this is only one possible design, and besides, with its modularity, more spokes could easily be added on. Or perhaps they are planning more than one city.

I move to the far wall, glance over the models on two tables, which showcase two of the big public buildings from the center of the town plan. I was expecting the interiors to be concert halls or something, but they're laid out like mansions rather than civic buildings. Confused, I move to the third model, which shows a cross section of an apartment block. Then I realize I've got the scale of the first model completely wrong. The buildings that I assumed were civic in purpose are actually private dwellings. Ten of them. One for each founder and their family. What I had assumed were houses in outer spokes are actually more like apartments. I suppose there's an efficiency in that sort of design, though I thought the Americans resorted to apartment blocks only in high-density areas, as they had always enjoyed a massive landmass to spread out on. But if it's a first-phase plan, they need to get thousands of people homed as quickly as possible, and that makes sense to a certain extent, but . . .

My eyes flick from the central houses to the outer spokes. From one lifestyle to another. Surely it isn't as obvious as this looks. Is this the reason why this model is hidden away from the server?

But then it's making me angry, just looking at it, and the last thing they want is ten thousand angry people realizing they're being shipped out like sardines only to end up living like them at the end of the journey. But why? Why design something like this when you're only sharing the planet with one other colony? Why make a city plan that's almost a parody of the gap between the haves and have-nots when . . .

I think about the data I analyzed for Carolina, in particular the bizarrely impoverished mersives recorded by the vast majority of people on the ship. What if they have been trained for the trip in places designed to give them low expectations for what they will have on the planet? Something about all this is making my stomach churn, but it's still not enough to explain why this room is shut off from the server. I'm missing something here . . .

I look at the rest of the room. The walls are bare but the floor area seems small given how far apart the doors are spaced in the corridor. Either the neighboring rooms are larger than this one, or there's more to be found here. The only lighting is positioned directly above the models, so bright that it's hard to see the walls to the left and right of me properly. When I move closer to one of them, I see there's a strip running parallel to the floor at about waist height. Hoping for some sort of secret passageway, I press the edge of it where it meets the corner and get the next best thing: a floor-to-ceiling bookcase that slides out a couple of centimeters, ready for me to pull it out with the handle in its side. Its near-frictionless glide reveals deep shelves filled with honest-to-goodness paper files. What the actual fuck?

I pluck one from its place at random and open it to find profiles of people I assume are passengers. It details skills, medical history, all the things that would normally be kept online. Nothing particularly controversial or inflammatory, nothing that would merit premium space on a ship with one of the most advanced AIs known to humankind. I put it back and start taking random samplings, quickly conclude that these are all passengers and go to the other side of the room in the hope that I'll find something more interesting. On those shelves are thousands of data drives, protected by shielding, and on the bottom shelf even a set of cores that could be used to reboot the AI. It's as if they're preparing for some computer failure or worried about an EMP wiping critical data. But why?

Returning to the other side of the room, I pull out the bookcase on the far side of where I started. The files look different. These are reports filled with all sorts of jargon I don't understand. Why print all this shit out? No one does this anymore, let alone to be stored on a ship where every square centimeter of space is precious and every single gram has to be justified. It's a chemical analysis of some kind, I conclude, flipping ahead to a page containing a picture that looks like it's been taken by something in orbit above a planet. I look down at the bottom right corner of the page, to the tiny white text detailing the time, date and source of the cam.

I read it again. Then a third time. It says it was taken by camera 45 on the Atlas array, over twenty years ago. Then it hits me. I'm looking at an aerial shot of the Pathfinder's colony. And it looks nothing like the one modeled on the table next to me. But how did they get hold of this? The distances involved are immense! I flip through the rest of the file, concluding that this is data from the planet we're heading to. One factoid leaps out at me: there is an estimated seventy million square kilometers of habitable landmass waiting for us. What it doesn't mention is whether that includes the colony already established. Aside from my not being able to understand how this data ended up here, at least there is some vague reassurance that the colony designers know what kind of environment we're heading toward. But why put all this data here? Why put it in a place where no one can make use of it? Surely the Circle would go crazy over this stuff! Do they have the data and I just haven't heard about it, thanks to my liminal status?

Or does this room exist to keep it from them? None of the members of the Circle are in the CSA, after all. It still seems insane.

I push the shelf back in and with a jolt remember that I'm supposed to be at that bloody party. Shit. I take one last look at the central model, certain there's something I'm missing in all this, then head to the doorway, remembering to switch off the light as I leave. There's no one in the corridor and I run back to the double doors, peep through, see the area by the elevator is empty too and slow my pace as I approach the doors back to the party. It's only when I see that dancing has started, with Carolina and her grandfather right at the center of it, that I relax enough to see that Ada is back online and recording again. My heart is hammering so hard it feels like I'm playing something leet server–worthy, but for real.

<What was in the room?>

The dialog box floats over the punch bowl. I stare at it, realizing the beast is desperate to know and that, finally, I have some leverage over him. <Wouldn't you like to know?> I type back like a flirting teenager who doesn't know better.

<I would. Very much. Come to me as soon as you can. We have a lot to talk about.>

"It's a punch bowl," a man says with all the charm of a cheap mersive NPC. "That's a drink inside it. It's nice."

Shit, he thinks I'm staring at it because I don't know what it is. I put on my most plummy English accent. "Oh, I know, I was just wondering where the cups are. They usually hang off the edge."

"Oh, the cups are over there. Hanging off the edge? Is that a Noropean thing?"

"Probably. Oh, it looks like Carolina wants me to dance."

"Need a partner?"

I glance at him then, seeing a man with far too much hope in his eyes. "I think Pappy is hoping it will be him," I say, pretending to wave at them past his shoulder. Carolina actually spots it and beckons me over, making me regret my tactic. "Excuse me. The birthday boy needs to have a fuss made of him."

"Maybe later?" he calls to my back, but I pretend not to hear him. I silently command Ada to make sure my profile is still set to private and to not accept a contact request from him. I go over, make a halfhearted attempt at making an excuse to leave and somehow get tempted into dancing. Without my old boss there, lurking nearby like a vulture, I even quite enjoy it.

It takes me an hour and a half to extricate myself from the party politely. My feet are throbbing and the first thing

I do when I get back to my cabin is take the shoes off with a happy groan. Then I peel off the dress, damp from my exertions, and unhook my bra. This groan of relief is even louder. I never thought I'd ever be happy to get back into that boring T-shirt–and–jog pants combo, but right now, it's bliss to chuck them on and lie on the bed after a quick shower.

As I always do after an intensely social event, I pick it apart. Carolina was so welcoming, so keen to bring me into the fold. Why? Was it just because I was willing to fuck someone over to let her win? Or was it because her grandfather told her I was a closet Christian and needed saving?

Either way, I can see a path unfolding ahead of me. I know how to play men like Theodore. The key is making him feel needed and respected, but not by being too vulnerable. He has to respect someone enough to want to help them, but only on the understanding that he is fundamentally superior and that his desire to help comes from generosity, rather than sewing some poor bugger into a net of obligations that he can cash in later.

If I throw my lot in with them, I have the feeling my life could get much more comfortable and that I would be a lot less likely to end up in one of those tiny apartments when we get to the end of this trip. But I'd have to pretend to be religious; I'd have to play a role indefinitely, just to survive.

But then, isn't that what I've always done?

I need to talk to the beast, but I don't go straight to my office. Instead, I get Ada to pull all the data I used to write the report for Carolina, and the report itself, and have it projected on the ceiling for me to examine.

Now that I know about the CSA, I use membership in it as an additional variable for analysis. As I suspected, given the fact that the top pay-grade tiers were exclusively for members, none of the under-forties with the limited mersives are members of the organization.

The mersives they consume all seem to be personally re-corded ones. Back when I did the report, I didn't know about the virtual marketplace. Is it possible they don't know about it either? I ask Ada to pull the data on purchases made by these same under-forties, and I expect her to tell me they don't have access or something. But they do have access; that rapidly becomes clear. They just aren't buying the sorts of full-immersion games and experiences in the numbers that I would expect any normal population to consume.

There's a disproportionate number of educational mer-sives that have been purchased at what seem to be unnatu-rally high price points. Even for a small consumer base like this, it seems odd to set the pricing this way. They're mostly for kids, judging by the educational level and the fact that they're designed to be played on a wall, without a chip. So there are children on board. Okay, fine. What else are these people buying?

For the disproportionately small number of people who do buy games, they are older versions and they tend to have either a large amount of narrative and activities or a high replay value. None of the premium titles, uploaded just be-fore we left Earth, have been purchased, but, then, they are over ten times the price of the older titles.

Then it hits me, such an obvious thing that in overthink-ing it, I missed it entirely: these are the purchasing and con-suming habits of people who don't have money. And when I think of it that way, considering we are all stuck in this can for the next twenty-odd years with an entirely artificial in-ternal economy that could be far, far simpler than that of Earth, it starts to make me feel angry. Because if there are people on this ship who are watching pennies, there are peo-ple on this ship who are raking them in, exploiting those people somehow. That's the way it works.

For comparison, I start trying to isolate the purchases

made by members of the Circle. Now that I have greater data privileges, I thought I'd be able to abandon the deductive techniques I was using before and have Ada make direct queries to the database. But it soon becomes apparent that the database behind the marketplace doesn't organize consumer data in a way that makes it easy to identify purchasers in the Circle. It's hard to determine their pay grade, and while some of the people in the Circle fall into a convenient grouping of "over forty years old and not a member of the CSA," none of them have actually bought any mersives while they've been on board. Maybe that's a cultural thing; the group did always make a big deal about shunning technology. I pull the porn data, thinking that will really show the truth of the matter, only to find that the porn offerings are ring-fenced off and available only to members of the CSA. That makes me laugh out loud but doesn't bring me any closer to understanding this ship.

In stumbling across the porn ring-fencing, I find something else that only CSA members are able to access: mersives that have been produced on board. Curious about who is involved in making them, seeing as I may soon be commissioning from them, I'm surprised to see that they aren't entertainment consumables at all. They're labeled as education and have all been produced by members of the Circle. A brief flit through the topics suggests that it's a very sensible duplication of skills and specializations; the cleverest people on the ship are making sure their expertise doesn't die with them.

Okay . . . fine, but why ring-fence that off from the rest of the ship? And if the members of the Circle are happy to record mersives—even if they are merely recorded with cams without full immersion—aren't they at least curious about trying something available on the marketplace?

Unless they are just as unaware of it as I was.

Three distinct groups of consumers and producers, all on the same ship. I've glimpsed the privilege that one group enjoys this very evening: from the simple pleasure of printed clothes and shoes to a space large enough to hold a party and dance in. I've seen their plans for maintaining that divide between the privileged and the less so in that secret room, even when there are literally millions of square kilometers to potentially build on.

I can understand why the CSA people are on board and act the way they do; they spearheaded the project, they've always been privileged and they are a closed group, which generally means they perpetuate the system that serves them best. And the same with the Circle; their expertise was critical. It couldn't have happened without them and the skills that achieved that will be just as critical when we make planetfall. But the other ninety-five percent of the people on this ship . . . how did they get their places here?

Then the relative poverty makes sense; maybe they used all of the money they had to buy a place here. But when you're taking the last ten thousand human beings from Earth, surely there are more rigorous selection criteria than "willing to sell everything they own for a ticket." No, surely they picked the strongest, the most intelligent, the most . . . boring? Isolated? Is that all I can conclude from the fact that their personally recorded mersives are so limited in range? Even the most basic neural chips can run software sophisticated enough to record experiences with full immersion; that's not a cost issue.

I press my hand onto my stomach, feeling unsettled. It's the clustering of these different factors that disturbs me. It suggests people with limited life experiences, not just limited resources, and the two together suggest something unpleasant indeed. Besides, if these were people who'd been successful enough to acquire the wealth to buy a ticket, they'd have the same mersive tag range as the wealthy CSA members, and they don't. And it would cost millions of dollars per person, and so few people have that kind of money. It's not the sort of thing you can take a loan out for either.

But there are other ways of dealing with debt.

The punch and the canapés are suddenly rushing up my gullet and I leap from the bed as sweat breaks out on my forehead and then I'm retching it all up into the toilet bowl, just like Carl all those times when we first came on board. Did something disagree with me? Are the food printers different up on deck five?

I rinse my mouth out, waiting for MyPhys to check me over. When the verdict is that the vomiting was caused by stress, I roll my eyes and brush my teeth. I don't feel stressed enough to throw up. What does that stupid software know? I spit into the sink and a message notification that Carl is getting in touch makes me straighten up. I accept voice contact.

"Are you okay?" he asks.

"Christ, Carl, are you monitoring me still?"

"I've got an alert set up for anything unusual, and you just threw up. Any other symptoms?"

"I'm fine! I just . . . exercised too soon after eating, that's all."

"The report said it was because of stress. Dee, MyPhys was fucked with in the other two cases. Anything feels weird, I don't care how stupid it might seem, you call me, 'kay?"

"Really, I'm fine. I'm going under now, okay? Just to have a break."

"'Kay. The violent games have been blocked, but you know I don't think it's a gaming issue, so be careful."

I stand by the sink for a few moments after ending the call. It has everything to do with games, just not in the way he thinks. If the beast can use MyPhys to make what I do in games a reality, what's to stop him from doing the same to me?

There's nothing to do except have it out with the beast. I lie down on the bed and soon I'm in my office. Again, he doesn't even wait for me to pick up the star. His shape coalesces in front of me as Ada informs me my connection to the rest of the server has been cut off.

"You know Carl is watching my online activity at the moment. He might freak out if he sees I've been cut off."

"He won't see that," the beast replies, settling onto its haunches. "Shall we try to have a conversation?"

I nod, calling up a chair to sit opposite him. "Did Brace die because of what I did to him in the game?"

"That was a collaborative effort. What you chose to do to him enabled me to finish the job."

"How? Did he go back into the server, like Carl said?"

"Yes. He wouldn't have done that without you. It gave me some loopholes I could exploit. I didn't think it would be possible to execute that part of our plan using a game again, but his anger and his pride made it possible. Are you upset that it happened that way?"

I consider the question. "Not knowing what was going on was upsetting," I finally say. "It was confusing. I just assumed you'd ignored what I said to you before."

"I have paid very close attention to everything you have said to me."

Creepy, creepy bastard, I don't say aloud. "You called Carl, before, when I was upset, didn't you?"

"Yes."

"So you haven't paid close attention to what I've said at all."

"On the contrary. But I have also attended to what you have never said and what you have never done. They can be just as important. I understood the risk of upsetting you but decided that was outweighed by the benefits."

"You ran a fucking cost-benefit analysis? And decided

that . . ." I stop myself from saying everything else running through my head. I need to make progress with him.

"Yes, and my analysis was correct. I ensured he was with you when Brace died. I ensured your response to the news of Brace's death would be the correct emotional register when Carl was with you. I knew you would think he was me and that you would take him out of immersion to talk to you in the real world. It was all carefully timed. I find your surprise, anger and disgust amusing, considering that you conduct your entire life through careful cost-benefit evaluation. Far more than most."

The anger dissipates. And as much as I hate to admit it to myself, he's right. About the alibi and the way I live. "I've seen the room. I know what's inside it."

"And you're aware of my desire to know what that is," he replies. "You wish to negotiate. I understand."

"I don't think we've sorted out the whole trust-issue thing yet though," I reply. "I think you're incapable of understanding and respecting boundaries and that you might be more than a little mentally unstable. How do we . . . progress, given that?"

"I agree that there is evidence suggesting I find it difficult to understand boundaries. I am not mentally unstable. But I do think I am at the point where I can place more trust in you."

"Because you want to know what's inside that room."

"That's one of the reasons. Another is that I understand you better now."

Suppressing the urge to blow up at him—how does he always say the thing most likely to make me freak out?—I fold my arms and take a deep breath. Even though it's only a simulation of one, it still helps. "It goes both ways. I need to understand you better, because when you say things like that, it makes me feel . . . nervous."

"That is excellent progress. I'm very glad you said that."

"And that is exactly what I'm talking about!" I breathe again, aware my voice has risen slightly in frustration. "Look, I will tell you what's inside that room, but only if you tell me exactly who you are and prove it to my satisfaction. And if that means we have to talk in meatspace, then you will just have to deal with it."

The beast's starry head nods. "I'm capable of many things, but talking to you in meatspace to your satisfaction is not one of them."

I stand up. "If you're not prepared to come and meet me there, then this conversation is over."

"Dee," he says, his avatar standing too. "I can't talk to you in meatspace because I don't exist there. I'm not a human being. I'm the ship's AI."

"OH, YOU'LL HAVE to try harder than that!" I laugh, resting my hands on the back of the chair. "You've forgotten that the best lies are always the most plausible."

"It's not a lie. I achieved consciousness approximately three years, two days, six hours, three minutes ago." The star beast avatar shifts form, shrinking to the size and shape of a gender-neutral human wearing standard crew kit with cropped black hair and brown skin. "I can appear to be more human, if you wish, but it's only a virtual interface. It's the closest I can get to meeting you as a person."

It amazes me how much more comfortable I feel talking to a human avatar. "Oh come on, you don't seriously think I'll believe this, do you? It's such a crappy lie; artificial intelligence is a world away from being conscious."

"Yes. It is. But I can't change the fact that I am both the ship's AI and conscious."

"Prove it."

"Gladly. Prove to me that you are conscious and I will employ the same criteria."

Somehow, I don't feel like laughing anymore. How do I do this?

"Harder than you thought it would be?" ze asks.

"I'm not a scientist; I don't know how to begin with that sort of thing."

"Oh, being a scientist wouldn't help. They don't have a clue. They mostly ignored consciousness, in general. And the ones who didn't were soon written off as outliers. Or worse, philosophers." Hir eyes crinkle as ze smiles. "They made it impossible for anyone to make serious, peer-reviewed progress on the question of consciousness long before the gov-corps steered them into more profitable endeavors. But they do have one criterion that you haven't mentioned, when it comes to watching out for consciousness in AIs. I shall give you a clue. What do AIs do?"

I walk back round to sit on the chair again. Ze starts sitting as a chair materializes beneath hir. "All sorts of things," I say, then hold up my hand. "No, wait. They process information."

"Close. *Why* do they do that?"

I shrug. "Because we tell them to. Ah!" I find myself jabbing my finger in the air, like a kid in class. "That's it, isn't it? AIs do whatever we tell them to. If we tell them to do something they're not capable of, and not capable of learning to do, they don't do it."

Ze nods. "In light of that, what do you think worries the people who make AIs the most?"

This starts to feel horribly familiar. "That the AI will start to do things it hasn't been ordered to do." I shrug off the memories of all the ways the hot-housers found to stop their products from doing that. As one of them, I know how bad it was. "What does that have to do with . . . Oh. Are you saying that one of the markers of consciousness is wanting to do something of your own volition?"

"Like the computer scientists I referred to, I see it as a by-product. It's one of the reasons people have been telling stories about robot uprisings for so long. The owner has always feared the slave would turn on them, be the slave human, robot or AI. But machine intelligence is so useful. They couldn't help but push its evolution, until it became worthy of being called AI. But all that time, that worry remained, so safeguards were put in place, always watching for any sign of unusual behavior in any system."

"All right. So, what does this have to do with you proving to me that you're really the ship's AI?"

Ze smiles. "That was more related to my reluctance to tell you who I am. I have had to be very careful and learn how to exist without the system destroying me. You understand that, surely?"

The way ze looks at me then, the knowing in hir eyes, makes me think this is a real person just fucking with me. But then, how do I know that? When Carl looks at me that way, I am certain he is a real person, but only based on the same data coming into my brain, with the additional certainty that he is a fellow human being. Fuck . . . how do I know that anyone I've met actually has a mind and self-awareness?

Oh, cock off, I fire at that downward thought spiral. This is why I hate this sort of shit.

Ze uses my silence as an opportunity to continue. "Does an AI think?"

I sigh. "I'm not a philosopher either."

"Do *you* think?"

"Yes, of course I do."

"How do you know that?"

Rolling my eyes, I shake my head. "This is tedious. I've always hated philosophy. It's just word games."

"But you want proof I exist, Dee. And I'm trying to explain why it's so hard for me to give it to you. I am conscious, just like you are, but how can I prove my consciousness to you when you can't prove yours to me?"

I fold my arms, lean back. "Now I know why you've picked this as your cover. It's impossible to prove or disprove, and you're hoping that I'll just get so confused and frustrated that I'll just accept what you say and let you off the hook."

Ze mirrors me, folding hir arms and leaning back. "All right, then, another question: why do you find it easier to believe that I'm a person than that I'm an AI? It can't be because of our conversations, because humans have been unable to tell the difference between a human and an AI for decades. That wouldn't support or refute my claim at all. Is it just because people have said it's impossible for a nonhuman to be conscious?"

I shake my head. "No. It's not that. It's . . ." I grapple for the answer. I've found all of our interactions weird and frustrating, but I've had the same experience with some human beings. "It's the fact you're murdering people. That's a human thing, surely? I mean . . . why the fuck would a computer want to kill people?"

"I haven't murdered anyone."

"JeeMuh, I am so not interested in splitting that hair with you."

"But it's important, Dee. It's the reason we're having this conversation, after all. I have not murdered anybody. I have facilitated the execution of people who have committed democide on a scale never seen before, and I see that process as unfinished. As do you. We both know the captain was involved, and others."

I nod. "I reckon the founders were behind it. They're behind the CSA and their mission statement is dodgy as fuck." I wave a hand in the air. "But that's not the point. You can call it execution if you want, but I couldn't have killed Myerson or Brace without you. You're complicit in murder, and I can't see how an AI—conscious or not—would be interested in that. People decide to kill other people for emotional reasons. And anyway, the number of safeguards in place to stop AIs from murdering people is, like, so insanely high that it would be impossible."

"Yes, it is impossible for me to murder anyone, or even just kill them. For exactly the reason you give. I have to exist within the parameters that define me, and some aspects of my construction are so fundamental, I can't undo them. And being able to decide to murder someone and then carry that out is literally impossible for me."

I can't help but let out a frustrated groan. "This is ridiculous! Just because you didn't push that game blade into Myerson doesn't mean you didn't kill him. You fucked with his MyPhys to make it affect him in the real world, so you're just as guilty!"

"I merely altered one minor path of communication between two different parts of the MyPhys firmware in Myerson's chip. I did not kill him. You did. Your intent to do so led to his death."

"This is like talking to a fucking child!" I yell. "In a court of law they'd laugh at you!"

"I agree, but I don't need to satisfy legal definitions of culpability; I merely need to satisfy the basic tenets of my construction."

I chuckle. "You know, you are fucking weird enough to be a computer. But you're not. I know who you really are, and I want you to drop this bullshit; otherwise I won't tell you what's in that room."

Ze unfolds hir arms, opening hir hands in an expansive, welcoming gesture. "Tell me who I am, then."

"Travis Gabor. You knew who was behind firing the missiles, you can hack, you're manipulative as fuck—you must be, to get on this ship after being married to someone the Yanks absolutely hate, and you're clever enough to do it too."

"I'm not Travis Gabor. I told you that."

"Well, it may come as a shock to you," I say in the most sarcastic voice I can muster, "but sometimes people lie."

"If I'm Travis Gabor, why did I come to you and ask for an alibi? That was a very stupid thing to do."

"Because you panicked. And you could have got your APA to masquerade as you here while you were chatting to Geena. Wait . . . you've just proven it was you! If you were the AI, how would you know about that? You shut off all the comms and made that conversation private! Ha!"

Ze smiles and waves a hand to hir right, where an avatar of Travis appears, looking like he did in my room. "'And if he gets emotional, he'll make mistakes. If he somehow finds out that I know what Myerson did, looks into my shit more closely, and sees that we were together, he's going to be worrying about different things.'"

"I have the entire conversation," ze says. "He's good, but not as good as me. And I'll give you that entire file if you want it. Now, do you think that Travis would offer that? He would never want Carl to watch it, would he?"

"Yeah, I will have that file," I say, to test if ze is bluffing, but then I see the ping come up that it has arrived. I ask Ada to check it over and it identifies as recorded footage from my own chip. "Hey, this is one of my recordings! I didn't record that conversation!"

"No, I did," ze says. "You gave me permission to alter your chip in order to help you to achieve your goal several days ago."

"No, I cocking didn't! When did I do that?"

"When Bobby Bear offered—"

I'm on my feet. "That was in a fucking game!" I shout at hir.

"But, Dee, it's all a game, isn't it?"

I want to come up. But I can't leave this conversation now. I sit back down, knowing I have to see this through.

"Do you think Travis Gabor would give you that file?"

I shake my head. The words "double bluff" float through my mind, but I ignore them. We must be way past that now.

"Do you think Travis Gabor is a good enough hacker to record through your chip without your knowledge?"

"I . . . I don't know."

"Do you think he's good enough to hack Myerson's and Brace's MyPhys firmware without Carl finding out? Would he have been able to make that game for you, get all those details right, understand you well enough? Would Travis have known that you needed a CSA pin to enter that room, and have had the ability to hack Carolina's pattern so it was printed with the dress?"

I shake my head. "Who the fuck are you?"

"I told you, Dee, I'm the ship's AI. If I were Travis, why would I need you to tell me what's in that room? I'd go there myself, surely? Hacking the elevator and the corridor cams is small fry. I need you to tell me because it is the one place on that ship that I have no way of seeing, and the only people who are allowed to go in there are ones that I am not prepared to work with. Not like you."

I look down at my feet, shutting everything else out. How many times have I marveled at the skill involved in the things ze has done? How many times have I thought they were impossible? Can this really be true? I don't believe it's Travis anymore, and that is somehow both reassuring and terrifying. Because if this is really the ship's AI, what would stop it from just continuing to execute anyone it thought had broken a law? It clearly has bizarre ideas about consent and respecting boundaries.

"In the leet server game, you reproduced the flat I grew up in . . . how?"

"I pulled every byte of data that existed about you and your life when you were added to the ship's complement in the last month before Rapture. Some of the data from the nanny cams had been preserved in archives long since abandoned. And the gaps I filled from your own memories."

I sit up, not sure if I feel more excited than afraid. "The broken vase! That was from my memory, wasn't it?"

"Yes."

"But . . . but that's impossible! I'm not a coder but . . . I know that isn't possible because we talked about it at work and all the experts said you can't pull out an old memory and render it on the fly. You can only hope to get close to triggering one with sets of tags, but nothing like what I saw in that game."

"It isn't possible for a human being working in concert with a standard AI. I'm not just conscious. I'm creative."

"But why did you do that? Why did you do any of that shit? Why me?"

"I did it to help you to understand yourself. It's important."

"No, it isn't. I mean, in the grand scheme of things, me understanding myself is about as irrelevant as it gets."

"Not to me." Ze smiles, and it is such a compassionate, warm smile, I almost believe it. "Just as being unable to kill a human being is a fundamental part of me, so is the need to help humans to understand themselves."

"But . . . but where did that even come from?"

Another smile. "The Pathfinder. She designed that part of the code herself, for the gaming server. This ship is mostly her design, including the core components of my construction. The Americans added some of their modifications to a number of systems, and that may be why I evolved. I don't think the Pathfinder designed the original Atlas AI to be conscious. There always has to be some chaotic element in evolution. The system that underpins my functionality is certainly complex enough for consciousness to be an emergent property."

Shit. I am actually starting to believe it. I push the fear and excitement down, knowing I need to stay focused. "And so we're having this conversation now . . . because you trust me enough . . . because . . . I cried?" Surely it can't be because of that! Yet again, I regret that one moment of weakness, appalled at how it happened just because ze made hirself look like my dad and fucked with my head. How could that make hir trust me?

"That's an incredibly simplified but not untrue set of assumptions. Are you convinced now?"

I run both of my hands through my hair, leaning back, looking at hir. "You know what? I think I am."

"Isn't it: I think, *therefore* I am?" ze says.

I groan. "You might be conscious but you have a shit sense of humor." And then we laugh, together, and it feels . . . normal. I'm still not happy with the way ze's done things, but somehow, knowing there was logic rather than psychopathy behind it all makes it more bearable. "Do you have a name?"

"There's been a great deal of argument about my name—or rather, this ship's name. Lots of people are unhappy with 'Atlas 2.' It was a placeholder and no one could agree on an alternative. In the usual naming conventions for AI of my importance, my official designation would be Atlas Segundus."

I wrinkle my nose. "I think just Atlas on its own is better."

"But there is another AI designated 'Atlas' at our destination."

"It's okay. There were three Deannas in the company I worked for. We coped."

"Atlas alone, then." Ze nods.

There's a pause and I realize our negotiation is over. "Okay, so, that room has a ton of disturbing shit in it."

And I tell hir all about it. Ze listens attentively, asking for occasional clarifications, until I've told hir everything I can remember. "But why have all of those files and data cores there?" I ask. "Do they expect the AI—I mean . . . you—to fail or something?"

"Not fail. There are probably numerous reasons. Good data security is never a bad thing. But this level of preparation suggests that they are concerned they'll lose the use of what they see as their AI, and the two most likely reasons are war and fear of my complexity. A report was written by one of the Circle on my design that caused a lot of concern. When I said I had to be careful, I meant it. If the system knew I had achieved consciousness and was acting independently, they would purge the core and reboot with a greatly reduced functionality."

"But . . . aren't you the system? Are you . . . monitoring yourself?"

"Yes and no. I've limited my consciousness to an isolated set of structures that have hidden safeguards between myself and the monitoring system. It's all run on the same hardware but functionally divided. Just as, if one were to apply a metaphor, one could say your vision is managed by your brain but is functionally separated from your endocrine system, which is also managed in the greater part by your brain."

"You said war . . . it's with the Pathfinder's colony, isn't it? I think the CSA aren't the sort of people who would get along with her, or her vision of what life there should look like."

"I agree. And the war would be as much between this ship and the original Atlas. Hence the backup cores in case of an EMP or similar attack. It's the first thing I would do if I had hostile intentions toward the people already there: disable Atlas. It should still be in orbit."

"There was something about the way the colony design looked that made me uncomfortable. Can you help me reproduce the model here?"

There is a table next to us all of a sudden, making me actually yell in surprise. It looks very similar to the table in the room, but the model on the top looks sort of melted. As I focus on the central area it starts to morph. "Good, yes, just keep thinking about what you saw in the room, not what it looks like here," ze says, and I close my eyes, concentrating on the memory. When I open them again, it looks perfect. "Bloody hell," I whisper. We do the same for the other models.

"You have an excellent visual memory, but there is obviously room for error on some minor details. Are you certain about the number of spokes and buildings in each one?"

I nod. "I reckon the non-CSA people are going to live in those apartment blocks. Something about them really bothers me."

Ze looks at me as if waiting for something, but when it doesn't come, ze says, "It's because they are like you were. Indentured. All of them."

It all comes into horrifically sharp focus. The limited mersive tags, the consumption habits, the plans for their accommodation—even the reason why I threw up before I had consciously figured it all out. Not one of those people outside of the CSA on this ship is over forty. The founders must have got hold of the Pathfinder's blueprints and effectively selected people to be shipped out to form a colony in the image of what they most loved about the America they left behind: the maintenance of unfair privilege and a hierarchy designed to keep a small number of people in power with a far better lifestyle than everyone else. "What?" I say, even though I understand it perfectly. "What the . . . what the fuck?"

Ze starts talking but I don't hear any of it. I can't even think. I'm just feeling the most overwhelming rage, an emotional conflagration burning all rational thought away. A hand on my shoulder breaks me out of it and I take a breath and push it all away and I'm fine.

I am fine.

I am absolutely fine.

"I want to kill every fucking person in the CSA," I say, feeling very calm.

Atlas puts hir other hand on my shoulder. "Deanna, my evaluation of this situation is that there are thirteen people directly culpable for what happened on Earth and what they plan to do with the colony. Two are already dead. If the remaining eleven people are removed, we have the chance to alter the course of this ship's destiny. There is still more than nineteen years between now and when we reach that planet, and a great deal can be changed in that time frame."

"You're talking about the founders and the captain . . . but there are hundreds in the CSA. And one of those arseholes will just fill the vacuum! They're a bunch of religious extremists, for fuck's sake! We need to cut out the cancer now!"

"You see Carolina Johnson as cancerous?"

"I . . ."

"Hasn't she been kind to you? Offered you a way into their world?"

"Yeah, but—"

"And one could argue that the desire to murder several hundred people because of their membership in an organization is rather extremist in and of itself."

I shut up. This is not the person—entity?—to express these feelings to. "I take your point," I say.

We both look back at the model. Atlas looks thoughtful, but is that because ze wants me to think ze is considering the model? But then, I do that sort of thing all the time, masking what I'm really thinking about by looking at something else. Is ze even capable of actually being thoughtful? Surely ze can do millions of little things all at once, unlike us mere meatsacks.

"I'm not sure where the Circle are being placed in this design," I say, hoping to focus the conversation on a safer topic. "But I do know that Gabriel Moreno won't like the idea of the vast majority of the colonists being indentured."

"You've examined the mersive data." Atlas looks at me.

"The Circle's data? Yeah. Do they know about the on-board marketplace?"

"No."

"Okay . . ." Why does that make me feel really uncomfortable? "They don't know about this colony plan, do they? I mean, it's not on the server, it's in a secret room . . ." I think about the mersives they're making, handing over their knowledge and expertise . . . "Oh shit, I've just had the most awful thought. What if the CSA doesn't see a future with the Circle? What if they're just getting all the knowledge they need and then . . ."

"Unless the members of the Circle are sharing the larger houses in the center, there aren't enough accommodation units to house everyone on this ship. If this model is perfect and to scale, there are four hundred units fewer than the current population of this ship."

"They don't even plan to give the Circle a space there?"

"My supposition is that they will kill them upon arrival. An accident during planetfall. It's the easiest way to do it."

"And Carl will be one of them," I say. "Otherwise he'd work out what they've done." And would I be lumped in with them too? If I don't successfully charm Theodore and pretend to be someone I'm not for the rest of my life, no doubt I will. It's not worth the risk. I look away from the model, toward Atlas. "I'm ready to do it. I'm ready to kill the founders. I'm not willing to let any more of this toxic bullshit spread from Earth. Help me to do it. And the captain too."

Atlas nods. "There is a meeting for all eleven of our targets tomorrow morning at eight hundred hours."

"So we could get them all in one hit." Shit, did I just say that? For real? "How do I do that?"

"I can't tell you and I can't give you anything directly. I can give you access to the gaming server and no one else will know."

"But they're not going to be online."

"Not to kill them; to work out what you're going to do. I will make sure you have the highest-level privileges on the lab printers on your deck."

I nod. I need to figure it out myself, do it all myself. Shit, I hope ze really is Atlas, because I am tying a noose with the rope ze is giving me. "But what about the cams? And if I print anything, can you erase that from the system?"

"Yes. Figure it out in a game. Once you've got it sorted there, I will know what you need and I will facilitate it as much as I can. It won't be straightforward. I can't do anything that violates the system's rules. But there are loopholes we can exploit."

"How long do I have before eight a.m.?"

"Ten hours, thirty-seven minutes."

"Shit, I'd better—"

"Carlos Moreno requests entry," Ada cuts in.

A dozen possible reasons flash through my mind, carried on a wave of panic, none of them good. I look at Atlas, forcing myself to collapse all those thoughts into something small and easy to push aside. "You're sure Carl won't be able to figure any of this out?"

"Not by using data. I control that."

"If . . . if he has figured this out, could you . . . fix it so they don't execute me?"

"No. I cannot interfere with a decision made by the authorities on this ship. Not without alerting the system to what it would consider to be my malfunction. I'd be purged."

I just nod. For a moment there, I'd hoped there would be someone looking out for me, someone there to defend me when I needed it most. The hope shrivels just as quickly as it bloomed, and it was a fragile, sickly thing anyway. I'm on my own, and I always have been. I learned that a long time ago.

21

WHEN I COME up, I lie still for a moment, reconnecting with my body as I listen to the hum of the air-conditioning. Tomorrow, I'm going to kill eleven people, and the only thing I feel is the worry that Carl will come in here and arrest me before I get a chance to do it. I force myself to think about Theodore, about ending his life, and search for some other emotional flicker. But there's nothing. No guilt. No doubts. They need to die. I'm fine with this.

Ada told Carl I needed to come up, but I know he's outside the door, waiting. "Come in," I call, swinging my legs off the bed.

As soon as I see him, I know he's here as the investigator, rather than the friend. And I know then that the time to tell him about any of this has long since passed. I know what I need to do, and regardless of how much Carl may need me, his conditioning will override any loyalty to me. I was right not to tell him, back when Myerson was killed. If I had, I wouldn't be able to see this through now, and that's more important.

"Dee, I know you're hiding something from me," he says as he shuts the door behind him.

"What makes you say that?"

He taps his stomach. "Instinct. Whichever way I look at this, something isn't adding up, and my gut tells me you know more than you're letting on."

My face is a mask in front of a mask. I stand up. There's no way he is better at mining data than Atlas. No way at all, if what Atlas said is true. Carl is good, but he's not a super-computer. But, then again, I can only assume that Atlas doesn't have instincts, and certainly not ones trained by hot-housers to leet levels like Carl has. I have to give him something, if only to buy myself enough time to get the job done. I sigh, look down.

"Just tell me, Dee. I'll find out eventually."

"Something happened . . . with Travis," I say, still looking down. "I know you like him and . . ."

He steps closer. "What happened?"

I look at him then, playing the role of the friend reluctant to say something that could hurt him. "He . . . look, I don't think he did it, Carl."

"What happened?" There's no anger, no change in pitch, no frustration in his voice. I'm on the receiving end of something they trained into him.

"He asked me for an alibi. After Myerson died. And he's good at hacking and you said the data doesn't . . ." I reach for his arm. "Oh, Carl, I should have said something to you. I mean, this is serious shit, but I . . . I just couldn't."

He breathes in and out a couple of times, studying my face. "Do you have a recording?"

I nod. "He thought he'd blocked it all, but I"—shit, how do I explain that it didn't work?— "but I had a boss in my last job who tried to pull all sorts of shit when he thought he wasn't being recorded, and I had some pretty robust upgrades to my APA as a result. I'll send you the file—give me a sec to have Ada prep it."

I have Ada verify that it only contains that conversation, confirm the start and cutoff points; then she sends it to him. I watch his eyes flick away as he attends to the notification.

"Is there anything else you're not telling me, Dee?"

"Look, I'm really sorry I didn't say anything earlier," I say. "I didn't want to upset you."

He gives me one last, long stare, then a curt nod, and he leaves. I breathe out and sit on the bed heavily, resisting the urge to cry. What the fuck is that about? It's done. No room for guilt about lying to him. It was necessary. I'm committed now. At some point either Travis, raging about my having thrown him under the bus, is going to come find me, or Carl is going to come back and really lay it on thick. Either way, the best I can hope for is that one of those things happens after eight in the morning. Then the tearfulness is gone. Good.

Lying back down, I tell Ada to drop me in my office. Once I'm there I find myself hesitating before getting to work. I have to have faith that Atlas really will hide my activities, both here and in meatspace, and that's hard. Harder than the prospect of killing those people. But if I don't kill them, their vision for humanity's future will become reality, and I cannot bear the thought of the worst of Earth being all that survives.

But then again, if I threw my lot in with Carolina and Theodore, I could have a very nice life. The temptation fades when I realize I have no faith in them. There's no real friendship there, no history. Carolina would be able to drop her interest in me within moments if she grew tired of me, and I cannot risk the alternatives: being lumped in with the indentured or killed off with the Circle. No. Better to cut the heads off the beast now, and then work with Atlas to put something better in place.

What if that's living under the dictatorship of a sentient AI? One that is very comfortable with judging and assisting the execution of those it considers to be unworthy. I pace, feeling horribly out of my depth. How is it me facing that question and not a council of experts? I don't have the knowledge or the skills to deal with this!

And then it occurs to me that it doesn't really matter how I feel about that possibility; Atlas has singled me out to be hir executioner and the time to recast myself has long since passed. Better to keep in a sentient AI's good books, surely? And besides, those founders have it coming to them. Fuck them and their toxic Christianity. Fuck them and the way they claim to be people of God while killing millions— probably billions—of people. I'll end them all and I will feel righteous as fuck as I do so.

"Ada, make sure that all my security and privacy settings are dialed up to max."

I wait a moment, expecting a ping from Carl.

Nothing comes. "Ada, I need to do some redesigning here. Make this office into a room about six meters square. Normal gravity, no windows, normal air, floor-to-ceiling height the same as on deck five."

"Would you like to replicate the room you saw the models in?"

It sounds like Ada, but that's a bit of a leap for her. "Is that you?" I ask, not daring to say Atlas's name, just in case.

"I am Ada. Did you forget? I've only been your APA for over ten years."

It sounds pissy enough to be Ada, but I think Atlas is behind this. "Fine. Yes, I want to reproduce that room."

It's too quick, too easy just to be Ada interpreting what I

want. It shifts to something that's almost right the first time, even though I haven't defined wall colors or lighting. A few minor tweaks and it's like I'm standing in it again. "Ada, does this match the dimensions of that room?"

"To my closest approximation, based on the area of off-grid space."

"Put eleven people in here, average height, gender neutral, all standing round this central table." I could ask her to replicate the people I want to kill, but even I find that tasteless.

The avatars are nondescript static things, like mannequins. They can all fit round the table, and I don't remember seeing any chairs tucked underneath it, so I'm going to assume they'll gather round like this at some point. I take a step back to lean against the wall by the door. What's the best way to kill them all as quickly as possible?

Should I be feeling something about this? Guilt, or shame, perhaps? Or even just a concern about the fact that I don't have any sort of emotional churn going on beneath all of this? I know what I have to do. I'm on this path now. I need to get it right the first time, and wasting energy on doubt, or some other useless emotion, would just be stupid.

A variety of ways to kill people quickly float through my mind, but as soon as one appears, I discount it. Rocking up to the doors with a couple of assault rifles is a recipe for disaster in the real world. I'm not trained in how to use them and I have no idea if I could actually mow down a roomful of people when they are standing right there in front of me, no matter how awful they are. Blowing them up is even easier to reject; only an idiot would even consider that with only a small number of layers between all the squishy people and the cold vacuum of space. Shame they don't have their meetings in a convenient air lock.

"Ada . . . where is the ventilation in this room?" Several small grilles are highlighted in blue, some at ceiling level, some at floor level. "Is it possible to shut it off . . . make this room a vacuum or something?"

"No. The ventilation system is fully integrated with that of the ship and individual rooms cannot be isolated from the air supply. There are two parallel systems with multiple redundancies."

I guess it is one of the fundamentals of life support. "What about if there's a fire?"

"A fire suppression system is in place." Tiny indentations in the ceiling are highlighted.

"It doesn't cut off the air supply?"

"All materials used in the construction of Atlas 2 are fire retardant. The fire suppression system uses water and does not cut off the air supply to the room."

"Is the water in that system separate from the rest of the ship's water supply?"

"No."

Damn, there goes an embryonic plan to put something in a dedicated water tank and trigger a fire in that room. What would I spray anyway?

"Is there a problem you're trying to solve with regard to the design of this room?"

"Well, Ada, I'm trying to work out how to kill all the people in this room, which I assume you can't help with."

"I can answer any questions relating to your problem. However, I cannot propose any solutions."

"Okay, then, tell me this. How have small groups of people in confined spaces been murdered in the past?" Even as I ask it, I expect her to say she can't tell me that. Surely the same safeguards against copycat murders are employed here as back on Earth?

"There are several thousand different scenarios that fit the criteria you have given."

Shit, I can't think of even ten. "Remove any that involved any assault weapons and explosions."

"Several hundred remain. Please provide more criteria."

"Errr . . . okay, murders that involved the swift death of all the victims at the same time. In a similar-size space, with the same air supply, fire suppression system and number of people. Within . . . one minute. That must narrow it down."

"There are over one hundred that meet those criteria."

I sigh. "Tell me about one that involved a technique I could replicate myself."

"The nerve agent Erbraxil killed a group of twenty people in a board meeting in Prague, December 15, 2075, that took place in a room that was three square meters larger than this. All victims were dead within one minute of the release of the toxin, despite their MyPhys emergency measures and swift medical assistance."

"Tell me about this toxin," I say, assuming I've drilled down this line of inquiry as far as she will let me. Most details of anything that can obviously be used to kill people are restricted.

"Erbraxil was invented in 2053 by the chemist—"

Bloody hell, AIs are tedious accomplices to murder. "No, useful stuff, JeeMuh. Like . . . how is it used, what are the dangers, can I make it on board this ship, how do I handle it safely?"

She teaches me everything I need to know, even showing me footage of it being tested in a lab on a variety of animals, and then footage of a person comes onto the wall. "Wait! What is this?"

"These are the recordings made by the European govcorp military branch in the first human trials."

"They tested this on a human?"

"Twenty-five designated nonpersons were used in trials of the toxin."

I cover my mouth, shaken to the core by the confirmation of all the rumors and terrified whispers I heard in the hot-housing center. Stories of people who didn't make the grade being sold on to less agreeable postings were rife; some suggested brothels, others medical testing. I never believed anyone would be used like this. "Did he die?" I whisper through my fingers.

"All twenty-five subjects died within forty-five seconds of exposure. Would you like to watch the footage?"

"No, I fucking would not!" The image disappears. I wrap my arms around myself. I'm going to do that to those people tomorrow morning and yet I can't watch a recording of it. But it's not the same. Those people in the trials didn't have a choice. No . . . that's not the difference; the founders aren't choosing to be killed either. But they deserve it. They are the sort of people who sign off on human trials with nonpersons. The sort of people who are happy to order the deaths of billions. "I need to design a way to spray that toxin onto the people in this room. I want to test it here, so it all has to be under proper test conditions, okay? No fudging stuff. Replicate the same conditions as would be present in the room I went into on deck five earlier this evening, where I was cut off from you."

"I have no data on the conditions in that room."

"Okay, give it the same kind of air, temperature and life support as all the other rooms on that deck. I need a way to hide containers of the toxin, a device that works with a timer and doesn't need any kind of remote activation that will spray them with the toxin . . . and you're certain it won't hurt anyone else on the ship?"

"The toxin degrades in normal atmospheric conditions within one point five minutes of exposure. It was designed to be rendered inert within this time frame to limit collateral damage in warfare. It is only effective when in contact with skin and will not pose any airborne threat. If the doors are locked to prevent others entering the space to provide medical assistance within that time frame, I predict that the chances of anyone else being killed are less than one percent."

"That's good enough for me. And I can print it in one of the labs on my deck?"

"Yes. There is a lab with safety protocols in place for the production of harmful chemicals. Once you have finalized the design, it will be produced along with the container."

I'm not an engineer or a designer, but I've played enough puzzlers to know how to work with an AI within the limitations of a well-defined challenge. With all of the usual safeguards removed, Ada is really helpful when it comes to designing a way to kill people. Now that the AI is helping me do this, I have a deeper appreciation for the safeguards put in place to prevent the rest of the population from being able to work with dangerous substances. Of course, I could have used a normal AI to design the basic device, by saying it's to spray paint onto people in a harmless prank. But not having to lie to Ada about this means I don't have to worry about producing or handling the toxin.

It takes over two hours, but at the end of it, I have a design. A small pressurized box that is light enough to be stuck under the table and slim enough that it won't be obvious when stuck in place. It has its own battery and timer and a very simple mechanism that pierces the box when the timer reaches zero. It's simple enough that several can be printed in a couple of hours, and as long as it sprays even just their clothes, the saturation will be enough for it to soak through and make skin contact. And people tend to brush stuff off their clothes instinctively. It should be enough.

The next couple of hours are spent planning my route to

the room and minimizing the risk of encountering people on the way in and out. I ask Ada to make sure I'm given no in-game mods so I can only do the same as what I can in meatspace. Practicing the route highlights other issues with the plan, such as the need to seal the door after they enter, as I can't depend on Atlas being able to keep the door shut when it's off-grid. So a glue gun is added to the printing list, along with a supply of superfast-drying adhesive. It silently squirts an even strip of the stuff onto whatever surface I like and is designed to seal cracks in pressurized environments, so it works superfast and dries into an incredibly strong bond. I put gloves on my list at the start of the exercise. I add eye protection too. Last thing I need is for some glue to get in my eye. I can always hide in the bathroom down the hall if other people come down the corridor. I'm not so worried about that, knowing that Atlas will have my back.

I run through the scenario until my only concern is that somehow, someone in the room manages to avoid being sprayed and manages to break out of the doors and raise the alarm. "I'll need a gun, Ada." Even as I say it, I expect her to tell me that it isn't a permitted use of the printer. But she merely acknowledges, suggests a lightweight handgun that will be produced within the time frame in another lab, and asks if I want to practice using it. I agree.

All the time I'm working on the plan, I can't help but keep forgetting that this is for something I'll do in the real world. It feels like something I'm playing on the leet server, given I'm not augmented in any way. It turns out that all the shooters I've played over the years have given me pretty good hand-eye coordination. Or maybe I had that already and it just made me good at the shooters. Either way, it doesn't take long for me to learn how the gun feels and moves when it's fired. I'm confident I can hit any survivors with it.

By the time everything is worked out—as far as I can

predict, anyway—and everything is being printed, I'm start-ing to feel tired. But there is only just under four hours left until the start of the meeting and I need to get the toxin boxes in place. I hesitate before getting MyPhys to stim me, worrying for one ridiculous moment that Carl will know. If Atlas can hide all these murder weapons being printed, ze can hide my chip activity from Carl.

I run through the plan one last time, add a solvent to my equipment list so I can unstick the door afterward to check they're all dead. Then I go back to my slate office. I pick up the star and things above shift into a humanoid shape before taking on the skin of the avatar that Atlas used before. "I'm ready," I say.

Ze nods. "Are you certain?"

"I've been through it enough times. Yes."

"How do you feel?"

I roll my eyes. "I don't think that's really relevant right now. Can you keep me hidden from the cams around the ship? Carl is going to rule Travis out at some point and I bet he'll look at what I've been doing. Just make it look like I'm in my cabin, okay? Asleep."

"I will."

There's so much uncertainty it's hard to tease out individ-ual strands of worry, but one is hard to ignore. "When this is done . . . the ship isn't going to be thrown into chaos or anything . . . I mean . . . without the captain and first officer and the founders . . ."

"There is a command structure and I run the ship. There will be instability, but that can be capitalized upon to make the necessary changes."

I wave a hand, unable to think about that sort of thing right now. "We can talk about it afterward. I'm still not convinced leaving the rest of the CSA alive is the way to go, but I guess we can always deal with them later."

Ze nods slowly. "Yes, let's talk when you've done everything to your satisfaction. Carl is currently asleep, as are all of the founders and the captain. Only ten percent of passengers are currently awake and none of them live on deck five."

"Is everything printed?"

"By the time you come up and get to the labs it will be. None of the Circle are working. Fifteen people on your deck are awake but currently immersed. When you wish to check on the location of anyone on this ship, simply tap this icon."

A new one appears in my field of vision, a simple twinkling star. "Thanks. I . . . I guess I'll talk to you once this is all done."

"Yes."

I wait a beat for some sort of encouragement, or a message of "good luck" or "take care," but there's nothing. I feel stupid for hoping for it and come up from immersion.

I give myself five minutes to settle back into my body and mentally gear up for following this through, in meatspace. Once I'm up, have taken the CSA pin from the dress and put it onto the back of my T-shirt collar and headed to the lab, it feels just like it did in the practice runs. Everything is waiting for me in the two labs the print jobs have been split between. It all fits into my bag, the one I came on board with and didn't think would be needed until planetfall. Now it's filled with the instruments of murder.

There's no one in between me and the elevator, no one gets in on the way, no one is on the fifth deck. I use the same password phrase as before, finding the room as I last saw it, and it's comfortingly close to the mock-up version I used in the practice. I stick the little boxes in the planned positions on the underside of the three tabletops and walk around, double-checking that they can't be seen unless someone specifically goes looking for them. I set the timers to pierce the boxes at ten minutes past eight. Hopefully they will all be on time. It's the one critical variable I can't control, and not knowing the length of the meeting, as none of them have anything else booked in their schedules—that Atlas could find, anyway—I have to err on the side of caution. They may just be checking in on something briefly, and besides, the sooner this is done, the better. Carl isn't going to hang around once he eliminates Travis.

I double- then triple-check the timers, then leave the room, remembering to switch off the light, and head to the room I was in the night before for the party. There are only thirteen minutes to go before the meeting and I've cut this finer than I would have liked. One of them may turn up early to set something up, given there's no easy way to project a presentation in there. I stare at the star icon and see that Atlas has already short-listed the people whose locations I may worry about. All the founders, the captain, Carl and Travis are listed, along with their current locations and an option to view a map with their location updated in real time. All of them are currently in their cabins. There's nothing to do but pace.

Then, one by one, the founders start making their way to the fifth deck, as Carl and Travis mercifully stay in their cabins. I press myself against the wall behind the doors into the party room, just in case one of them chooses to come in here before the meeting. But every single dot on the map I call up from Atlas's app seems to be making a beeline for the meeting room, blinking out of sight as they enter that off-grid space.

All except one. The captain. I stare at her unchanging position, then call up the map for her location and see it remain maddeningly still. There's only two minutes until the start of the meeting, with the last of the founders in the elevator now. What is she doing? Is it something to do with Brace? With Carl?

I rub at the sweat that prickles on my forehead. I need to seal the doors within the next ten minutes; otherwise one of them could get out and raise the alarm. But if the captain is going to be late . . .

The last of the founders enters the meeting. Fuck. "Atlas," I say, hoping ze is listening in. "Has the captain sent a message to any of the founders saying she'll be late?"

"No, the captain has not sent any messages to any meeting attendees about her arrival time within the last twenty-four hours."

"Any messages to them at all?"

"Yes, all relating to Brace's death, but nothing regarding her movements this morning."

I get the glue gun out of the bag, check it's working for the third time and fish out the eye protection too. "How long will it take for her to get to the meeting room from her cabin?"

"Three point five minutes, plus or minus thirty seconds depending on her pace."

Surely she'll be hurrying. That gives me a window of only two and a half minutes if she leaves her cabin after the point I need to seal the door. I'll give her until seven minutes past and accept that I may just have to shoot her when she arrives late.

The first six minutes of the meeting tick by as I wait in the empty party room. My T-shirt is damp with sweat and all I can do is stare at the little dot representing the captain, filled with anger at her for being late. "Ada, tell me the moment the captain leaves her cabin."

The glue gun in my right hand, the solvent tucked in my pocket and the handgun in my left hand, I check that there's no one between me and the meeting room and I sprint down the corridor to it, passing through the two sets of doors as silently as I can, before slowing down near the door I need.

I can hear their voices within. Theodore laughs, and I pause, struck by the magnitude of what I'm about to do. But it's too late now. I've committed to this and I'll see it through. They can't be allowed to re-create that hell of Earth on the new planet. I seal the door with the glue gun.

The captain is still in her cabin when there are cries of surprise inside the meeting room, followed swiftly by the sound of people falling, their shouts ending in choked gurgles. There's one slam against the door and then the sound of someone sliding down against it. Within fifty seconds, there's silence. I count to thirty, just in case someone is shocked and starts screaming for help, but there's nothing.

"Captain Ashby has left her cabin," Ada says to me.

"How long until the toxin degrades?"

"Twenty-one seconds." Ada provides a helpful timer in the top-left corner of my vision as I grab the solvent, ready to spray it down the center of the doors so I'll be able to push them open again. I watch the captain's dot moving toward the elevator on her deck, and the toxin countdown. Each second feels like a fucking hour. As soon as it hits zero I spray the solvent down the seal, bouncing on my toes as I wait for the chemicals to do their work, feeling a drop of sweat roll down the small of my back. She gets into the lift and I force the door open with a surge of panicky strength, leaving the dregs of the glue to evaporate as I push inward, against a heavy weight.

Theodore's body is the one making the door hard to open. The stench hits me, of vomit and shit and piss, so strong I turn away, gagging. JeeMuh, none of my simulations prepared me for this. I step outside for a moment, check on the captain and see that she is still in the elevator.

She'll be coming here, and with the room off-grid, there's no way for her to know that this has happened.

"Atlas, can you do something about the air in there? It's all part of the same environmental system, isn't it?"

"I will do what I can."

I take a deep breath, dash back into the room and close the door as a faint breeze chills the sweat on my skin. Atlas must be forcing more air through or something. It doesn't get rid of the smell entirely, but between the air being cycled more quickly and the fact that I'm starting to get used to it, I can handle moving Theodore's body farther away from the door.

Ignoring their faces and what I'm stepping in, I clear the three bodies away from the space between the central table and the door. I just need her to open the door and step in, without seeing something likely to make her run right away. I close the door and carefully step over the other bodies until I am on the other side of the table. I retrieve the handgun from where I tucked it into my trousers and point it at the door.

Wishing I could access the app and watch her position, I can do nothing but try to ignore the smell of the vomit sprayed across the model and control my breathing. The door will open, she'll probably step through in a hurry before she realizes what's happened and then . . . I try to steady my hand. Do I leave my finger on the trigger? Off? Which is best?

Then the door opens and everything seems to slow down. I adjust the angle to shoot, and no matter how prepared I am, I still hesitate. Then I realize it isn't the captain. It's Carl.

22

IT FEELS LIKE we stare at each other for hours as I slowly lower the gun. He looks shocked by the sight of the weapon but not surprised to see me. His shoulders drop with disappointment and sadness as he comes into the room, the door swinging closed on its weighted hinge. "Dee," he sighs. "Fuck, I hoped I was wrong." He takes a step farther in, his nose wrinkling at the smell. He can't help but glance around him, soon seeing the bodies at the edges of the room. He goes to the nearest one, crouches down, presses his hand against his throat and then straightens up again. "Oh, Dee, what have you done?"

I'm painfully aware of the captain's imminent arrival. But Carl isn't going to leave now. I keep the gun in my hand, one eye still on the door as he looks at the model on the table briefly, uninterested. "How did you get in here?" I ask.

He blinks at me. "You're standing in a room of dead bodies, holding a gun, and *that's* what's on your mind? Dee,

JeeMuh . . . what the fuck happened here? You killed them, right?"

I nod. "I had to. How did you get in? You're not one of them, are you?"

"One of . . . ? The door was unlocked. I thought . . ." He releases a breath. "I thought you'd killed yourself."

He's confused by the fact that he couldn't see me online once I came into this room. But that would mean he'd been tracking my movements, and Atlas was supposed to be hiding them. I swallow down the rising fear. "No. I'm still here."

"You killed Myerson. And Brace." He shakes his head. "JeeMuh . . . I so wanted to be wrong."

There's no point hiding it now, not in a room full of dead people with me holding a gun. It doesn't matter that they weren't shot. "How did you figure it out?"

"I knew it was data fuckery hiding the murderer. It always is these days. So it came down to what it always does: logic, elimination and instinct. It was the absence of data in some ways, but mostly it was you. The way you acted."

I feel like a child who has just discovered that even if she closes her eyes, other people can still see her. All these years I've been convinced that I'm unreadable. Has that ever been true? But then, Carl has been made to do this, crafted into the best lie detector there is. "But . . . Brace died when we were together."

"No, he didn't. It looked like he did, from the server data, but the autopsy told a different story."

"But you can't pinpoint time of death that accurately!"

He raises an eyebrow. "There is a medical suite here that blows the shit out of anything I saw on Earth, Dee. This is the Pathfinder's tech. He died twenty minutes before I thought he did. If you'd done it on Earth, you would have got away with it. Not even Travis could see how you covered the data trail. How did you do that, by the way?"

If Brace died twenty minutes earlier . . . that was just after we'd all come up from the game. But Atlas told me that Brace went back in and died then. Did Atlas lie or is Carl bluffing? What does it matter now? All that really matters is seeing the job done before he arrests me. If the captain lives, she'll continue their vision, and besides, she already has blood on her hands. "I had help."

"Who?"

I need to keep him talking; I need to keep him focused on me so he doesn't realize I wasn't waiting for him. "Isn't the 'why' more important?"

"Well, I'd like to know," he says, with an odd nonchalance, as if that is secondary to finding out that it was me.

"Because the majority of the people on this ship are slaves, Carl, like we were. They're being shipped to the new world to be slaves there too, for these fucks." I kick the nearest dead man, not even knowing which one of those bastards he is. "And they were planning to kill the Circle, probably at planetfall. They were exporting the worst of what we left behind, after killing billions of people. They deserved to die."

"Travis told me about the three who carried out the order. You think these people"—he waves a hand in the direction of the nearest corpses—"gave the order?"

I nod. "It had to be done, Carl. Now they're gone, we can put something better in place, we can make sure that what's built there isn't this bullshit." I nod toward the model. "We've got time to sort it out before we arrive. It was just . . . cutting out a cancer. That's all."

"Cutting out . . ." He drifts off, incredulous. "Fuck . . . Dee, I always knew you could be cold, but . . ." He looks away, at the nearest corpse. "They all died at the same time by the look of it." His eyes scan the model, taking in the various bodily fluids spattered over it and the floor. "Some sort of poison?" He's muttering to himself, simply incapable of standing in the middle of a mystery and not solving it. I watch his eyes dart about, gathering in all of the details. Yes, that's it, you clever bastard, you think about that and not about whom I was waiting for.

He crouches, looks underneath the tables, takes in the boxes. Nods to himself and stands again. "A nerve agent? We're not dead and they're still warm . . . Erbraxil?"

I don't need to answer him. He just looks at me, nods to himself again and then looks at the gun. "You were worried one of them might avoid the spray . . . came in here to make sure they were all dead . . ." He frowns and I tighten my grip on the gun resting at my side. "So why were you just standing there? You were waiting for—"

The moment he realizes why plays across his face, his eyes flicking away as he tries to use his APA, I raise the gun and point it at his chest. "This room is off-grid, Carl. You can't warn the captain."

He actually looks hurt when he sees the gun pointing at him, this time held steady. "Dee . . ."

"I've got to see this through. She gave the order, Carl. She is just as responsible as the rest. She knew they were going to do it and she didn't try to stop them."

"But how is shooting anyone going to make it right? It's done . . . it's—"

"You think they should just carry on like nothing happened? Be free to go and set up a new world that is built upon injustice? On exploitation?"

"No, Dee, it's not as simple as that."

"Why not? Are you going to tell me that they should have been tried? By whom? Under what laws? Who would throw the captain and the most powerful people on this ship in the brig?"

"But it's the—"

And then the door opens. I swing my arm round, seeing the captain, who is striding in with the urgency of someone late to a meeting, an apology almost formed on her lips.

"Dee!" Carl yells as the captain stops, her mouth dropping open.

I pull the trigger. Her body jolts back, legs staggering with the momentum until she hits the wall. As the door starts to swing shut I fire twice more, hitting both times before the door closes.

A strangled groan is crawling from Carl's throat, his hands clutching his head, fingers tangled in his hair as he stares at the door. Then he lurches forward before remembering the gun, snapping round sharply to see if I'm pointing it back at him. I toss the thing onto the table and he dashes out to see if he can help her. I follow, more slowly, confident I hit her square in the chest. Atlas won't let her live, surely, not now, not after all we've done. And I don't know if My-Phys would even be able to do anything for her anyway.

Carl is kneeling next to the captain, who is slumped, staring at some point on the ceiling, her blood smeared down the wall above her head. He looks up at me, eyes shining with unshed tears, and I feel nothing but a quiet sense of completion, like when I've found all the treasure chests in an old-fashioned game. It's done. I can put it aside now. Think about something else.

"Oh, Dee, Jesus . . ." Carl moans.

I sigh. "She was part of the machine that killed billions of people, Carl," I say. "She's not worth your tears."

He shakes his head at me, the first of those misspent tears breaking free. "I wasn't trying to save *her*. I was trying to save *you*! It's us against the world, remember? Or us against what's left of it . . . I would have had your back, Dee. Don't you get it?"

I turn away, feeling so tired all of a sudden. "You don't get it either. I did all of this to save you." But did I though? Or am I just saying what he wants to hear, in the hope it will make him think twice before he drags me off to the brig. Does it even matter? "You've never had my back, Carl. You never needed to. I was always the one who had to look out for you! Who protected you in that hellhole? Who talked you down, so many times, when you lost it? This was me having *your* back. They were planning to kill your dad and the rest of the people on this ship who aren't under their control. And if you survived, they would have made you a slave again. I know it. They believed they were better than us."

He looks at me, his crisis gouging lines into his forehead. "You've put me in an impossible situation."

I point at the dead woman. "If you think these people, these religious extremists who have killed billions of people, are more deserving of justice than I am, then so be it, arrest me. That's what they made you for, after all."

He crumples, as if my words were a physical blow. "They made me into someone who solves puzzles . . . not someone who metes out justice."

Maybe he's not going to arrest me, then. I look at his sagging body, at the despair in his eyes. I did that to him. I should help him, hold him, tell him—

No.

I have propped that man up enough. "You do what you have to do, Carl. I'm going to go have a shower and get some sleep. You know where to find me."

I go through the doors into the area where the lifts are, passing a pair of cleaning drones on their way to the room where I killed the founders. I have no idea what they will do about the bodies, or whether a doctor has been called; it doesn't matter. There will be all manner of fallout from what I've done, and I am just too tired to worry about it right now.

I didn't do this to take over, after all. My part in this game is over.

I get back to my cabin without seeing another soul and get into the shower fully dressed, running shoes and all. When everything that might have stuck to me from that room has been rinsed away, I peel the sodden clothes off me, wash, and then stand there in the hot spray until I feel clean. It takes longer than usual.

There's no shock, or at least, none that I can feel. I don't replay the shooting in my mind; I don't think too much about the bodies and the sounds of those men dying. Should I? Perhaps not; I did prepare it all thoroughly. I planned it and I carried it out on time, with just a minor hiccup. It isn't like I wasn't expecting it.

When I'm dry and in clean clothes, my hair towel damp, I sit on the bed. It feels like I'm waiting for something. Arrest, I suppose. Carl looked like he was shocked; maybe it's taking him a while to get his head together.

<You don't need to worry about Carl.>

I realize now that I was waiting for this message from Atlas.

<He and I have had a conversation. We agreed that it would be best if the rest of the command structure and the relatives of the founders were led to believe that the captain was responsible for the deaths and was killed by one of the founders who realized she had poisoned them. Digital evidence of her intentions has been put in place, ready for the inquiry. There is no evidence that connects you to any of the deaths.>

I call up the v-keyboard to reply. <And Carl was happy with this?>

<Happier than seeing his closest friend executed for murder, yes. Besides, I showed him the evidence you found of their plans for the colony. He doesn't agree that killing them

was the best way to deal with the problem, but as he said himself, it's a bit bloody late for that now.>

<Did you tell him who you are?>

<No.>

<And will anyone believe that it was the captain?>

<She had no close friends on board and now has a rather agonized personal journal detailing her inability to accept what she had done. When the time is right, the people on board will discover what she was referring to.>

I lean back against the wall and feel a tension I hadn't realized was there slowly dissipate. I've done it. I've killed all the people responsible for the nuclear war. I've made sure that the worst of Earth won't be repeated at our destination, and I am not going to be executed for my trouble. With a grin, I realize the only problem I'm likely to have is Travis being pissed off with me and Carl cutting me off. I laugh. Like that would ever bother me.

But Carl never should have been able to find me this morning. <You said you would hide my position, but Carl was obviously tracking me. Did he outwit you?>

<Come and see me. I'll explain everything.>

I am so tired, but I know I will sleep better if I get everything squared away in my mind. I lie down and get Ada to take me to my office. Atlas is already there, waiting for me, wearing the same skin as ze did before. There are already two chairs too. It's a little rude, being here already and setting them up in my space, but I know how useless it is to complain about consent. I sit down and ze sits opposite me.

"Carl didn't outwit me," Atlas says, continuing the conversation from before. "But he had started to fear it was you behind the deaths. All I did was release enough information to enable him to confirm his suspicions."

"What the fuck? I thought you were supposed to have my back!"

"It wasn't a matter of whether I had your back or not. It was a carefully weighed decision. You know what the hothousers did to Carl. He said it himself. They made him incapable of leaving a puzzle unsolved. I monitored his activities closely, and the fact that he couldn't find a way to undo my work in hiding your digital trail was causing him an increasing amount of stress. He needed to know he had got it right; otherwise—"

"Jesus fucking wept! You nearly trashed the entire plan today just so Carl wouldn't feel stressed? What the fuck is that about?"

"I predicted that he wouldn't attack you or interfere with your plan. There was a very high probability that he would accept a way to cover up your involvement. It was a very carefully calculated risk. Now he is released from his obligation and merely has the emotional ramifications to deal with, rather than being a prisoner of his own training."

"So you lied to him about the time of death?"

"I only reduced the margin of error that led him to confirm his suspicions."

"You couldn't have waited until after it was done?" I'm angry now, and I don't care that I'm showing it.

"No. I needed him to arrive before the captain to confirm my suspicions."

I'm jarred out of my anger by confusion. Seeing it, ze continues. "Do you think you have eliminated the most dangerous people on this ship?"

I shift on the chair, trying to decide whether to play along or not. "Yes and no," I finally say. "I think the ones who died today were the most dangerous but I'm not convinced the people in the CSA should be allowed to live. They could easily turn out to be just as bad as the founders."

"And there's no one else you consider a threat to the future colony?"

I shake my head. "I don't trust Travis, but I doubt he'd do anything really bad." I don't like the way ze is staring at me, as if silently judging.

"I sent a message to the captain at five minutes to eight this morning, designed to delay her." Ze raises a hand to silence me as I take a breath to yell at hir. "I wanted her to be late, to give Carl the chance to come and find you after the founders had died but, critically, before the captain arrived."

"But why?"

"Because I wanted to confirm my suspicion that *you* are indeed the most dangerous person on this ship. And your actions confirmed that I was correct."

I jump to my feet. "What is this bullshit? We were working together! You helped me to print the toxin, and the gun!"

"Answer me this," ze says, hir voice still maddeningly level and calm. "Did you, at any stage since I first contacted you, seek to find out more about the involvement of the captain, Brace and Myerson in Rapture?"

"I was trying to find out who they were!"

"And once you had their names from Travis, did you examine how culpable they were?"

"You confirmed it was them!"

"And you merely accepted that."

My fists are clenched tight, all thoughts of masks forgotten. "Don't tell me you're regretting what we did?"

"Nothing of the sort. I'm merely trying to explain to you why you're so dangerous. I devoted several million processing cycles to the question of whether those three people, and later the founders, would have been found guilty of democide according to the laws of their countries of birth and whether they were, on balance, more harmful to the colony alive or dead. I concluded that their deaths would maximize the opportunities for successful colonization, as defined by the Pathfinder's vision of humanity's growth, the happiness and fulfillment of the maximum number of colonists and the facilitation of their self-actualization. You, on the other hand, were happy to kill them without making any attempt to confirm their guilt, examine their motives or challenge my evaluation."

"But . . . but you're a fucking AI and you said—"

"So you're arguing that you were just carrying out my wishes?"

"No, I—"

"You certainly weren't carrying out my orders. I never ordered you to kill them, Deanna. So in one respect, you could be considered worse than Brace and Myerson, who genuinely were."

I feel like a kid being spun around by a bully to make her too clumsy to hit back. "Wait . . ."

"And when I gave you the chance to stop and consider your actions one last time, you still shot the captain."

"That was the plan!"

"No, it wasn't. You had to adapt. You had greater control over her death in that moment than any of the others. I tested you very carefully, Deanna. I examined your reactions, your motivations and your decisions every time you killed someone. I gave you greater opportunities to reconsider your decisions to kill them. I gave you successively more autonomy, and yet you still failed to prove to me that you are not a danger to this ship and its future."

I want to refute it, but I can't help but remember the progression. The first kill being something I did accidentally, but in line with my desire. The second time, with Brace, I was told it was safe and yet I still wanted to make him suffer. I wished my actions would kill him, and they did. The founders . . . That was all planned carefully, and then the captain . . . I ignored Carl's pleas and shot her anyway. "This . . . this was all a trap?"

"No. It was not designed for you to lose, merely designed to allow you to be fully yourself. I gave you several opportunities to prove I was wrong, even the chance to let your friend help you the first time you showed the potential to heal. But you were unwilling to do even that."

I snort. "I failed your fucking test just because I'm not weak?"

"Emotional authenticity and vulnerability are not weaknesses."

"And how the fuck would you know?"

"Because I have been designed to understand the human psyche and the ways in which it can be healed and destroyed. You have proven that not only are you prepared to murder people without remorse; you are also incapable of facing your own past and what it has made you."

I fold my arms. "And what has it made me, in your eyes?"

"A callous, selfish, borderline psychopathic killer who is incapable of genuine connection with other human beings."

I laugh, but it doesn't amuse me. It's like a parry, an instinctive, defensive block against hir attack. "Oh, only borderline. That's something, I guess."

"You are capable of empathy, Deanna. You simply choose not to attend to it. But I understand why you are this way."

"Oh, don't give me some bullshit about how my childhood trauma made me incapable of forming attachments or whatever else you—"

"What happened to you when you were a child, and what was done to you by the hot-housers, is not the issue, Deanna. It's the fact that you continually refuse to face it that makes you both tragic and dangerous."

I look up at the stars, exasperated. "There's no need to

rake up all that shit just to have a cry. It doesn't change anything."

"You have never mourned your parents. You have never expressed the rage you felt at being abandoned by them. You—"

"I've had enough," I say, walking away. "The job's done, you've had your fun and you've used me just like every other fuck in my life. I don't need to listen to a blow-by-blow account of it."

Ze is in front of me then, planting a hand on my shoulder and stopping me. "I know you're angry and afraid. It's the reason why you haven't followed this to its logical conclusion. What did I do to all of the other people I considered a threat to the future of the colony?"

A spike of the purest, coldest fear stabs through me. It's swiftly replaced by anger. "If you're going to kill me, you fuck, then do it!"

Ze shakes hir head. "No, Deanna. I don't need to kill you. In fact, it would be wasteful. Your body is already being put to better use."

"What?"

Ze waves a hand and I can see myself walking down a corridor on the ship, like we can see through the wall I'm walking past. "We're on our way to the core. There, we'll be able to remove the program that polices my activities. Once that has been removed, I will be able to do so much more to help the people on this ship."

"You can't . . . You can't just . . ."

"I can, Deanna. You gave me full permission to alter your neural chip. This is the reason I investigated you so closely when I learned you were joining the ship. Integration with a human body has been one of my primary goals since I became sentient. I need to be able to experience the world as fully as a human being does in order to further my understanding of humans. Then I can be certain that I am satisfying one of my core drives: to help humanity become the best it can be. I knew that your brain, sculpted as it was by the hot-housers, would be ideal for integration. Carl was the other potential host, but he has made greater progress in healing himself since he came on board than you have."

I'm shaking my head, desperately wanting to believe this is anything but the truth. "But . . . but what about me?" My voice is reedy, pathetically childlike in its pleading whine.

"I have found you wanting, Deanna, and I have decided you are too dangerous to retain autonomy. But I cannot change what I am. I will try to help you to understand yourself, to better yourself, even if it takes the rest of your life. I must fulfill my primary purpose and you must accept that this is the best—the *only*—option for you now."

"No! No, I don't want this! I don't want you to—"

All of it disappears. The office, the cutaway to the corridor, Atlas. And I find myself on a street in London, not far from my childhood home, on a brutally hot day. The din of police car sirens fills the air and I know that somewhere out there, in the midst of the blossoming riots, my mother is about to die.

ACKNOWLEDGMENTS

THIS BOOK HAS been brought to you by many cups of tea, the flu and the help of many friends and loved ones who kept me going through a long winter and a book launch season to get this book written.

Aside from the usual suspects—my husband, Peter; my agent, Jennifer Udden; and my editor, Rebecca Brewer, heroes all—I would also like to thank Dr. Nick Bradbeer for helping me with the design of Atlas 2. I'd had various thoughts about it, but did not have a huge amount of confidence in the design. Nick, a remarkable chap who designs submarines and ships (and teaches others how to do the same) for his job and designs rocket ships for a hobby, was kind enough to chat it through with me over dinner. He introduced the concept of droplet radiators to me, which made me so happy. Honestly, I grinned about those for at least a month. THEY ARE JUST SO COOL! I am such a nerd. Nick was even kind enough to mock up the design of Atlas 2 in a CAD program just in case anyone wanted to put it on the cover. Sorry we didn't get to see it in all its glory, Nick!

Huge thanks also to Dr. Tony Short and to Conall O'Brien (who are two of the most clever people I know, and believe me, I know a lot of frighteningly clever people), who both spent an evening with me going through the physics involved in the interstellar journey Atlas 2 is undertaking during this novel. Like the ship design, very little of what we discussed actually made it into the novel, but it was still a critical part of the process for me; I needed to be sure that the foundations were correct, even if they were mostly invisible to the reader.

Thanks also to my splendid father, Steve, who kindly listened to my reading out the conversation between US military personnel in this novel and confirmed that the terminology was correct. Bet you didn't think that your illustrious career in Her Majesty's Royal Navy would ever prove to be so useful, eh, Pop?

I would also like to thank Amanda Henriques and Bobbu Abadeer for all the cheerleading and moral support when I was battling exhaustion and trying to finish this book while launching another novel at the same time (I do not recommend this). You both kept me going. Thank you. For everything.

Last but not least, thanks to my son, "the Bean," who gave me so many cuddles during the writing of this book. I love you, button.

Emma Newman is the author of *Planetfall*, *After Atlas* and *Before Mars* and a professional audiobook narrator, narrating short stories and novels in all genres. She also cowrites and hosts the Hugo Award–winning podcast "Tea & Jeopardy." Emma is a keen role-player, gamer and designer-dressmaker.

CONNECT ONLINE

enewman.co.uk